# The
# Devil
# You
# Know

ELAINE EWERTZ

For the dreamers

*Those who don't believe in magic will never find it.*
Roald Dahl

Song lyrics page 49 as well as "Cecilia" and "Aiden" poems author's own.

Copyright © 2015 Elaine Ewertz
ISBN: 0692558799
ISBN-13: 978-0692558799

Cover design by Henry Louis
CEO 17 Media Co.
17MediaCo.com

**eSquared Press**
**Orlando, Florida**

# CECILIA

Merciless ragged bones on fire
Lies, innocent lives on the wire
From the depths of her own private hell
She takes a punch, her lips swell
But she hides, hides it all away
in the mirror, watch as her hips sway
She thinks she is free
Surely gone of misery
Oh but it has just begun
A battle so close to won

This page intentionally left blank

# ONE

**Tuesday March 18, 2014**

Cecilia's heart was a bass drum, pounding so hard she could feel the beat in her fingers. She sank down to her knees on the hard tile of the bathroom floor. *God, no, please. Not another one. I don't have time for this,* she thought. She opened and closed her hands, trying to squeeze away the pins and needles. A bead of cold sweat trickled down her forehead to the bridge of her nose.

She shivered, wondering how she could feel both cold and hot at the same time. Then, like clockwork, the ugly, bubbling nausea began and she felt a rising pressure start in her stomach and travel up through her chest to her throat. She stood on shaky legs and swung open the stall door, where her breakfast came back up quickly and painfully, her stomach acids burning her nose, her eyes watering.

She hadn't bothered to close the door, so when she was finally done, she heard a gasp behind her.

"Oh my God, Dr. Harper, are you OK?"

Cecilia craned her neck to see Lizzy standing behind her, her eyes wide and mouth open. She rushed forward and held out her hand. "Here, let me help you."

Once she had gotten to her feet, Cecilia sat in the chair next to the sink. "I just need a moment. I'll be fine." She leaned back and closed her eyes.

"Let me get you some water," Lizzy said. Cecilia felt a gust of air as the door swooshed open and she heard Lizzy clomp down the hall, her white clogs squeaking on the linoleum.

Lizzy returned with a small Dixie cup and placed it in Cecilia's trembling hands. "You should go home. We can reschedule the rest of the day or have Dr. Patton see them."

Cecilia looked up at Lizzy and the green and pink polka dot pattern of her scrubs seemed to join together, creating jagged lines instead of dots. She closed her eyes. "No, I'll be all right. Thank you, Lizzy. Just give me five minutes. I'll be right out."

When finally her breathing returned to normal, she stood up in front of the mirror, swept her long chestnut hair into a bun, adjusted her navy Ann Taylor blouse and smoothed her tailored charcoal-gray slacks. Taking her white lab coat off the hook, she shrugged it on, listening to the voices in the hallway a few feet away.

"Has anyone seen Dr. Harper? Erica in room three is still waiting."

Cecilia heard hurried footsteps. "I don't know, she's been disappearing all day. I can't find her. . . " The voice trailed off down the hall.

Another impatient, muffled voice floated through the air. "Well, I don't know how she's able to function at all. . ."

As soon as she opened the bathroom door, she saw Harriet standing across the hall, talking to another nurse. Harriet was a veteran nurse of sixty-four, who, despite her children's pleas, refused to retire. Hearing the door, she turned quickly to Cecilia, her eyes wide. "Are you OK?"

Cecilia forced a smile and walked to the desk. "I'm fine.

Just had a rough morning."

Harriet frowned. "You look pale."

"I *am* Irish."

"That may be, but you don't look well. Why don't you go home, Doc? We've got you covered here."

Cecilia ran her hand over the cold surface of the steel desktop. Taking a deep breath, she squared her shoulders. "I appreciate it but that won't help. I need the distraction. I need to stay busy."

Harriet cocked her head, short copper spikes tilting to the side. "You are stubborn, Doc. But if that's what you need, I get it. Just promise you'll let me know if there's anything I can do."

"I promise. I'm feeling better now anyway. Who's next?"

Harriet paused for a beat. Finally, she smiled and said, "All right, Doc, but I'm keeping my eye on you." She handed over the chart. "Erica Somers is in room three. Your post-surgery follow-up from last week."

Cecilia made it through the rest of her day on autopilot, zooming around the office until late afternoon when she saw her last patient. She closed the door to her office and sat on the small green plaid sofa by the window. Her eyes darted to the stack of charts on her desk, then the sound of rain falling on the pavement outside diverted her attention. Staring at the window, she watched the water fall in droplets and long streaks down the glass, the liquid shimmering red, yellow and green with the changing colors of the traffic lights on Lakeside Drive. Then the colors blurred together as she felt warm tears escape down her cheeks. As she wiped her face, movement outside the window caught her eye.

A young couple, hand in hand, strolled down the sidewalk under the cover of the building's overhang. They were illuminated by streetlamps several yards away. The woman wore a white dress with large black flowers and kept tucking her strawberry blonde hair behind her ear as the breeze kept gently lifting it into the air. Their faces were radiant but maybe it was just the glow from the pale yellow lamps on the side of the old brick building. Cecilia watched as the woman smiled lovingly at the man. Smiling back, he brought her hand to his lips and kissed it.

Unable to watch any longer, Cecilia jerked her head to the right and closed her eyes, wiping them once more with the back of her hand. When she turned back to the window, she saw a face reflected in the glass that she barely recognized. The corners of her mouth were turned down, faint black streaks crept down her cheeks and dark half-moons filled the space below her eyes. A loud crash of thunder made her jump and she rubbed her arms, feeling goose bumps. The *tick-tick-tick* of the clock seemed louder as she realized she was the only one left in the building.

Glancing up, she saw that it was nearly eight o'clock. She needed to do notes. She needed to work on her research. She needed to go to the lab down the street to do more trial runs on the medication she and Dr. Patton were testing on brain tumors. She rubbed her eyes and yawned. *I'll come in early tomorrow*, she thought as she packed up to leave.

Later that night, Cecilia curled into the fetal position and pulled her comforter over her head, forming a cocoon of warmth. March had been unseasonably cold so far. But, she refused to get up and turn on the heat knowing she could never go back to sleep once out of bed, even in the middle of the night. Nightmares had prevented any sort of quality sleep lately anyway, so she wasn't sure why she even bothered. As she tried to will herself to sleep, she felt the familiar fear return like a houseguest who had worn out his welcome long ago but refused to leave. Her chest felt cold and tight and she knew that even though she was exhausted, sleep wouldn't be coming anytime soon. She sighed and turned on her bedside lamp. Staring at the small orange bottle, she thought of how much she hated taking pills. It made her feel weak, like she was cheating. But the Ambien would kick in almost immediately and so desperation won.

Slipping into unconsciousness, she found herself in her favorite coffee shop, standing a few feet from a man with jet-black hair and a tall muscular build. It was strange because she couldn't seem to make his face come into focus. It was a little blurry, like a portrait that got wet in the rain, a water droplet landing precisely over the face, the edges beginning to bleed until it ruined the entire picture. She felt an odd attraction to him, and even without seeing his face, she felt compelled to move toward him. *If I can only get closer, maybe I can see him better.* Seemingly reading her thoughts, the man stepped closer.

At that exact moment, Cecilia heard a loud knock at the door.

Her mind a sea of murky confusion, she turned around to face the doors of the shop but no one was there.

The thunderous knocking continued and finally, in a crescendo of confusion, Cecilia awoke from her dream. Her heart thudded in her chest as she realized someone was pounding on her front door. Maybe a neighbor was expecting a late night visitor and had the wrong house. She stared at her ceiling, waiting for the person to give up.

But it didn't stop. "Seriously?" she said, snatching her phone from the nightstand, ready to dial 911. She crept slowly down the stairs, careful not to make a noise. Leaning into the front door, she squinted through the peephole, then jumped back, her heart beating frantically.

What—She tried to slow her breathing as she stood perfectly still, her hands turning to ice. *What the hell was that?* she thought, feeling her chest tighten. It looked like some kind of monster. It was several months too early for Halloween and if that was a mask, it was a damned good one. Covering her mouth with her hand, she hoped he—it?—had not heard her gasp. She dared to take another peek and judging from the slow smile that formed on his grotesque mouth, he had heard her. His teeth were like a shark's, sharp and pointed, and his eyes were the deepest and darkest red she had ever seen. His skin was as pale as the walls of her house. She looked away and closed her eyes. It felt as if the earth had stopped turning on its axis. There was only utter stillness, complete silence except for the low hum of the refrigerator several feet behind her. Goosebumps had formed on her arms and she rubbed them frantically as she searched for a plausible explanation. It was either a nightmare or someone playing a prank. *Probably my stupid neighbor, Ben. But there is no way a monster is standing outside my door*, she thought.

When she dared to inch closer to the peephole again, the inhuman, pallid face was gone. She stood like a statue wondering what to do. Call the police? And tell them what? There was a monster outside her door? That would go over well. It was probably just Ben the Stoner messing with her. He was known around the neighborhood for getting high and pulling pranks on people. Shaking her head, she trudged back up the stairs to her bedroom.

∞

The day that followed was the day that never seemed to end.

The front office had double-booked her all day, and as was the norm, one patient would wait calmly in the exam room and another would come out and start complaining to the nurses. Running on fumes and two Americanos, Cecilia did her best to calm them down them by the time she got into the room. There was something she noticed that always seemed to fascinate her: the patients who were upset would be rude to the nurses but not to the doctor. Cecilia had a feeling it had to do with a small pad of blank paper with Spring Lake Medical Group printed at the top. They were usually nice to the one who gave them their much-needed medication.

She had no surgeries scheduled for the day and was both disappointed and relieved. Doing a surgery would allow her to get out of the bustling office and into a quiet operating room where she could listen to music and go into her state of flow, her happy place she always went to when she performed a surgery. But, going home and crawling into her feathery bed, burrowing under the cool cotton sheets and drifting away to oblivion sounded pretty tempting, too.

Around five in the afternoon, she was wrapping up her day and getting ready to leave when she heard a nurse yell, "Code blue!"

She ran out of her office and into Room Four where she found an elderly woman laying on the table, clutching her chest, her breathing shallow. It was Mrs. Stapleton, a seventy-three year old widow that had been Cecilia's patient for several months. Her husband had died two months ago and she had come into the office complaining of chest pains three times since then. Cecilia had ordered tests but they had come back normal. Cecilia's colleague, Dr. Patton, had tried to convince Cecilia to let him treat her instead, but Cecilia had refused. She found the older woman's presence a comforting reminder that she was not alone in her pain.

"We've already called an ambulance to transport her to the ER," Lizzy said. "Her BP is 152 over 98."

"OK." Cecilia leaned down to the woman. "Can you hear me?"

The woman's eyes fluttered open and closed. "Yes. . . my chest. . . " She writhed on the exam table, making the paper sheet crinkle under her. "Don't ever get old," she said, straining to form words. "And may you go before the love of your life does. It's—" She paused, squirmed a little and took in a sharp breath. "Torture."

Cecilia placed a hand on her arm. "We're going to get you to the hospital right away. You're going to be fine." She used her stethoscope to listen to her heart. It was slightly tachycardic but nothing alarming.

Suddenly, Mrs. Stapleton grabbed Cecilia's arm. Her grip was weak, her cold hand the texture of paper mache. "You're going to fall in love. He's out there."

*What an odd thing to say,* Cecilia thought as she held Mrs. Stapleton's hand.

A few seconds later, the paramedics burst into the room with a stretcher. Cecilia moved out of their way as she relayed the vitals. It most likely was not a heart attack, but the protocol was to call EMS immediately with a complaint of chest pain. The medics raced down the hall to the elevator and a moment later, Cecilia watched out her office window as they lifted her into the back of the ambulance and sped off, the sirens wailing and lights flashing.

She stood staring, her hands resting on the cool marble windowsill, long after the sirens faded. The woman's words replayed in her mind on a loop. *He's out there.* It was strange, how the words were hopeful but her tone had been anything but. It almost sounded like a warning. She sank down into her chair, closed her eyes and let out a long sigh.

Lizzy stopped at the doorway. "Do you think she's going to be all right?"

"I think so. Her BP was elevated but not to a dangerous level and her heart sounded fine. It could have been anxiety. It looks like a heart attack sometimes. Let me know what you hear from the ER, OK?"

"You got it," Lizzy said.

As she was driving home, she remembered her rude awakening from the night before. Ben, her stupid neighbor. She made a mental note to have a little talk with him the next time she saw him. But if he did it again tonight, she would call the police and let them handle him. Pulling into her driveway, she looked over at Ben's house. It was such an eyesore in the neighborhood. He refused to give it a fresh coat of paint despite the fact that it was peeling, revealing the dark grayish wood underneath. He would let the grass grow until Damian, the high school kid across the street—on orders from his mother no doubt—would trudge over and offer to cut it for twenty dollars. Ben would laugh, hand him a wad of cash and tell him to "go for it."

If it was Ben knocking at her door at night, what were the odds he would keep coming back? He would probably be off bugging someone else. She gave a last look at his house before going into her own and locking the door.

Standing in her kitchen, she randomly opened cupboards and then the fridge. Nothing looked appetizing. She couldn't imagine eating. All she wanted was sleep. So she turned off all the lights and climbed the stairs to her bedroom where she hastily undressed, threw her clothes to the floor and fell into bed.

Then it started. She was getting used to hearing Ben's thumping techno music at night (which, when she mentioned it to him, the young "entrepreneur" who smoked weed all day, had corrected her in his haughty way, saying, "it's called *house* music"). *It sounds like music they play in hell,* Cecilia thought. *Good sound track to torture someone by. Satan's playlist.* She reached for her earplugs on the nightstand.

Tonight, there were no nightmares. Instead, a tall man with large, striking brown eyes and inky black hair stood before her. He was equally attractive and odd-looking, the type of face that would draw stares from both men and women who wouldn't know why they could not look away. He was almost otherworldly, like he couldn't have been human. Was this the same man she had dreamt about the night before? She couldn't be sure, as she had never seen his face clearly until now. He walked towards her, and as he stepped into the light, she stared, mesmerized.

His dark eyes shone with tiny sparkling gold flecks, seemingly on fire, and burned into her own wide clear blue eyes with an intensity that made her want to look away. As he came closer, he gave her a slow smile—

Bang! Bang! Bang! Her delightful dream came to an abrupt stop as she jolted upright, her feet tangled in the sheets. "All right, Ben," she said as she trudged down the stairs. "This is going to get ugly, you little shit."

Ben would probably go away if she ignored him. But she

knew she wouldn't be able to go back to sleep until she found out for sure, because, what if it wasn't Ben? Tiptoeing to the peephole, she reluctantly peered out. As soon as she saw it, she jumped back, bumping into the entryway table, knocking over an empty glass vase. It tipped over and fell to the floor, rolling on the rug until it came to a stop against the baseboard. Stunned, she backed up and leaned against the wall for support. Taking a deep breath, she glanced back at the door but didn't dare look through the peephole again.

"Ben, you're not funny. Go home," she called through the door, trying to disguise her growing terror.

"I do apologize for interrupting your dream."

Cecilia jumped again. *That's not Ben.*

Shivering, she felt the hairs on the back of her neck stand on end. The deep baritone, almost too loud, yet melodic and smooth, sounded like it was coming from everywhere. Or, at the very least, from the walls of her house. She had never heard anything like it. It was terrifying and it wasn't that it didn't sound human. It sounded *super*human, like a man who had been genetically engineered, had been altered somehow to be an upgrade to mere mortal men. The voice was strong, resonant, and confident. Her heart galloping like ten thousand horses, she closed one eye and looked through the peephole again. His jagged, sinister laugh sounded like the loud rumble of an engine running over shards of glass. "Yes, that was me. Again, I'm sorry, but this won't take long, I just want to have a little chat." His dark eyes sparkled and a trace of a smile danced on his lips.

"I don't know what you think you are doing, but if you don't leave right now, I'm calling the police!" she yelled through the door.

His expression changed to a mock surprise and then to a pout. She stared, wondering why she couldn't look away.

He lowered his head and gazed up with deep red eyes. "You should really hear me out. I know something that you think *no one* knows. I know your big secret, Cecilia." He paused, smirking. "I mean, *Dr. Harper.*"

"OK, I'm calling the police now!" Cecilia's hands trembled as she fumbled for her phone on the table. *How did he know my name? How can he see me?* she thought.

"Oh, no need. No need. I'll leave. Sweet dreams, doctor." In an instant, he was gone.

Cecilia remained frozen, staring at the door. *I have to call the police and they are going to think I'm crazy.*

Cecilia decided to call the nonemergency line to report the incident and the woman on the other end had been speechless when Cecilia had given her the description of the man.

"And this is the second time this has happened?"

"Yes. He knocked on my door last night but didn't say anything. Just now, he said he wanted to talk. He knows my name. He said my name." Cecilia put the phone on speaker, sat it on the table and massaged her temples.

"And you're sure you don't know this person?"

"I'm positive. His voice does not sound familiar at all and like I said, he must be wearing some kind of Halloween makeup or something."

"OK, we are sending an officer to drive by your house. He's going to drive by a couple times to look for anything suspicious. His lights will be on so it should scare off anyone who may be up to no good. In the meantime, lock all your doors and keep your phone nearby. If he knocks again, or anything else unusual happens, call 911 immediately. OK?"

"Yes, thank you."

"You're welcome. Call us back if you need us. We're sending an officer who was in the area. He should be driving by any minute now."

About two minutes later, Cecilia saw flashing lights shining in through her living room curtains. She pushed them aside slowly, almost expecting to see that face again. Instead, she saw a patrol car creeping by just in front of her house. She stood and watched as the officer passed, disappeared from sight, then passed by twice more. Satisfied that her creepy visitor had left, she decided to go back to bed. As she made her way up the stairs, they creaked under her feet, giving her a small heart palpitation and a cold shiver up her spine. *Relax,* she told herself. *The creep would have been scared off by the sight of the police car and if he's smart, he won't return.*

This reassurance did little to calm her nerves, however. After all, he knew her name and what she did for a living. But she had never heard that voice before. Another chill traveled through her body when she remembered his words. *I know your big secret.* It was impossible. The only thing she could think of—no. There was no way. No one knew about that. *It could have been a patient I treated in the past. Brain tumors can cause their behavior to become erratic. That has to be it. It's the only logical explanation,* she thought.

She decided that if he knocked on the door again, she would call 911, then ask his name. Maybe he would give her some sort of clue as to who he was. Having a plan relaxed her enough that she was finally able to fall asleep, but not until well after four in the morning.

# Two

**Sunday October 26, 2013**

Rick swallowed the last gulp of his Jack and Coke and slid the tumbler, empty except for an ice cube the size of a postage stamp, onto the coffee table. His eyes followed the glass as it slid a few inches across the slick surface. A crumpled pack of Newports was lying next to a dirty glass ashtray which contained at least fifteen butts and silvery-gray ashes were scattered across the table. He leaned back on the couch, propping one foot up on the wooden coffee table – a wedding gift five years ago – causing it to sway forward. One of the four legs was broken (a result of one of Rick's angry outbursts a few months back) and about to give way at any moment now. He moved it back and forth with his foot, slowly at first, then faster and faster until Cecilia stepped forward and grabbed the edge. The drink glass had fallen off the table, rolled over and spilled the few remaining drops of pale brown liquid onto the rug.

"Rick, please," she said. Her hands began to tremble, an involuntary reaction she had developed in the past few months since Rick had spiraled out of control.

He looked up at her, his eyelids drooping, a sloppy smirk on his face. "Aww, does thaaat. . . bother yooooou. . . my princess?" he slurred. "C'mere, I'll. . . I'll make you feel better." He grabbed for her but fell back onto the couch when she took a quick step back. "Whatever. . . bitch. . . . . . didn't you come to get your shit? Get it and lea—"

"Yes, I did. But, I need to know where my crystal vase is. The one my grandfather gave me. Please, Rick. You know how much it means to me. Just tell me where you put it."

*Are the pills not affecting him at all? I just need to get out of here before this gets any uglier,* Cecilia thought. She wrung her hands together, trying to stop the shaking.

"I think. . . I think I'll. . . k-keep it. You owe me that much, you selfish bitch. You divorced me, remember? Why should I give you. . . " he snarled at her as he struggled to stand up.

Cecilia took two steps back. "You think you can. . . get away from me?" He lost his balance and fell back onto the worn-in brown sofa. "If I wanted. . . to get you. . . I could. I just don't. . . I don't care. . . Fuck, the room's s-spinning. . . " He pushed his matted light brown hair back which caused it stand up, waves haphazardly strewn in different directions. His bloodshot eyes slid closed.

"You're drunk, Rick. Please just tell me where it is and I'll leave."

"No shit I'm drunk. . . and I took a couple of those p-pills. . . those happy pills," he said, opening his eyes.

Cecilia's heart accelerated. *He still has the Xanax? I threw them all out. I only gave him one.*

"How many did you take?"

"Oh. . . only a couple. . . Fuck, I'm so dizzy. . . "

*So he's only had three total. It's not enough to do him any harm. Okay.* She took a deep breath. "Go to sleep, Rick. I'll be back some other time for the vase."

After packing up the rest of her things, she returned to the living room where Rick was unconscious. Careful not to wake him, she quietly moved her boxes to the door and turned to look around the room of what had once been a happy home. Cat toys were scattered across the hardwood floor, untouched for the last two weeks after Tigger had run away. Rick had never liked the fat orange cat, so he had been relieved when they came home one day and Tigger was nowhere to be found. The cat had been a comfort to Cecilia though, especially after Rick had started falling asleep on the couch, leaving her alone in their king size bed. Tigger had spent every night curled up with her, purring by her side.

Photographs with a thin layer of dust lining the top of the frames sat on shelves above the sofa. They were pictures of the couple taken during a happier time, a time that seemed strangely distant now. Her eyes lingered on one of them. The photo was taken on their trip to the Keys a few years ago before they had moved to Florida. In it, they were sitting at an outdoor table with thick slices of Key Lime pie in front of them. Rick had a smudge of the pale green concoction on the corner of his mouth. Cecilia had tried to wipe it off but Rick insisted on taking the picture with the blob of pie on his face. They had been laughing as passersby watched them acting like silly teenagers.

She started to walk over to grab the pictures, but decided against it. Where would she put them? Besides, she knew damn well what she would do if she took them home: Pull them out from time to time and stare at the memories of the past, cry, torture herself with thoughts of what could have been. There was no point in holding onto something that no longer existed. Best to make a fresh start, wipe the slate clean and move on. She said a silent goodbye to the house and then her eyes found Rick, snoring softly on the couch. *He'll sleep it off and just be really hung-over in the morning*, she thought as she locked the front door. Walking to her car, she heard the rustling of trees in the empty lot across the street. It was too dark to see anything, but she could have sworn something was moving in the spaces between the old trees and overgrown shrubs. Since she and Rick had bought the house, every now and then she had seen a deer in the woods. There had even been reports of bear sightings in their neighborhood.

Rushing to the safety of her car, she buckled her seatbelt and looked at the house. It was odd to think that just a short time ago she had been excited and filled with joy at this view. Now she shivered at the thought of the man now lying asleep on the couch alone, a man she didn't know anymore. They had only been married five years. She shook her head and started the engine. *How did this happen? Love really is blind.*

## Two Days Later

"You've reached Rick Harper. Please leave a message after the tone. *Beeeep.*" Cecilia pressed "end" on her phone and turned her full attention back to the road. *Now, he won't even return my calls. And the alcoholic bastard changed the locks the day after the divorce proceedings. I just need to get a couple more things from our old house, mainly the antique vase Gramps gave me on my thirteenth birthday.*

Just then her phone vibrated but it wasn't Rick. On the other end was a voice she had never heard. As she listened to the voice, she heard the reluctance, the gentle sensitivity, the quiet way bad news is delivered as if saying it sweetly will soften the blow. She felt herself sinking into darkness, quicksand enveloping her entire being, drowning out the last ounce of hope from her body.

She pulled off onto the shoulder of the highway and pushed the red triangle above her radio to turn on her hazard lights. "He overdosed," the voice told her. "His friend found him when he didn't show up for work this morning."

Cecilia dropped the phone onto the floorboard of the car, crawled over to the passenger side, opened the door and lurched out onto the concrete. The thick, grimy smell of exhaust fumes filled her nose and cars whirred by her like a swarm of angry hornets. A semi-truck sped past, the wheels making a *clunk-clunk-clunk* sound as it flew over bumps in the road. Nausea hitting her like a tidal wave, she began vomiting and felt her body convulse as she knelt onto the black pavement. Soft grass was a few feet away but she wanted to stay close to her SUV, hidden from view. In between heaves, she could still hear the voice rising from the floorboard, a distant crackle, worried and concerned, "Dr. Harper? Are you still there? Are you OK?"

The world was spinning. The warm, rough pavement scraped her knees and hands, but she barely took notice. Passersby called out, yelling, "Get up lady!" and "She's drunk!" Horns honked, headlights flashed in the early hours of the evening, when the sun had already completed its slow descent and a dim pink-gray light still covered the earth. But to Cecilia, the world was dark. The sun had shone for the last time and each and every object she saw was obscured with a thin, black veil, a quiet, grim agony that was hers and hers alone.

For three days, she had stayed in bed and tortured herself with memories from her failed marriage. There had been good times. They had once been happy. It wasn't that she would have taken him back, but she longed for the better days. The days before his mother died. He had always loved to drink, but never to excess. And he did have a nasty temper, but she never would have guessed in a thousand years he would turn violent. She thought that if she could go back in time she could somehow save their marriage and save him.

Then she had forced herself to get up and face the world, telling herself that Rick had already done the damage that night. He had killed himself. He had already taken enough pills to overdose. She was able to lie to herself and get through the day but the truth was always there, right beneath the surface, taunting her. *I'm probably going to hell*, she thought. *But, what can I do? Spend my life in prison for something I may not have even done? I'm a coward, God forgive me. But I just can't lose everything I've worked for.*

# THREE

**Thursday March 20, 2014**

Cecilia stood in line at Brewed Awakenings in a daze. Trying to wake up, she took a deep breath, inhaling the earthy, sweet smell of fresh coffee that filled the air. She glanced at the locals, mostly dressed in business casual, and some wearing their winter gear: thin wool scarves, knitted hats, and boots, even though the temperature had now reached fifty degrees. It was a stark contrast to Cecilia's tailored black blazer and four-inch Louboutin pumps.

She wasn't a fan of this little town. Sure, it was beautiful here, and the beach was ten minutes away, but it was a little more relaxed than she cared for. She missed the fast pace and the impersonal, cosmopolitan feel of New York. As soon as she saved enough money, she was going to move back, start over, and put the past behind her—maybe buy a house just outside the city. The sooner she could get out of here, the better.

She stifled a yawn. Having had no sleep for the past two nights was really taking its toll. But the worst part was the reason. Fidgeting with the straps of her leather bag, she saw in her mind's eye the pale evil face she kept seeing outside her door.

She tried to stay patient as the elderly woman in front of her struggled to place her order. The barista was offering the woman too many choices: Pike Place, French Roast, Blonde Roast. The woman just wanted a damn cup of coffee. Cecilia decided to use this time to piece together a logical solution to her problem. For what felt like the first time in her life, she wasn't sure how to handle a situation. Rick had always criticized her for being a control freak.

*Rick*. Just thinking his name gave her a strange surreal feeling, as if she were floating, drifting through a life that wasn't hers. Lately she felt as though she were playing a part in a movie and any minute now the director would yell, "Cut!" Some mornings she awoke and for a split second, she thought she was lying in bed at her old house and expected to see Rick next to her. Then her eyes would open to see her small pale blue bedroom, the curtains the wrong color, the door on the wrong side of the room, and she would be caught in a flurry of momentary panic until she came back to reality. Then when she thought about how she ended up alone in a small house in downtown Spring Lake, the panic returned.

She shook her head to snap out of it and forced herself to focus on the problem at hand. If her monstrous visitor returned tonight, she would call the police. Hopefully, he would stick around long enough to be caught. When her coffee was ready, she took it and turned around, only to bump squarely into the man behind her.

She mumbled a "sorry" and tried to quickly step aside, but when she met his eyes, she couldn't look away. His eyes were brown and penetrating, like large, omnipresent orbs holding the answers to life's mysteries. It was jarring. The sharp fingers of sunlight reached into the window shining directly onto his face, lightening his eyes a shade, giving them a bronze glow. It was like nothing she had ever seen before. To say that he stood out among everyone else in the store would be a drastic understatement. He looked like he had been dropped onto Earth from another planet.

He was striking. His porcelain skin was a sharp contrast to his jet-black hair. She stared unabashedly, taking in his tall, lean frame. She guessed him to be in his mid-thirties, although it was hard to tell. He had that ruggedly handsome look that made it possible for him to be older, but Cecilia didn't see a single wrinkle on his face. His pouty bow-shaped lips suggested an ancient sadness, like a man who knew too much, but his eyes sparkled with an expression of quiet bewilderment, as if he were constantly amused by human behavior. He also looked vaguely familiar, but she could not think of where she had seen him. When she had bumped into him, she had gotten a whiff of his scent, sweet and woodsy, as if he had just been sitting next to a fireplace. She felt instantly attracted to him and felt her face flush slightly when he held out his hand and smiled, his eyes like glowing embers. He somehow managed to appear both wicked and shy at the same time.

"No, pardon *me*. I'm Aiden."

She accepted his handshake and mentally scolded herself for her reaction to him. It was not like her to blush like a schoolgirl when in the presence of an attractive man. She was a grown woman—a respected doctor—for God's sake. His rosy lips quirked up into a barely noticeable smirk as she looked him over. His black long-sleeved Henley shirt was just tight enough to show off his toned chest and shoulders, and his faded black jeans fit him like a glove. His square-toed black cowboy boots were worn and scuffed around the edges.

"Cecilia," she said as she shook his hand and smiled.

"Cecilia," he repeated. "What a lovely name." He spoke quietly, and Cecilia detected a slight rasp in his voice. His tone and soft words suggested an intimacy that made her feel shy. It was unnerving. "Thank you."

One corner of his mouth turned up in a half smile that seemed almost mischievous. She managed a warm smile in return and said, "You don't look like you're from around here, Aiden." Judging from the color of his skin, he hadn't seen the sun in years.

His quick smile was that of a naughty boy who had been caught stealing but was fully confident he could charm his way out of trouble. "Beautiful *and* observant." Slight pause. "You could say I'm fairly new to the area."

"I see. Well, welcome." *He has dimples when he smiles. Jesus, help me. I've got to get out of here,* she thought.

"Why, thank you." His eyes burned into hers, almost expectantly.

At a loss for words, Cecilia said, "Well, I'd better get to work. It was nice meeting you, Aiden."

Disappointment flashed across his face. "Likewise, Cecilia. Maybe we'll bump into each other again," he said, smirking.

Smiling, she gave a quick nod and rushed out the door. What was it about him that had her so flustered? No one had ever thrown her off this way before. She barely escaped a fall on her way out the door as she tripped over the rug. *Perfect,* she thought. She felt the rising swell of embarrassment start in her chest, work its way up to her throat as it tightened, then up to her face as it reddened with heat. Grateful her back was to him, she pushed her way quickly through the double doors.

Sitting in her car, Cecilia felt faint. The strangest thing was that he looked vaguely familiar, but she couldn't place where she had seen him. *Those eyes,* she mused. She had never seen that color before: dark, golden brown with a hint of shimmering bronze. *It's as if I've seen him before, but only in my mind...* She froze. Suddenly remembering her dream from last night, she jerked her head up to see him watching her. He was sitting by the window, sipping his coffee, a book in hand. His expression was slightly amused, but there was something dark just beneath the surface.

Regardless of how attractive he was and how polite he had been to her, she could not help but feel darkness—an air of danger surrounding him that warned her to stay far away. There was also this tiny thought in the far recesses of her mind that she had seen him before, but not just in her dreams. She brushed it off, forced herself back to the present, and drove away.

Elaine Ewertz

# FOUR

The waiter set two more margaritas on the table. "Here you are, ladies." El Rico's was slammed for a weeknight. All the overworked, stressed imbibers piled in right around 5:30 p.m. for their after-work drink. It was the best option in Spring Lake if you wanted decent food and drinks. It wasn't New York, but it would have to do.

"Thanks, handsome," Amber said, smiling, looking at the young blond waiter from under her lashes. "Cheers!"

"Jesus, Amber!" Cecilia laughed and shook her head. "He's young enough to be your son!"

"So? Did you see how he blushed? So adorable." She watched him as he walked back to the kitchen. "Hey, as long as they're legal…"

"Cougar."

"You know it," Amber said as she smiled and tossed a blonde curl over her shoulder.

Cecilia had met Amber at Columbia, where they both completed their undergraduate degrees. Both were accepted to the same medical school and shared all of life's ups and downs, including Cecilia's recent divorce. Unlike Cecilia, Amber had always wanted to live in Florida, so when Cecilia and Rick announced their move, Amber decided to move too. The woman could be impulsive.

Amber was gorgeous, a tall, leggy blonde with turquoise eyes. She always turned heads when she walked into a room. She seemed oblivious, but Cecilia knew better. How could you not notice people staring at you everywhere you went? Men smiled at her, and women gave her dirty looks. Amber seemed to enjoy both. Cecilia got plenty of looks as well, but somehow not as many dirty looks from women. She thought it was because she was a brunette—not as threatening as being a blonde.

"So how is work going?" Amber winked at her cougar cub as he walked by again.

Cecilia smoothed her hair and smiled. "Crazy. Hectic. Couldn't ask for anything more. It's exactly what I need."

Cecilia had wanted to be a doctor since she was fifteen. That was the year her grandfather died of glioblastoma, which was a very aggressive type of brain tumor that usually had a grim prognosis. Cecilia and Gramps had been close, spending summers together fishing at the lake near his house. She had a relationship with him that she didn't have with any other member of her family. She could talk to him about anything, and he never judged her, never criticized her the way her parents had. In fact after his death, when Cecilia told her parents of her dream of becoming a neurosurgeon, they told her to choose a more realistic goal.

She had worked her way through school, paying her tuition as she went, graduating with honors and her pick of medical schools. Now she spent her free time conducting research and publishing papers in well-known medical journals. Never satisfied, she dreamed of one day finding a drug that could slow the growth of brain tumors or inventing a more effective surgical procedure.

"That's good, hon. Keeping busy is the best thing for you now. After what happened you just need to be distracted for a while. It will get easier."

"I hope so." She took a deep breath, pushed her shoulders back. "It will. Last year when things started to go downhill with Rick, I prayed for patience." She paused, noticing Amber's expression. "I know, I don't usually pray, but I did and my mind is so muddled with thoughts and worries that I can't tell if I got what I asked for. I know I got many more challenging *opportunities* to be patient. I guess that's how it works."

Pausing again, she let out a small laugh. "I'm afraid to pray for strength."

Amber smiled, tilting her head to the side. "I get that. But, you are very strong. You have no idea. And you know I've always got your back, CeCe."

Cecilia smiled and looked down at her glass, taking a sip.

"I mean it," Amber continued. "No matter what. Although if you killed someone. . . " She gazed at the ceiling, her eyes narrowed, then looked back at Cecilia. "Yep, I'd still have your back then. He probably deserved it." She laughed.

The clinking of glasses and plates from the kitchen suddenly seemed louder. A waiter appeared from around the corner and zoomed by with a tray piled high with food. The cacophony of sound intertwined with the heavy scents of Mexican spices, cheese, beer and the sweetness of Cecilia's margarita. She closed her eyes.

"Hey! You OK?" Amber looked worried.

"Yeah, I'm fine. This drink just hit me hard I guess!" She forced a laugh. "It has been a while since I've had any alcohol."

Amber laughed. "We really must build up your tolerance. It was much more impressive in college."

"Right." Cecilia laughed again. "Well, I'll work on that."

"I'll help." Amber tossed back the rest of her drink. "You ready to go? Or do you want to stay and—"

"No, definitely not. I should go," Cecilia said.

"Yeah, yeah. We do have to work in the morning like responsible adults," Amber said before motioning to the waiter for the check.

∞

Cecilia climbed out of the cab and tried to infuse as much grace and dignity into her walk to the front door as possible. It had been a long time since she had been drunk, and her tolerance for alcohol was practically nonexistent.

Looking into her bathroom mirror as she hastily washed the makeup from her face, she noticed her normally bright blue eyes were dull and red-rimmed, and her skin was paler than usual.

As she got ready for bed, she thought about the past year and how her life had changed dramatically in just a few short months. She had joined Spring Lake Medical Group when she and her then-husband, Rick, had moved to Florida the previous summer. Having just completed her residency at Columbia University Medical Center, she had hated the thought of leaving New York, but Rick was offered a grant to earn his MBA at the University of Central Florida. He had wanted to go into marketing and thought a graduate degree would help land him a job. She had reluctantly agreed to move with the understanding that they would eventually move back.

She missed New York ever since the day they had made the two-and-a-half-hour flight. Spring Lake was a small, sleepy beach town on the east coast of Florida, and Cecilia had not been impressed from the moment they had arrived. Stepping off the plane, she had instantly hated it. It was the air, so hot and humid. And people moved at a turtle's pace here. She grew impatient with the slow drivers and the fact that no one seemed to be in a hurry to get anywhere.

But she had decided to give it a chance for the sake of her marriage. Rick was going to earn his degree and their lives were going to get better. The two had met during their junior year and fell in love almost instantly under the harsh fluorescent lights of the Columbia University library. Spending countless nights talking more than studying, they stole kisses in the far corner by the dusty copy machine, long after everyone had left. Her family didn't approve of Rick and had urged their only daughter to hold out for someone better. Cecilia desperately wanted to prove her parents wrong. But her hope turned to sinking disappointment when he dropped out after one semester. It was just one of many things they fought over in the final year of their marriage.

*"My heart's just not in it, CeCe. I don't know what you want me to do!" Rick threw his hands up.*

*"What do I want you to do? You're unbelievable. We changed our whole lives— uprooted and moved down here so that you could get your degree! You know I didn't want to move here."*

*She was leaning on the kitchen counter, her arms crossed over her chest.*

*"Well, the world doesn't revolve around you, Cecilia! Did you ever stop to think that maybe I wanted to move here? New York City is no place to raise a family."*

*Cecilia laughed. "Oh, now we're having a family, are we? How are we going to afford that? The plan was to move here temporarily, so you could get your degree, which might I mention, is free, thanks to a grant. I can't believe this." She shook her head.*

*Rick slammed his drink down, causing liquid to splash onto the table. "You're so fucking smart, aren't you? Got it all figured out. You're so much better than I am. You are a doctor, after all, and you make three times what I make. It's funny how you seem to forget who supported you during med school!"*

*"You've got to be kidding me! I took out massive student loans and borrowed money from my parents too. And I don't think I'm better than you. I just want you to follow through on this. You quit your job to go to this program. Now you drop out? What now?"*

*"Don't worry about it! I'll figure it out."*

Elaine Ewertz

*"Will you? You need help, Rick. You've been drinking more and more lately. It's getting out of control."*

*"My mother died. Give me a fucking break!"*

*"Three years ago," Cecilia said quietly.*

*Rick's eyes widened, and he moved as if to stand. "What? What did you just say?"*

*"I know what happened, honey. It was horrible. It is incredibly sad, and I'm so sorry, but you need help. This is not what she would have wanted for you—"*

*Rick stood, knocking over the chair. "How dare you! You condescending bitch!" He lunged toward her.*

*She took a step back. "Don't hit me, Rick." She tried to walk away, but he grabbed her arm and threw her onto the floor. She landed with a thud, clutching her elbow as he stood over her.*

*"Get up!"*

*When she didn't move, he laughed, grabbed his drink from the table, and drained the glass.*

*"Oh, don't be so fucking dramatic." He walked over, held out his hand impatiently. "Come on, stop this. You're acting crazy."*

*"Get away from me," she said quietly.*

*He shrugged and walked away. "Suit yourself."*

At the divorce proceedings a few months ago, Cecilia had watched speechless as Rick had put on quite the show, charming everyone at the courthouse, flashing his sparkling white smile, running his hands through his wavy brown hair. Before her court date, Amber had desperately urged her to tell her attorney about the abuse. But Cecilia knew that it would only open Pandora's Box, and it would be her word against his. Everyone in town thought he was the perfect husband. She thought it best to just cut her losses and move on.

But when he and Cecilia sat in front of the judge with their attorneys, Cecilia froze when his attorney claimed Rick had supported her while she had gone to medical school. She had tried to argue, but neither she nor her attorney had been prepared for that. They had no defense, no way of proving

30

otherwise. Rick showed steady employment for those four years while Cecilia could show none, except for money given to her by her parents. She was ordered to pay alimony for up to three years to give Rick time to earn his degree. The economy still hadn't fully recovered since the Great Recession of 2008, despite what the "experts" on television said. Marketing jobs were few and far between but Rick had the ability to be successful. He was smart, creative, and great with people. The problem was that he had lost all motivation once a bottle of Jack Daniels became more important than anything else.

In the strange way that life can sometimes change at the drop of a hat, she found herself no longer needing to worry about paying alimony. Although, if she had it her way, she would happily pay it for the rest of her life if it meant Rick would still be alive. If anyone found out what really happened last fall, Cecilia's life as she knew it would be over. There wasn't a chance in hell that the police—or anyone else, for that matter—would believe her side of the story.

Falling into bed, her body felt heavy. Closing her eyes, she brought the covers up around her shoulders but after a few minutes, she felt hot and pushed them off. Her hands felt clammy and suddenly her chest was tight. She forced herself to take several deep breaths to prevent another panic attack. It didn't help. Kicking the covers completely off, she reached over to the nightstand, switched on the light and pulled a bottle from the drawer. Staring at the bottle, she knew what the pills inside would do. They would make her go to sleep. But the thought of taking one made her feel sick. *I deserve to feel this way. I let him die*, she thought.

The red numbers on her nightstand read 1:34. The alarm was going to go off in five hours. She wrenched the cap off the bottle and dry-swallowed a tiny white pill. *Now think about something else, anything else, until this kicks in*, she ordered herself. His face popped into her mind. Dark eyes, pale skin, wild black hair. It was the man she had bumped into at Brewed

Awakenings. *Aiden.* She thought of their short conversation and the way he made her feel uncomfortable with his closeness, the way he spoke to her as if he knew her.

Then he was right in front of her and she knew she was dreaming. Under her skin, she felt cool silk sheets and a few inches away, Aiden lay on his side, his head propped on his hand. His deep brown eyes studied her. She looked down at his hand resting on her thigh then around the room. The walls were a rich cream color, the silk sheets a deep crimson. Eerie and gothic paintings adorned the walls, and just above the mantle hung a large tiger's head.

Then her eyes met his again, he half-smiled and traced his hand lightly over the outline of her body as she lie naked on her side, facing him. The fireplace crackled near the foot of the bed, casting a soft orange light onto their pale flesh.

"I love this," he said, tracing the curve where her waist met her hip. "So beautiful and soft. Amazing."

She shivered as his fingers left goosebumps in their wake. Needing more, she leaned into him, kissing his neck until he roughly pulled her close, leaving no space between them. He kissed her passionately, his hand entwined in her hair, pulling gently, sending a tingle down her spine. After a few moments of sheer bliss, Cecilia was confused when he pulled away, his expression turning pensive.

"It feels as though you're holding something back from me, as if you're hiding something…"

"No," Cecilia said, trying not to sound desperate. "I'm not hiding anything, Aiden. Please…"

Aiden narrowed his eyes then gave a half smile as his fingers slowly—painfully slowly —traced her inner thighs, working their way up, up… Cecilia moaned.

Bang! Bang! Bang!

Cecilia slowly awoke, frowning as she realized her dream was over.

Bang! Bang! Bang!

*Damn it, not again!* In her drunken stupor she had almost forgotten about her nightly visitor. She sat upright in bed, frozen in terror for a moment. She knew what she would see when she looked through the peephole.

But she saw nothing.

After almost falling down the stairs in the dark, she had looked through the peephole half a dozen times. There was no one there. As she made her way to the living room window, she heard it again. And again, as she peered out the window once more. Except the last knock hadn't come from the front door. It sounded like it was behind her. She leaned onto the entryway table for support and took several deep breaths in succession, looking around the room, hoping to find an answer somewhere in the shadows.

Walking to the back door, she began to dial 911. She heard movement behind her and stopped in her tracks. It sounded like it was coming from the hall closet. She backed away and dialed the number, her hands shaking. Tiny red letters appeared at the top of her phone: No service. The doors were locked, and there was no sign of a break-in. She ran to the front door and looked through the peephole.

Nothing.

Going into the living room again, she pushed aside the window curtain. It provided a clear view of the porch. If there were someone out there, she would definitely see him.

But the porch was empty. The wilting flowers hanging in a pot from the ceiling were perfectly still, as was the palm tree next to her driveway. It was almost too still—lifeless—making her feel silly for being so frightened. The eerie silence of her house magnified the beating of her heart, which she could now hear in her ears. She stayed where she was, listening for a sound. Looking down at her T-shirt, she saw the fabric moving slightly over her heart.

Taking a deep breath, she checked her phone again. Still no service. She decided to go knock on Ben's door and ask to use his phone. It was probably nothing, but it was better to be safe than sorry. There was just a small problem. The front door wouldn't open.

Confused, she locked and unlocked it several times. It was stuck and wouldn't budge. She cursed and heard a sound behind her. It sounded like the hall closet again, but she decided to harness the power of denial and check the back door. There was no one on the back porch either.

Standing motionless for a moment, she stared at the closet door. The white paint was chipping along the sides, and on the doorknob hung a sign that read, "Neurosurgeons do it better." The hanging sign appeared to move slightly, but it was a stationary movement, a *maybe-I-just-imagined-it* movement, much like watching ceiling fan blades slowly come to a stop. They could still be moving infinitesimally, but it is impossible to tell. *Maybe my mind is playing tricks on me,* she thought, and sincerely hoped this was the case. But then she could swear she heard movement inside the closet, so her little dance of denial began waltzing toward the edge of a cliff.

*Oh, this is ridiculous*, she thought. *There is no one in the closet. Just open it up, and you will see.* Turning the knob, she pulled the closet door open and saw nothing. Just as she was about to turn on the light, she saw the hanging coats move slightly, and then everything went black.

# FIVE

"Cecilia." She heard her name spoken quietly by a male voice. "Open your eyes, love."

It was a voice she had heard before, but in her daze, she could not remember where. Her head throbbed and she was afraid to open her eyes. A dark, smoky scent wafted through the air, like a forest fire burning a few miles away. Mixed in with the smoldering fire was a subtle sweet scent, like a fifty-dollar vanilla candle.

"Open your eyes." The voice said again but with more authority.

She hesitated, frozen with fear. Feeling her hands bound behind her, she tried to move, writhing in the chair. She opened her eyes, expecting to be face to face with the evil visage that she had seen outside her house for the past two nights. She started to scream, but stopped, her struggle with the rope coming to a halt when she saw his face. Leaning back casually in the chair across from her, his espresso eyes sparkling in the faint light from the kitchen, a trace of a smile played on his lips.

"Aiden?" She stared in disbelief. "What—"

"You remembered my name." He smiled. "Hello, Cecilia."

He looked so relaxed, so comfortable in his own body, one ankle crossed over the knee of the other leg, his hands clasped over his waist. He was wearing a black V-neck T-shirt with a black leather motorcycle jacket that looked expensive but slightly worn, black jeans, black leather boots and a black fedora. The only thing he wore that wasn't black was a dark brown leather tribal necklace with a strange symbol made of turquoise and red stones. After taking all this in, Cecilia looked back up into intense eyes to find him watching her steadily.

Seeing that she was still speechless, Aiden went on. "Don't be afraid. I just want to talk."

"So, you broke in, knocked me out and tied me up?" Her words came out in a rush.

He laughed quietly. "Not the usual way to go about having a conversation with a beautiful woman, I know. I'm sorry, I'm a little unconventional."

"Get the fuck out of my house!" She tried to sound commanding, but failed, her words coming out in a squeak instead. She thrashed in the restraints and opened her mouth to scream when Aiden appeared in a flash, standing above her. His presence was so dominating that she couldn't find her voice.

"That's better. Now, I'm sorry I had to do it this way but I needed a captive audience. I know you're scared—"

His quiet, condescending tone helped her find her voice again.

"Leave me alone! Get out now, you fucking asshole!" She forced herself to yell louder, hoping a neighbor would hear her screams.

He kneeled down so they were at eye level. "Where's that sweet girl I met at the coffee shop?"

She flinched away. "I know you're scared," he said, his voice dropped to a whisper. "But, this is not going to help you. Do not yell at me or disrespect me. And I will do the same for you. I'm not here to hurt you. In fact, by the time we're through, I think you will be quite happy with the way things turned out."

"I seriously doubt it," she said under her breath.

Anger flickered in Aiden's eyes for a moment, and then he surprised her by laughing. "And this is what I love about you. Even frightened out of your mind, you still manage to make a sarcastic remark."

"What do you want?" she asked.

"Why, do you have somewhere to be?" When she didn't answer, he went on. "Are we going to be calm now?"

"What do you want?"

"You see, that really doesn't matter. All of this hinges on what *you* want, darling Cecilia." He slowly walked back around the table and sat down.

"Well, I'd love for you to leave."

"No, try again," he said, his face placid.

"Why are you here?"

He ignored her question. "I look a little different on this side of the door, don't I?"

"Who are you?"

"We'll get to that. I thought this," he said as his strong, yet graceful hands made a sweeping gesture from his face to his legs. "Would make it easier for us to talk. You like?" He raised an eyebrow.

When Cecilia simply turned her head away, he said, "Don't answer that. I already know."

"Oh my God—"

"No, not him, but close." Aiden interrupted.

"You are one sick son of a—"

"Seriously?" he interrupted again. "Knowing what I am and what I am capable of, you have the nerve to speak to me that way?" He shook his head. "You are delightful, Cecilia."

"Actually, I don't know what you are and I don't care what you are capable of."

He paused, raising his eyebrows. "I think you have an idea of what I am but you don't understand it. We'll have plenty of time to sort that out. And as for what I'm capable of, you will care very soon."

"This is not possible. I'm just having a nightmare," Cecilia said, almost to herself.

"Hmm. Speaking of which, did you enjoy your dream tonight before you were so rudely awakened?" His eyes sparkled, a flicker of gold in the dim light from the kitchen. "Tequila seems to agree with you."

She felt her face flush with anger and embarrassment. She turned her head away, on the verge of tears.

"You look just like someone I knew a long time ago. Although, you're much more beautiful than she was. I wonder, though. . . " He appeared to think for a moment. "Does your head hurt? I can make that go away. All you have to do is ask nicely."

"Fuck you."

"So soon? Why, Cecilia, how very forward of you."

She turned her head facing the wall, stubbornly avoiding eye contact. When she looked into his eyes, it was as if she could feel him reading her thoughts, hearing her innermost secrets.

Aiden sighed. "So stubborn. You have a headache, I can feel it. And it's going to distract you from what we need to talk about. You're going to want a clear head for this." Aiden waited, watching her expectantly.

"Of course my head hurts!" It actually hurt terribly and she couldn't think straight. He was right about one thing: she needed to think clearly, but so that she could figure out how to get out of this.

"Please make it go away," she said as sweetly as she could manage.

"Good girl. Now, look at me."

She met his eyes and in a split second, the pain was gone. She couldn't believe it. What was he?

"Now, let's get to why I'm here. Although I think you must have an idea."

"I really don't."

"Don't lie, Cecilia," he said in a warning tone. "You're up to your neck in lies lately, aren't you? Lying to those you love and care about. How long can you keep this up? Surely, it must get old."

"I don't know what you're talking about. This is ridiculous. Please just leave me alone. I have to get up in a few hours."

"For what? Work? That's really important to you, isn't it? In fact, I would venture to guess that it is the most important thing in your life. Being a doctor, saving lives." He paused for a beat. "Kind of ironic, though, don't you think? I mean, considering..." He let the word hang in the air.

"Considering what? I don't see any irony here, only a creep who has been harassing me in a Halloween mask for the past two nights and has now broken into my house." She regretted saying it, but she knew he was probably going to kill her anyway so what did it matter?

"A creep? That's what you think of me? I'm hurt," he said, feigning a sad face. "You know, your haughty little attitude would normally piss me off, but you're so damned cute when you're trying to act tough. And please stop thinking I'm going to kill you because I'm not. The last thing I want is to hurt you."

"So you can read my mind?"

"A Halloween mask," Aiden said under his breath, shaking his head slightly, his eyes wandering around the room, then meeting hers again. "Not exactly. I can sense how you're feeling. Let's just say I'm highly intuitive."

"You're *intuitive*?"

"I'm a Cancer." He smirked.

"How did you cure my headache?"

"Oh that's simple. I'll explain later if you really want to know. Let's get to the point, shall we? Let's talk about your little secret."

"I don't have a secret."

He made a tsk-tsk sound. "Where's your husband?"

"I don't have one. We are divorced."

"Ok. Where is your ex-husband?"

"How should I know?"

He grinned. "Oh, Cecilia. You underestimate me. I can make you tell me but that would defeat the purpose. I need you to be honest with me. I can keep a secret. No one has to know. So let's try that again: Where is he? Rick, I believe was his name."

"How the hell should I know and what do you care?"

He shrugged. "Ok, if that's how you want it." He slid his chair around the table so that he was directly facing her.

"What are you doing?"

"Close your eyes."

She ignored him and stared.

"Close your eyes, Cecilia." Something in his tone made her reconsider. She snapped her eyes shut.

Her mind was suddenly full of images not unlike her dream from just an hour ago. Aiden was on top of her in bed, kissing her, moving slowly down her body, leaving a trail of kisses down her stomach. He slowly slid his hand between her legs, parting them slightly, touching her most intimate area. In spite of herself, she was starting to feel aroused and angrily shouted, "*Stop!*" When he didn't stop, she begged, "Aiden, please…stop," She was panting, looking at him pleadingly. Her eyes filled with tears and she looked away in shame.

# Six

A few moments passed in silence as he sat in front of her. Cecilia had never felt so confused in her life. She hated him now, and the memory of being so attracted to him—in the coffee shop, in her dreams—infuriated her. *Look around*, she told herself. *He broke in and tied you to a chair. Don't think for a moment he's not going to kill you.*

"I told you I wouldn't hurt you, Cecilia. But I have other ways of making you cooperate."

"By raping me?"

"I didn't touch you."

She shook her head. "You know damn well what you did."

"I only took scenes from your own dream, your own mind. I just continued where you left off. There's no shame in pleasure, sweetheart. I can give you pleasure like you never imagined."

When she shook her head and looked away, he continued. "Not just in *that* way...in every way possible. I can make you very happy."

"Really? Because this isn't doing it for me." Cecilia jerked her head around, motioning to the rope and the chair.

"This is only temporary. I just need to know that I can trust you. We have something very important to discuss. Something that, depending on your answer, will change the rest of your life. It can either be very good or very bad. The best part? It's totally up to you."

Cecilia glared. "This is insane. How do you know about my ex? This has to be some kind of a trick."

"No tricks. But, I can and will change your life, one way or the other. I see that you still don't believe me, so let me produce some evidence. I want you to trust me, too, of course."

Cecilia's heart accelerated and her eyes widened before she could hide her reaction. In Aiden's hand was a prescription pill bottle, which he shook.

"Oh, look, there are still a few left. Surprising. Prescribed to Rick Harper, 1223 Magnolia Lane, alprazolam, half milligram."

"Where did you get that?"

"Does it matter? This is the drug that was found in Rick's system during the autopsy."

"I know. He overdosed."

"Wrong. Try again."

"What? He overdosed. He had a problem. It started with anxiety and I recommended he see a doctor, a friend of mine that I went to school with. He prescribed him Xanax just to help him sleep at night. But, Rick lost his job, dropped out of school, and just…completely changed. He wasn't the man I married. He started drinking and taking more of those pills."

"Nice story, now the truth, please."

Cecilia jerked in her restraints, stomping her foot on the tile floor. "That is the truth! What do you care? Why are you here?"

"Cecilia, the truth," he said.

She looked through the doorway into the kitchen. Her butcher knife was on the counter in the wooden stand. Her pepper spray was in the drawer under the microwave.

"Is there something you need from the kitchen?" Aiden asked. "Some water, perhaps?"

She shot him a dirty look.

"You're going to have a nasty hangover in the morning." He stood from his chair. "Let me get you some water."

He disappeared around the corner and she could hear the clinking of glass then the refrigerator door open. "I think I'll have a glass myself if that's OK," he called out.

Looking down at her hands, she saw they were shaking. *Such a thoughtful murderer. He's going to hydrate me first,* she thought. She scanned the room for her phone, thinking it was probably on the floor next to the closet door.

He walked back in, sat down his glass, then stepped around the table and leaned on the edge of the table in front of her. "Here," he said, holding the glass to her lips. "Drink. You'll thank me in the morning."

Leaning forward, she took a sip then pulled away.

"No, no, you need more than that. Come on, one more."

She took a big gulp and he seemed satisfied, setting the glass on the table. "Let me know if you want more," he said and he sat back down in his chair. "Now. You were going to tell me the truth about what happened?"

"Fine. I didn't tell any of our friends, no one. No one knew what was really going on. He had them all fooled. I was so loyal to him, trying to help him. But he treated me like shit and even started hitting me and knocking me around when he would drink. Still, I protected him. I didn't tell anyone. I thought he would eventually come around and get better. I took his pills from him, threw away all the alcohol in the house. But nothing changed. I tried for so long to help him. I tried taking him to a treatment center, but he refused. In fact, when he found out where I was going to take him, he beat the crap out of me. He blamed it all on me, telling me I wasn't a good wife, I didn't support him, I was too focused on my career. Of course, if it wasn't for my career, we wouldn't have been able to pay the bills or even eat. One night, he beat me so bad I blacked out. That's when I filed for divorce. I couldn't take it anymore! What the hell was I supposed to do? Then he has the nerve to ask for alimony! As if I needed to *pay* him after I'd already supported him for so long!" She felt her entire body shaking as the tears began to flow down her cheeks. "As usual, he was drinking and taking Xanax. He took too much one night." She paused and took a breath. "Why do you care about any of this?"

Aiden ignored her question and leaned in closer. "I believe you. But, you're still leaving out a big part of the story. He didn't overdose himself. You did."

"Really? And what makes you think that?"

"Do you know who did the autopsy?"

She shook her head. "I never saw the report. I didn't want to see it. I already knew what happened."

"Of course you did. But, if you had seen the report, you would have seen the name of the medical examiner."

"So?"

Aiden gave her a half smile and slowly pointed to himself. Cecilia only stared.

"Well, where are my manners? I didn't formally introduce myself. I'm Dr. Aiden Black, Chief Medical Examiner for District Three." He held out a hand and then pulled it back, shrugging his shoulders.

"You're telling me you did the autopsy?"

"Yes, ma'am," he said, pulling out a piece of paper from his coat pocket and slid it across the table.

After quickly scanning the report, Cecilia looked up at Aiden. "So, you're the medical examiner. Great. It still doesn't explain anything."

"Allow me. When I did the exam, something told me it wasn't an accidental overdose or even a suicide. Then I started to question who would have a motive to kill him. I did some searching, starting following you." He paused, noticing her glare. "I'm sorry, but I had to. Something wasn't right. Having the power to get into peoples' heads doesn't make me a mind reader. I had to figure it out. Then when I found out you were ordered to pay him alimony, well there was your motive."

"Why didn't you just report his death as suspicious? They would have come for me by now. You could have saved yourself a lot of trouble."

"Where's the fun in that? I like a good mystery. Plus, I'm intrigued by you. I wanted to meet you for myself."

Cecilia lowered her head. "I can't take this anymore. What do you want?"

"I want you to tell me the rest of the story. I found roughly fifteen milligrams worth of Xanax in Rick's system, which would be a nearly fatal dose on its own, but mixed with alcohol, well you know the rest of the story. But he didn't take all those pills himself that night. Tell me, did he have some help?"

Several moments passed before Cecilia spoke. "A few days after the divorce proceedings, I stopped by the house to get the last of my belongings. He was drunk—no surprise—but he was so out of it that I was able to get my things and leave."

Aiden raised his eyebrows. "That's it? That's all that happened?"

"Yes. Why?"

"I just find it surprising that knowing his history of alcoholism and violence, it was that easy for you to retrieve your belongings and get out without so much as a scrape. You two didn't even fight?"

Aiden was watching her so intently, it was making her nervous. "We argued, but like I told you, he was drunk. More than usual. He was almost incoherent and could barely move, let alone stand up and attack me."

Cecilia jumped when Aiden shoved his chair back from the table and stood. He began walking into the kitchen, raking his hand through his hair. Then she heard him sigh loudly as he turned back around. "You're lying to me and I find that incredibly insulting. I know you were there that night. I know Rick was drunk already when you arrived. What you are not telling me is how he went from drunk to dead." He walked back to Cecilia and leaned in, resting his hands on the tabletop, his face a few inches from hers.

Cecilia straightened in her chair and leaned forward. *Don't show fear*, she thought. "You weren't there, how could you possibly know what happened?"

At this, he grinned but didn't move. After a moment, he said, "You're leaving out a rather important part of the story and I will give you one more chance to tell me the truth."

"I told you the truth."

"My patience is wearing thin, Cecilia. What did you do?"

"Nothing!"

He leaned yet even closer until his eyes were so close to hers that she thought their eyelashes might touch. Her vision disappeared and she saw only blackness. Then she felt as if she were transported into her old house. Glancing around, she saw her old kitchen with a few dirty dishes in the sink. She walked into her living room and gasped. Rick was lying on the couch, choking, vomiting, his body convulsing. He was having a seizure. Turning away, she covered her mouth with her hands and began to sob.

When she re-opened her eyes, she was back in her apartment, tied to her dining room chair, Aiden sitting across from her, watching her, his face calm.

She sobbed, her shoulders shaking. "I. . .I only wanted to calm him down so I could get out of there without getting hurt! I tried so hard! I loved him so much! I don't know why…" She stopped, out of breath, leaning over. "I'm so sorry. . .so. . .sorry. . ."

Aiden was silent for a moment. "So you're telling me it had nothing to do with the money?"

Cecilia began sobbing again. "If I could go back, I would have happily paid alimony forever! I don't care about the money! I didn't mean to kill him! I—oh God."

Aiden was quiet, his gaze steady and patient on Cecilia for a few minutes. She looked up at him, met his gaze and then dropped her eyes in shame.

"That's all I wanted," he said gently. "You just opened up to me and told the truth. Now we are getting somewhere."

"How did you know? And how did you. . .put me back in my old house?"

"I was watching you. And I took your mind back to your old house on the night that he. . ." He trailed off and cocked his head to the side sympathetically.

*God, he is so manipulative*, she thought.

"Yeah, but you're still not going to leave me alone, are you?" she asked, her body slumped over in the chair, the rope pulled taut. "What are you going to—"

"Shhh. . . " Aiden leaned closer to Cecilia and wiped a tear from her cheek. "I told you, I'm not going to hurt you. And I'm not going to turn you in. You have nothing to be afraid of. I'm going to give you everything you've ever wanted."

"What? Why?"

"I've been watching you a long time, Cecilia. I've wanted you from the moment I laid eyes on you."

She leaned back in the chair. "So what you want in return is...me?"

"Why is that so difficult to believe?"

"Oh my God, you're insane. I don't know you. I don't trust you. Either you're playing tricks on me or you're not even human, but that's crazy."

"I completely understand. But you will learn to trust me. I can be very patient. I want to earn your trust. I know we've gotten off to a rough start, but I will show you nothing but kindness. I will be very good to you. I only ask that you hear me out."

"You call this a rough start?"

Aiden cocked his head to the side but said nothing.

Cecilia looked around the room, weighing her options. "Ok. I'm listening. Not that I have a choice," she said, frowning.

"On the contrary, love, I am giving you the choice of a lifetime."

"I said I'm listening."

"What do you dream of, dear Cecilia?"

When she only narrowed her eyes and didn't answer, he sighed. "I can see you like to play this game. Keep me guessing. Well, luckily, I already know the answer. I'd just prefer to hear it from you." He paused. "No? Ok. You are great at what you do. You are an amazing doctor. Compassionate, intelligent, full of empathy for patients in your care. But, you are only human. You want recognition, fame, power. You want more than to just show up every day and go through the routine. You do research in your free time, you've published a few papers in well-respected medical journals, but it's not enough for you. And why should it be? You are smarter than that. You could do so much more. But how? What if someone were to help you out with that? Make it just a little easier? Now, before you argue with me, remember, no one makes it big without some help. Well, that's what I'm offering you. A little shove in the right direction."

"I want to succeed for more than just the recognition. I have other reasons, too."

"I'm sure you do. I can still help you."

"And how can you do that?" Cecilia asked.

"Well, I have power that most people don't have. The way that I made your headache go away? That's child's play. I could do so much more."

"Because you're not human."

"Not entirely."

"It could have been a coincidence that my headache went away."

He laughed. "Seriously? Now, you're doubting me. I didn't want to do anything to scare you because it's very important that you trust me, but if you insist on seeing more…"

"I do."

He spread his hands in front of him. "Ok then."

Suddenly the room was alive with sound. Cecilia recognized the song as being from her favorite band, The Redheads. Thunderous guitars assaulted her ears, the singer's voice so clear, the rhythm so distinct. It sounded exactly the way it would in a small theater. But it was as if she had never truly heard the song fully until now. For a moment, she forgot where she was, forgot she was tied to a chair in her dining room, sitting across from a monster who may or may not kill her.

*When did it get so hard, girl*
*Did I really have it that easy before*
*I thought it was rough then*
*Trade one of those days now I will*
*Let's build a house made of steel*
*Paint it red and say how do you feel*
*I'll never leave, never see the light of day*
*Would you have it any other way*

She looked around frantically. "What…how…"

"Look at your stereo." Aiden watched her carefully.

The stereo's screen was black. It wasn't on.

"Where is that coming from?"

"It's difficult to explain where it's coming from. Just enjoy it." He paused for a moment, listening. "I happen to really like that band. You have excellent taste, Cecilia." He leaned back, smiling, as he adjusted his hat.

"I don't understand. I don't understand how you are doing this."

"You don't need to."

"I need to understand *something*."

"What?"

"Anything!" Cecilia said. "I don't understand any of this!"

"You really like being in control, don't you? As soon as you hear me out, you can be in control again. Well, to a certain extent, of course," he said, flashing a devilish smile.

"Ok, let me get this straight. You are offering to help me become successful?"

"Yes and more."

"I already am successful."

He paused. "Yes you are, but you want more. Don't pretend that you don't."

"Of course I want more, but I don't need your help."

"Maybe not. But, if you refuse, I can amend my report and take the evidence in and well, you know what will happen after that." He shrugged.

"You don't have any evidence other than a pill bottle."

"It has your fingerprints on it," he said.

"So? I lived there. Anything in that house could have my fingerprints on it."

"That's true, but I may have other evidence, you will never know, will you?" He paused. "I have nothing but time, Cecilia. Do you know what the statute of limitations is on homicide in this state?"

Cecilia narrowed her eyes. "There isn't one."

"That's right." Aiden nodded. "In 1996, Florida eliminated the statute of limitations in homicide cases. And as a bonus, in 2010, the governor signed a bill into law which eliminates the statute of limitations for civil cases for wrongful death by homicide. So, as I said, I have nothing but time."

Cecilia searched the room, trying to think of a way out. Her eyes rested on the flowers at the center of the table, the whitewashed antique china cabinet behind Aiden, then the window across the room. There was no way out. Not tied to a chair. Not with a man twice her size watching her every move. *Just go along with it, agree with him. Maybe he'll leave,* she thought.

"And all you want from me is to be yours?"

"Yes, I want you to be with me, live your life with me as my wife."

*Oh dear God. I can't even pretend.* "Well, that's not going to happen. I don't know who you are or how you manage these mind tricks but you need to leave."

Aiden leaned forward. "I know this has to be overwhelming for you. Which is why I'm going to give you some time to think about it. You should know all the facts before you agree. I will give you anything and everything you want. I can help move things along in your career, help propel you to achievements you've only dreamed of."

Cecilia rolled her eyes. "I don't want your help."

"The beautiful doctor doesn't believe me." Aiden leaned back in his chair and smiled. "You're very ambitious. You want worldwide recognition for your work. I can help you with that. Do you want to travel the world? I can give you everything you've ever dreamed of. All I want in return is your love. Just give me you. Give me a child. That's all I want. That scary face outside the door? You will never see him again. The only face you'll ever see on me is what is right in front of you now." He paused. "Do you think you could live with that?"

"I think you're insane." She jerked around in a futile attempt to free her arms. "You know nothing about me. Untie me now!"

"Not just yet." He raked a hand through his hair. "I understand. I will give you time. I can be patient but don't keep me waiting too long. I will be back soon and I will expect your answer. You need to rest now, Cecilia, love. Think about my offer. Think about what your life could be like."

He stood quickly and with a flick of his wrists, released her from her restraints. She sat frozen for a moment. "Don't try anything, either, love. I will know. Don't try to tell anyone. They will just laugh. And don't try to run away. I will find you."

He winked and kissed her on the cheek. "Until I see you again." He disappeared down the hall in a flash and Cecilia heard the front door close a fraction of a second later.

She stood slowly and went to peek out the window to make sure he was really gone. Then she spotted her phone lying on the entryway table. Taking it, she went and sat on the couch. She couldn't move. She sat for ten minutes, trying to convince herself to call the police. After all, a man had been hiding in her closet, waiting for her to come home. He had knocked her out and tied her up, interrogated her. He hadn't hurt her though. She scanned her body and saw no bruises or cuts, felt no pain. *How did he knock me out?* She felt her head. There was no tenderness, no knot that would indicate he hit her on the head. More importantly, what would she tell the police? That a man claiming to be the county medical examiner broke into her home? That he made her confess to aiding in the murder of her ex-husband?

And what if he really was the medical examiner? It was a gamble. And the strangest thing of all? She believed Aiden was telling the truth. Either way, he had the upper hand. She plugged the phone into the charger. *I need to call the police*, she thought. Eyeing the phone on the hallway table, she suddenly felt her eyelids going heavy. It was as if she had been drugged. *That asshole*, she thought as she felt herself beginning to slump. She dragged herself to the couch and gave up the fight to keep her eyes open. *Need to call. . .*she thought as she faded out.

# SEVEN

Sitting across from Amber at El Rico's the following night, Cecilia contemplated telling her the whole story. She hadn't told anyone yet, not even about the knocks at the door in the middle of the night. She hadn't called the police yet either. *I need to figure out what he is,* she thought. *If he really has evidence, I go to prison.*

And as open-minded as Amber was, she was still likely to think her best friend was crazy. Cecilia decided it was best to keep it to herself for now, at least until she made a decision. Amber was talking but Cecilia had missed the last few words, deep in her reverie.

"So, is that OK?" Amber asked.

"What?"

Amber laughed. "Earth to Cecilia! I invited a new co-worker to join us tonight. Is that OK?"

"Oh, of course! Sorry, I just—"

"There she is now!" Amber stood from the table and motioned the woman over. She was beautiful in an understated kind of way, with rich brown hair and doe brown eyes. She looked like she just stepped off the set of *Mad Men*, wearing a flowery vintage dress and faded brown ankle boots, her hair curled to perfection, framing the sides of her face. The two hugged and Amber made the introductions. Dr. Katherine Porter had just joined Amber's dermatology office and was in her third year of residency.

Two glasses of Cabernet later, the topic of conversation turned to dating. Cecilia tried to focus on the conversation and not on the dilemma she now faced. She wanted to forget about it for a while, pretend that her life was normal, if only for one night. She could think about Aiden and his deal later.

Katherine had been single for two years (which Amber made clear she thought was far too long) and the two were in deep discussion.

"...I've been hurt before, like everyone else. But by some miracle, I am still hopeful. I can still be open, vulnerable. I can let someone in. Because the way I see it, what's the point otherwise? To be genuine and authentic, well, that's all there is. It's all that matters. So many people are cynical. They've been hurt and they act like they are the only ones who have had their heart broken. They go out and date but they put up a wall. They are closed off and refuse to let anyone in. They go through all the motions, but why? You can't find love with a wall up, even if you are going out, smiling, laughing, playing the part. Sometimes I try to put a wall up, but I can't. When I meet someone I like, I end up letting my guard down and showing my cards and then he loses interest. What is wrong with this world that I have to play games in order to be in a relationship? It's so sad. Maybe I'm a naïve hopeless romantic, but take it or leave it, that's me. I won't apologize for being real, for being honest. And any man that doesn't see what a gift that is, having a woman who is honest, trustworthy and open." She paused, pushing a stray dark curl from her face. "He's not worth it. He doesn't get it. If he wants the games and the drama, let him have it. There are plenty of women out there who can provide that."

"I think you're taking it too seriously, sweetie," Amber interjected.

"I don't. Don't get me wrong, I don't think I'm this great prize—"

"I think you're putting the pussy on a pedestal," Amber said.

Cecilia laughed and shook her head. "Amber, come on."

Amber threw up her hands. "What?"

Katherine's cheeks flushed scarlet. "Ok, well maybe I am. But I don't think I'm better than anyone else. For all I know, I could be wrong and that would explain why I don't have a boyfriend."

Amber cleared her throat loudly.

"Amber stop! Behave! The woman is pouring her soul out to us," Cecilia said.

Amber put her hands in the air as a sign of surrender.

Katherine continued. "I just can't help feeling like, I don't know, if I stay true to myself and what I believe, maybe one day it'll be worth it. Maybe one day someone will come along who gets it. I want it to be meaningful. I don't want to just settle in order to avoid being alone." She sighed and took a sip of her wine.

"I think she's got it right," said Cecilia.

"OK, OK, I just think you need to lighten up, Kat! We all want the fairy tale happy ending, but in the meantime, have fun. That's the way I see it." Amber shrugged and downed the rest of her wine in one gulp. "I mean, look. This is why I date younger men."

"This is why she's a cougar," Cecilia said to Katherine.

"Yes, I'm a cougar. And do you know why? It's fun, yes, but the younger ones are still moldable and sweet. And if they do lie, they are not very good at it. They have not had a lot of practice. Whereas the older ones, oh let me tell you," she said, pausing to hold her empty wine glass up to the waiter. "Anyone else need a refill?"

As the waiter filled their glasses, Amber continued. "The guy I dated a few months back? Fifty years old, handsome in his own way I guess, but wow was he a walking midlife crisis! All he needed was a yellow Corvette and he'd be set! Know what I mean?" She tossed her head back and laughed. "He was so insecure and needy. Needed constant praise and reassurance. It was exhausting! He wanted to monopolize every minute of my day. I'm surprised he let me go to the bathroom alone. I'm serious! He was like a man-boy, an incubus, preying on women like some middle aged balding devil. In fact, I'm pretty sure he did me while I slept. He didn't sleep! I think he was constantly high on cocaine and Viagra or something! Jesus!" She shook her head, her blonde curls bouncing on her shoulders.

Katherine and Cecilia burst into uproarious laughter, drawing the attention of the other customers in the restaurant.

"And the thing looked like a soft-boiled egg covered in flesh-colored Band-Aids."

"Ew!" Katherine covered her mouth, looking mortified.

"Oh, dear God," Cecilia said.

"I'd wake up in the middle of the night to feel the bed shaking. He would be jerking himself off, but it was the strangest thing. He would do it for a few seconds and then pause like he needed a break. It was like," she said, making an obscene hand motion. "Jerk, jerk, jerk…pause…jerk, jerk, jerk…ughhh." She shivered.

"Maybe his wrist was getting tired. You should have helped him out," Cecilia said.

Amber threw her a look and Cecilia put her hands up in surrender. "Hey, just a suggestion. You could have finished him off then you could have gone to sleep."

"Yeah, but that's the thing! He would have been at it thirty minutes later anyway! He'd be spooning me, then I'd feel him poking at me again, just sneaking it in there, like 'Here it is baby'," she said in a singsong voice. "Listen, I love sex as much as the next girl, but damn, I need to sleep at some point! He needs someone who isn't human."

"He needs a blow-up doll," Katherine suggested.

"Yes!" Amber pointed at Katherine. "Exactly. I should have just put an Inflatable Sally next to him and gone and slept on the couch."

Cecilia and Katherine burst into laughter as Ryan appeared at the table, smiling. "Ladies? Anything else?"

"I don't know, what time do you get off?" Amber batted her lashes.

Cecilia watched as his face turned a deep red and he stammered. "Well, I—"

"Amber! Stop it!" Katherine nudged her then looked at Ryan. "I'm sorry. We're leaving now."

Ryan seemed to have recovered and smiled at Amber. "OK, I'll get the check."

"You're bad," Cecilia said to Amber, then took a deep breath, stretching. "This was just what I needed, girls." Cecilia smiled warmly at Amber and then at Katherine. "And it was so nice to meet you Katherine. I hope we can do this again soon."

"Oh wow it is closing time, isn't it?" Amber checked her watch. "Time flies! Yes, let's do this again soon. Tomorrow night?"

Cecilia rolled her eyes but laughed. "We'll see."

Elaine Ewertz

.

# EIGHT

The next morning, Cecilia awoke to the sound of dogs barking. It was probably Maggie and her friends having their weekly "doggie play date" as they called it. She groaned and rolled over to check the time. It was 8 a.m. Her body felt like lead as she dragged herself out of bed and peeked through the window curtains. Maggie and two other women were perched in patio chairs in her front lawn holding coffee mugs. Maggie's little white dog (Cecilia had no idea what breed it was; she just knew it was small, white and fluffy and had an annoying high-pitched bark) was running and playing with two other dogs about the same size. Every few seconds, one of the women would toss a toy in the air and the dogs were lunge and jump for it at once. Cecilia had never understood why people loved dogs so much. They always had a weird smell, like sweat and dirt.

Normally, Cecilia would have a list of tasks to accomplish on Saturday, her entire day planned. But today she felt lost and had no idea what to do.

She decided to go for a run, thinking it would help clear her head. She was getting tired of the jumbled thoughts that had been racing through her mind for days, thoughts of Aiden and his offer. He knew her secret. She had to do *something*. She couldn't sweep it under the rug and pretend it didn't exist. He was going to come back eventually and she needed to be prepared.

It was a warm clear day and she rolled the windows down as she made the fifteen minute drive to the beach. She was not a beach person, but because it was only sixty degrees, Cecilia guessed the beach would be mostly empty and she wanted to be alone.

As she ran, she stared at the water, the foamy waves crashing against the sand just a few feet away. Past the breaker, the sea was glassy and sparkled like millions of tiny diamonds. A flock of about five or six seagulls glided along the surface of the water, so close that it seemed they were touching it, but they remained perfectly parallel to the surface. After a while, they slowly flew up into the endless sky, traveling farther away until they looked like tiny black dots against a blue canvas.

Cecilia was struck by the beautiful simplicity of it. She wondered how it must feel to be able to fly away from a place if you decide you're no longer happy there. To have nothing tying you to the Earth. No mistakes, no shame, no guilt, no complicated situations. Just total freedom.

She breathed in the cool salty air, listening to the waves crash against the shore. A few people who must have been tourists were out, wearing T-shirts and jeans, kicking off their shoes to dip their toes in the water. It must have been cold because the woman screamed as a small wave lapped up to her ankles and she ran on tiptoes onto the dry sand.

Jogging further down the shoreline, she saw a pretty young mom and a black-haired little boy. The little boy was giggling, running into the lip of water where it would creep up the sand every few seconds with the tide, then retreat back, leaving tiny sparkling pink and beige shells in its wake.

Cecilia smiled as she slowed to a walk. *He's adorable*, Cecilia thought. He was wearing a green Ninja Turtles sweatshirt and black jeans. His mop of curly black hair bounced as he pulled on his mother's hand, saying, "Mommy! Can we go swimming? Pweeeease? Pweeeease?" His big brown eyes looked up at her in anticipation.

His mother shook her head. "It's too cold, honey. You'll get sick."

"But *Mom*! Just for a few minutes! Pweeeease? Just for two minutes." He held up two fingers to his mother's face and stared at her with wide, pleading eyes.

She began to kneel down and talk to him but he took off into the water.

"Aiden!" his mother yelled after him.

Cecilia's heart sped up. *Aiden?*

The boy's mother began chasing him into the water, but he didn't stop. He was beginning to get to the breaker, where it would be easy for him to be sucked into the undertow.

"Aiden! Stop right now!"

His mother was frantic now, looking around. "Help! Someone help!"

Cecilia was already running over to the water. The mother's eyes darted from her son back to Cecilia several times.

"He just ran in!" The young mother was on the verge of tears. She couldn't have been over twenty-two years old.

"We'll get him," Cecilia assured her and raced into the freezing water after him.

At that moment, the little boy fell down into the water. Cecilia dove and grabbed him in one motion and carried him back to shore, which thankfully was only a few feet.

She laid him on the sand and saw that he wasn't breathing. She leaned over him, getting ready to start CPR, when he began choking up water. He recovered quickly and looked up into Cecilia's eyes and smiled. Cecilia jumped. His eyes were exactly the same color as Aiden's. But it was more like they *were* Aiden's eyes. And the knowing smile he gave her appeared to be from someone much older than five or six years old.

"Oh God, thank you! Thank you!" The woman picked up her son and hugged him tight. "I'm so glad you're ok, sweetheart. Don't ever do that again, ok? Promise?"

"Yes, Mommy, I promise."

The woman looked back at Cecilia. "I don't know how to thank you. You saved his life."

"No need, anyone would have done the same. I'm just glad he's ok."

Cecilia walked back through the sand to the boardwalk, still shaken over the boy and his eerie resemblance to Aiden. *His eyes were the same...and that smile. . .* She shook her head. *Aiden is becoming a popular name these days*, she told herself. She turned to look back but the boy and his mother were gone. She stopped, puzzled, searching up and down the beach. They were nowhere to be seen. It was as if they had disappeared into the ocean.

Making her way back up to the boardwalk, she almost tripped over a large conch shell. She bent down and picked it up, turning it around in her hands. It was beautiful and fully intact, unlike all the fragments of shells strewn across the sand. Spiraling up to the top were several horns in perfect symmetry. The flared lip opened up to a smooth pale pink interior and she held the opening to her ear.

When she was eight years old, her parents had taken her on a trip to the Keys and bought her a conch shell from a gift shop on the beach. Her mother had told her to hold it to her ear and she would hear the sound of the ocean trapped inside the shell. She had carried the shell with her for weeks after returning home to New York, believing that she was hearing the ocean each time she pressed the shell to her ear. She had been fascinated with the idea that memories of sound could be kept inside a shell for eternity. When she had started third grade that fall, she had looked it up in a science book in the library, determined to find out if it was really the sound of the sea in the shell. She had been sad when she discovered that it was really just ambient noise from around her producing that sound and that she could hear the same sound when holding a plastic cup to her ear.

Glancing one last time up and down the shoreline and still wondering where the young mother and boy had gone, she decided to close her eyes and pretend that it really was the sound of the ocean coming from the shell. Standing still with her eyes closed, she felt the warmth of the sun and the gentle breeze and felt herself relax as she listened. Then her body jolted as she felt something begin to crawl into her ear. She dropped the shell and batted at her ear and the side of her face. She heard a slight buzzing then saw to her right something black flying away. Feeling a chill go down her spine, she shivered and ran up to the wooden steps.

After going home to change clothes, she decided to go to Brewed Awakenings to treat herself after her workout and the stressful way it had ended. Sitting with her coffee, scanning the day's newspaper, her mind kept drifting back to the mother and son on the beach. Where had they gone? It didn't make sense. And what was that *thing*—

She jumped when she realized she wasn't alone at her table.

"Hello, Cecilia." Aiden was sitting across from her, relaxed as usual, wearing a dark green Henley shirt with the top few buttons undone, dark worn-in jeans, and his signature black boots. She noticed he was still wearing the strange tribal necklace.

"What a surprise," Cecilia said, her voice unsteady.

"Is it? I told you I'd be back soon. You look amazing," he said, looking her up and down. "Just finish a workout?"

"I bet you already know the answer to that," she said.

He laughed, lightly and carefree. "I do. You're glistening. It's beautiful. How was the beach?"

"How do you know I was at the beach?"

"You smell like saltwater and sunshine," he said as he leaned in closer. "So have you thought about our discussion?"

"I have, but I don't know how you expect me to give you an answer to this. I don't know you and your blackmail isn't going to work. Just turn me in if you think you have enough evidence."

He leaned back, raising his eyebrows. "Calling my bluff, I see. I knew I liked you. You're right. You don't know me. Because if you did, you would know that I will turn you in. I have enough evidence to ensure that you will spend the rest of your life in prison." He paused, looking her over. "Well, the pretty ones don't seem to ever get the maximum sentence, so you might be looking at twenty years, maybe less for good behavior."

Cecilia rolled her eyes. His smug arrogance was getting really annoying.

"Actually, you might get off completely. Remember the young mother in Orlando who killed her little girl? Well, we know she did it but she walked. And you killed your abusive ex-husband. The jury might have sympathy for you. Or they may say you're a doctor and you should have known better." He shrugged. "It's a gamble."

She shrugged back. "So turn me in."

He smiled. "You have balls, Cecilia. I have to hand it to you. You either think I won't do it or you're willing to risk being locked up for a long time." He paused. "But, I don't want to see that happen. Like I told you before, I want to earn your trust. And I do understand your reluctance. Why don't we get to know each other a little more?" He held out his hand, waiting for hers.

"No, thank you."

Aiden sighed. "Let me take you to dinner. Let's just talk. Give me an hour, that's all I ask. You can ask me anything you like. If you still don't accept my offer, then I'll do as you ask and leave you alone."

"But you'll still take the evidence to the police. You'll open an investigation if I don't accept your. . . offer."

His eyes widened. "Well, yes, Cecilia," he said, as if he were addressing a small child.

*Fuck. He's serious.* She hesitated then took a deep breath. "What the hell. Fine. Dinner it is."

∞

After deciding on a simple blue dress and black boots, she curled her hair but then brushed it out. "This is not a date," she told her reflection in the mirror. She tried to think of it more as a business meeting and this was really just a formality anyway. She was no doubt going to prison if he made good on his threat, and there was no way she was going to agree to his crazy deal. *But I have a lot of questions*, she thought. *He's going to tell me once and for all exactly who or what he is.*

Elaine Ewertz

# Nine

When Aiden knocked on her door at precisely 7:30 p.m., she opened it to find him looking even more dapper than before. He was wearing the same body-hugging faded black jeans he had been wearing when they first bumped into each other at Brewed Awakenings, the jeans that had helped to inspire her dreams that night. Under his dark gray fitted wool coat, he wore a black button down shirt. And of course, he was wearing those black leather boots. He stood on her porch with a beautiful bouquet of flowers in his hand. *Stop thinking about how attractive he is,* she told herself. *You know nothing about him except the fact that he's capable of breaking and entering and blackmail.*

"Hello, beautiful. Are you ready for me?" His voice was a low growl and the way he said this sounded vaguely suggestive, but his eyes gave nothing away.

"This is not a date."

His eyes twinkled. "Of course, Dr. Harper, how silly of me. What is this, then?"

"It's a business meeting."

"I should have been able to tell by the dress." He raised an eyebrow.

"Sarcasm. Original."

"A snarky woman. Original."

She narrowed her eyes and stared at him.

He laughed, shoving the bouquet at her. "Take the damn flowers."

She snatched them and went to the kitchen to put them in water. She caught herself smiling as she filled the vase. *Stop grinning like an idiot*, she told herself. *He's trying to trick you. Manipulative bastard.*

"Thank you for the flowers," she said as she met him at the front door.

"You're welcome," he said. "Do you like French cuisine?"

"Love it." She locked her door and began to descend her porch steps.

He held out his hand and she hesitated, staring at it.

"Oh, come on. I won't bite."

His hand was so warm. Almost hot. She felt instant electricity and a not-unpleasant tingle go down her spine. He led her to his cherry-red car, a type she had never seen before. It looked like it was the from the 1950s and had a heart-shaped grill between two round headlights.

"Wow," Cecilia said. "What is this?"

"It's an Alfa Romeo Cabriolet. Do you like it?"

"It's beautiful."

"I don't take it out much, just on special occasions." He opened the passenger door. "Hop in."

They rode in silence most of the way listening to music. Cecilia studied the car's radio. It looked old, with large white numbers on the dial and round silver knobs on either side but it looked like there was a CD player too.

"Is this the original stereo?"

Aiden smiled. "Looks original, doesn't it? No, I found this great company that makes custom car stereos that fit and blend into vintage cars. Here." He handed her his iPod, which was connected by an auxiliary cord to the stereo. "Be the deejay."

As she scrolled through his music collection, her jaw almost dropped at the sheer number of songs he owned. She recognized many of them but there were several she had not heard of.

Picking a random playlist, she settled back into her seat and enjoyed the eclectic mix of music. He had everything from Mozart to Robert Johnson. She was glad for the music to focus on because she didn't want to talk for fear that she wouldn't be able to resist barraging him with questions. She would save that for later after she'd had some wine and gained some liquid courage. Glancing over, she took in his profile, wondering if he had any idea of how nervous he made her. She was trying desperately to cover it up but she had a feeling he knew exactly what kind of effect he had on her.

*And I'm going on a da*—to dinner – *with a man trying to blackmail me*, she thought. *Nothing wrong with this picture at all!* She almost laughed at the sheer absurdity of it.

Aiden gave her a strange look. "Something funny?"

"No, not at all," she said, as she glanced at him, biting her lip.

"Hmmm…being coy again, are we?" He stopped just short of a smile so she wasn't quite sure if he was amused or angry.

She shrugged. "Just thinking to myself."

"Hmm," he murmured.

Chez Francois was exquisite. Simple, yet elegant artwork adorned the walls and soft classical piano filled the air. The black grand piano was wedged in the corner of the room, next to a large window. A man with small silver glasses perched on his nose and gray hair sat behind the piano, smiling to himself as he played Beethoven's Fur Elise. The streetlamps shone into the window, casting light onto the reflective surface of the piano and onto the glasses perched on the man's face, creating a glare and making his eyes look like two glowing white orbs.

Aiden suggested the baked brie appetizer and a bottle of white wine to start. He was quiet, studying the menu.

*OK, time to start the inquisition*, Cecilia thought. But, she reconsidered as she glanced across the table at Aiden. Why was he so intimidating? She decided to have a glass of wine first.

The brie was magnificent and after a glass of the most amazing sauvignon blanc Cecilia had ever tasted, she was feeling bold. "So, Aiden, what do I have to do to get you to give me some real answers?"

"Ah Cecilia, you shouldn't ask questions like that," he said.

Cecilia rolled her eyes. "Seriously, Aiden. You said I could ask you anything."

He waved his hand. "Ask away."

"You said you weren't human. What are you?"

Aiden raised an eyebrow. "Ah, straight to the point. Well what do you think I am?"

"Are you a vampire?"

He made a face. "That is so pedestrian, Cecilia. Tell me you have a better imagination than that." He glanced to his right. "Hold that thought. The server is coming."

The young blonde placed their entrees in front of them, seared scallops for Cecilia and sea bass for Aiden. Her ponytail bounced as she looked back and forth to Aiden and Cecilia, asking if they needed anything else. Her eyes lingered on Aiden after he answered. Finally, she left and the two were quiet as they tasted their food.

"Mmm." Aiden closed his eyes a moment. "This is amazing. How is yours?"

"It's wonderful," she said, taking another bite.
"Good, I'm glad you like it. Ok, let's continue. Where were we?" He squinted, as if deep in thought. "Oh, yes. You were asking if I was a vampire. I am most definitely not. But if I

were, being the medical examiner would be quite interesting. Any other ideas?"

"Are you a demon?"

"Do you think you'd be alive right now if I were?"

"I don't know! You could be dragging this out for your own amusement."

He paused to consider. "True. But I assure you I'm not a demon. But you clearly think I am something evil."

"It might have something to do with the face I saw through the peephole or the fact that you snuck into my home and knocked me out, tied me up—"

"Alright, enough! You've made your point. And I didn't knock you out but we can talk about that later—"

Cecilia jumped forward in her chair. "Yes you did!"

"Calm down, you're going to cause a scene. I will explain that later. I never hurt you. Never would."

"You're such a liar!"

"Cecilia," Aiden said in a warning tone.

"*Aiden,*" Cecilia said mockingly in return. She snatched her purse and got up from the table.

"Where are you going?" Aiden asked, leaning over, catching her hand in his.

"Bathroom," Cecilia snapped and wrenched her hand out of his grip.

Alone in the bathroom, Cecilia needed to think. *What am I going to do? Run? He will find me. He will never leave me alone! At best, he will turn me in and I'll spend the rest of my life in prison!* Taking a few deep breaths, Cecilia desperately searched for an answer. *Ok, just keep calm,* she told herself. *Find out what he is and then go from there. Try to ignore the fact that he is a cocky son of a bitch who may be truly evil.*

Returning to the table, she noticed Aiden looked concerned. "Are you OK?" he asked.

"Considering the circumstances, sure, I'm great."

As the server refilled their wineglasses, Cecilia noticed the woman was staring admiringly at Aiden, trying to catch his eye. *You can have him*, she thought. *Good luck*.

When the server walked away, Aiden leaned in and took Cecilia's hand. "I understand this entire situation is stressful for you. Please don't walk away. I know that you just want to know what exactly I am and then you will decide whether it's bad enough that you would rather spend life in prison than with me."

"Aren't they the same?"

Aiden looked wounded. "That's how you think of this? That life with me would be prison?"

Cecilia was taken aback by his sad expression. Either he truly had feelings or was a very good manipulator. "At this point, yes. How can I be sure you will follow through on your promise?"

Aiden leaned back in his chair and shrugged. "I guess you can't be. But all I'm asking is that you give me a chance. Let me explain where I came from and what I am. Then you can make your decision."

"Ok, fine. I'm listening."

"Let's clear this up first. I didn't knock you out. Not physically, anyway."

"Let me guess. You used your special powers," she said, taking a bite of scallop.

Aiden leaned in, narrowing his eyes. Cecilia noticed they seemed to turn a deeper shade of brown, but it could have been the dim lighting. "You still doubt me. Tell me then, what is your explanation for what you've seen?"

"I can't. But there has to be a logical explanation. I just don't know what it is yet."

"Come on, you're a neurosurgeon. Use science to explain the things I've done. How did I cure your headache? How did I make you black out? How did I get your favorite band to play in your house without the stereo?"

"God, Aiden, I don't know. But I'll figure it out."

"Good luck with that."

The two were silent for a moment, staring each other down. Finally, Cecilia lost the battle. "Ok, then, tell me what you are. I'll try to keep an open mind."

"Do you know anything about Celtic mythology?" he asked.

"Like Celtic gods and goddesses? Woodland fairies and men with swords on white horses?"

Aiden laughed. "Well there were fairies and men with white horses. Today their descendants still walk the earth."

"So, you're telling me you're a fairy?" Cecilia tried but failed to keep a straight face.

Aiden rolled his eyes. "No, Cecilia, I'm not a fairy. My family line dates back to Celtic gods around the third century."

"So, you're descended from a Celtic god."

"Yes, I am."

Cecilia raised her eyebrows.

"Is that so hard to believe? I mean, you had quite the reaction to me upon our first meeting." He cocked his head to the side, as if recalling a fond memory.

"You are so full of yourself!"

"Oh, Cecilia, I'm only kidding with you."

"No, you're not."

He shrugged and gave her a devilish smile.

She smiled back in spite of herself, then noticed his necklace again. "Your necklace. I've never seen anything like it. What is that design?"

"It's a Celtic knot, but probably looks different to you because this was the original design from the second century. I've had it since I was a child." He ran his long, graceful fingers over the deep garnet knot centered over a flat turquoise stone. "My father passed it down to me when I turned nine. That's when a child of a Celtic god begins to fully develop his abilities. In other words, that's the age when I inherited his unique gifts and they started to make themselves known. I've had to replace the leather cord several times over the years, but the stone never fades."

"Who were your parents?"

"My father is a god and my mother was human."

Cecilia stared for a moment. "You're a demi-god? Seriously?" She looked at her wine glass. "What is in this?"

Aiden frowned. "I'm serious. Look at me."

Cecilia looked into his eyes, now glowing in the flickering candlelight.

"You asked me what I am. I tell you and you make a joke out of it?"

"It's just hard to believe. I didn't think those stories of ancient mythology were real."

"Well, some are, some aren't. But you shouldn't have any trouble believing me. I've shown you enough, haven't I? Or do you need more?"

"No, that won't be necessary. I've seen what you are capable of."

He laughed now, soft and low. "On the contrary, you haven't, dear Cecilia."

After a moment, Cecilia asked, "So is that why you have these special…powers? From your father?"

"My father is a very powerful man," Aiden said.

"Where is he?"

Aiden leaned back and cocked his head to one side, his eyes roaming the room. "He could be anywhere." He smiled and met Cecilia's eyes once again. "He travels the world. Of course, he's seen it all a thousand times over, but he never grows bored of it. He writes me letters, refuses to talk on the phone most of the time." He laughed. "He's old-fashioned."

Cecilia forced a smile.

"You have more questions." Aiden waved his hand, motioning her closer. "Out with them. They are eating you alive."

She leaned forward. "How old are you?"

"Well, I'm much older than I look."

She shivered. "Hundreds of years?"

Aiden nodded and pursed his lips in a way that seemed to say 'close enough'.

"Ok. So, your powers. What are they exactly?"

"Well I inherited those from my father. To say my father had many talents would be an understatement. Some of those were supernatural, but not all. He was greatly respected for being a powerful warrior, druid, carpenter, mason and poet. As far as the *powers*, as you call them, he rarely used them and only when he needed to. He could see inside people, feel what they were feeling, easily decide whether they were being truthful, even influence them to feel or think certain things."

Cecilia furrowed her brows. "Oh, really?"

"Yes, and I did inherit that from him, but my abilities aren't quite as strong."

"But you have them," Cecilia said.

"I do, but like my father, I do not like to use those gifts unless I absolutely need to for three reasons: one, I think it makes life way too easy and takes the fun out of it for me. I like a challenge. Two, if I want people to trust me, it is best I use them sparingly and three, it would make me stand out too much and that could mean serious trouble for me. I have to be on this planet a very long time and I do not need to be ostracized for being some freak of nature."

Cecilia thought for a moment. It was interesting the order in which he placed those reasons. "What is your father's name?"

"His name is Lugh."

"That sounds familiar. Wait, so if you are the son of an ancient Celtic god, that would make you over a thousand years old! Why are you still alive and they are not? Are you immortal?"

"No, I am cursed."

"Why?"

"I angered someone greatly and in return, she cursed me to live for eternity. It's a very long story, Cecilia and we will

Elaine Ewertz

have plenty of time for stories. There is so much I could tell you right now but we would be here for days."

"She? A woman cursed you?"

Aiden smiled. "Yes. She was a goddess. Her name was Elara."

"Elara. Ok." Cecilia sighed and shook her head. "What I don't understand is. . . well, you're immortal. You will live forever if nothing—or no one—kills you. How have you managed to stay alive for so long? I mean, a car accident, a plane crash. . . "

"I guess I'm very lucky."

"Aiden, please. Stop being so vague. If you want me to trust you, you have to tell me the truth. Because the odds—"

"The odds of me surviving this long are impossible. Is that what you mean to say?"

"Yes! Even with your incredibly heightened sense of. . . .of intuition. . . there are other things you cannot control. When you're face to face with someone, sure, you can manipulate their mind, but what about everything else? How have you stayed out of harm's way all this time? Are you indestructible?"

"In a sense, yes." He paused. "Why? Are you plotting to kill me?"

"No, I just need to know. It doesn't make sense."

"Ok, what if I tell you this? I was living in London in the 1940's and had been out drinking with friends one night. We were walking home when we were approached by a gang of thugs. They tried to rob us and one of them had a gun. We fought them off but I was shot in the chest—twice. It should have killed me. George—my closest friend at the time—knew what I was, knew that I would survive, so he took me home and stayed with me until I was better."

"And how long was that?"

"I recovered completely within two days."

Cecilia narrowed her eyes. "That's impossible," she said.

Shaking his head, Aiden said, "You really are quite the skeptic, aren't you? With everything you've seen, you still don't believe me, do you?"

"I'm just trying to wrap my head around this—"

"The beautiful neuro-scientist needs more proof. Not a problem."

Aiden picked up a steak knife and sliced it through his palm.

"Oh my God! Aiden, you're insane! What are you—" Cecilia looked around the restaurant, but none of the other guests were looking in their direction.

"It's OK, Cecilia. No one saw that." He held out his hand to her.

Now, look. That's real, is it not?" He wiped the blood away with a napkin and Cecilia saw the red gaping wound.

"Yes. I can't believe you just did that!"

"Ok. Now, watch. It should take about two minutes." He rested his hand on the table, keeping it open. She leaned in to study the cut, grabbed a napkin and wiped more blood away.

"That's deep. You'll need stitches—"

"Wait. Now, look." He wiped the remainder of the blood away and Cecilia could not believe her eyes. The wound was no longer open. It was closing, the new pink tissue forming a small white line down the center of his palm.

Cecilia's jaw dropped. "I. . . I can't believe it." But, when she saw Aiden's expression, she corrected herself. "OK! No, I believe it. I believe it. Don't cut your arm off or anything. It's just. . . wow." She stared at Aiden, wide-eyed. "I'm just. . . I'm going to need time to process this."

"Not a problem. I'm just glad you finally believe me. I was afraid of what I was going to have to do to convince you."

"No need for that. . . " she trailed off as she picked up her fork, shaking her head.

When they were finished, the server cleared the table and left the check which Aiden picked up quickly sliding his card inside the small leather folder.

"Thank you, Aiden."

"Anytime, love."

The two sipped their wine in silence for a few minutes and Cecilia noticed Aiden was studying her closely.

"What are you thinking?" Aiden narrowed his eyes.

Cecilia glanced around the restaurant, her eyes lingering on an older couple sitting side by side in a booth by the window. They looked happy and in love, the lines on their faces a roadmap of their life together.

Aiden followed her eyes. "Is that what you want? To grow old with someone?"

Cecilia met his eyes, reluctant to answer. "Yes but. . . I want my career too. It always seems as if I'm asking too much, like I have to choose."

"Why should you have to choose?"

"Men don't want a woman who is ambitious and driven. It scares them."

Aiden raised his eyebrows. "Really? I find that hard to believe. It's a very attractive quality."

"Well believe it or not, it never seems to work. It drives them away."

"It doesn't scare me," he said quietly. "I'm not intimidated by a strong, successful woman. Like I said, it's very attractive. It makes me want to be with her all the more."

"I guess you're different, then." She looked down at her hands and she caught herself twisting her pale pink manicured fingers nervously.

She made herself stop fidgeting as she met Aiden's eyes once more.

"You could say that," he said as he gave her a knowing smile.

Somehow she knew he was quite aware of the effect he had on her. She found it disturbing because she liked to think she was always in control of herself, but with his super-human intuition, nothing escaped his notice. Whether that was good or bad, she hadn't decided yet.

Cecilia gave a little body shake, trying to snap out of it. "Why am I telling you this?" She shook her head. "I'm tired, we should go."

"You're telling me how you feel because somehow you sense you can trust me."

"I don't know about that."

Aiden slowly reached across the table, taking her hand in his. "I think you do."

Cecilia let him hold her hand for a moment then quickly pulled away. "We should go. I'm sorry, but I'm tired and it's been a long day."

"That it has. I'll take you home."

Passing all the newly familiar streets, seeing the little diner where she and Rick had gone when they first moved to Florida, she felt a wave of sadness. It brought back a flood of memories of Rick, and the happy times they shared before everything had gone horribly wrong. She thought of how different her life was now, how lonely she was, despite having friends and a thriving medical practice. She felt a tear escape and quickly wiped it away.

Aiden looked over immediately. "Cecilia. What's wrong?"

"Nothing. Just been a long day and I need some sleep, that's all."

"No, there is something on your mind. I wish you'd tell me what is making you so sad right now."

Cecilia let out a loud sigh. "Nothing, Aiden."

"You're crying. It's not *nothing*."

"I guess I'm just reflecting on everything that has happened over the past few months and now. . . and I feel. . . overwhelmed." Cecilia bit her lip and looked out the window.

"I understand. Anyone would feel overwhelmed in your situation. You've been through a lot. Everything is going to be ok, Cecilia."

"As long as I accept your terms, you mean," she said under her breath, but of course Aiden heard.

She saw him clench his jaw then take a deep breath. He glanced over and his eyes surprised her. Gone was the devilish twinkle and in its place was a deep tenderness and compassion. It took her off guard. She caught herself staring then swallowed and blinked, forcing herself to look back out the window.

The rest of the ride home was quiet. Aiden appeared to be giving her time to process the entire situation: him, the deal he was offering, his superhuman abilities, and the fact that he had just shown her a softer side of him.

When they reached her house, he walked her to her front door and kissed her forehead. "Call me when you're ready," he said before leaving.

# TEN

A month passed and Cecilia did not hear from Aiden once. No phone calls, no unexpected visits. She knew better than to think he was gone for good, but it was clear he was giving her the time she needed. It was only a matter of time before he would be back.

It was the end of April and the weather had gotten hot. Amber had talked Cecilia and Katherine into going downtown for lunch and shopping. Cecilia gazed up at the clear blue sky as the three walked down Main Street. The afternoon sun peeked through the palm trees lining the cobblestone street, the shiny copper of a new penny catching Cecilia's eye as it sparkled in the light.

"See a lucky penny, pick it up!" Amber said.

"What? Oh." Cecilia bent down and picked it up, stared at it.

"You OK, honey? You seem distracted."

Cecilia nodded and smiled. "Oh, no, I'm fine. Just work stuff, I guess."

Amber squeezed her friend's arm. "I know, but it's Saturday. Try to forget about it for a while. You can worry about that stuff on Monday."

"You're right."

"I know I am!" Amber glanced at the store to their left, Island Chic Boutique. "Look at that dress! Let's stop in here," Amber said.

"Really, Amber?" Katherine raised her eyebrows.

"Oh, don't give me that judgy look! It's beautiful. I have to try it on."

Cecilia looked at Katherine. "You think that's skimpy? You should see her closet. I don't know how she does it, but she manages to pull it off."

"I guess. . . " Katherine sighed as the three walked into the store.

∞

"God, he's such a liar!" Amber was ranting about her latest dating disaster. "That's the last time I go out with an attorney. I'm serious! And he's so insistent on his lies. He really should be an actor. When I accused him of lying, he kept saying, 'I'm telling the truth. I'm so focused on the truth, it's all I care about.' Good God. It's the truth according to Ray, which is a twilight zone, seventh circle of hell crock of shit!"

"Why don't you take a break from dating for a while?" Katherine asked, shaking her head.

Cecilia laughed. "As if that would ever happen."

Amber shrugged, thumbing through a rack of summer tops. She looked up to the speaker on the ceiling. "Wow I haven't heard this song in forever. I love it." She started to hum along.

Katherine stared.

Amber sighed. "Oh, the young. It's Paul Simon, dear. We need to broaden your horizons."

Katherine rolled her eyes. "Don't try to change the subject. Seriously, why don't you take a break from men? It doesn't seem to be working out well."

"Are you suggesting I try women?" Amber raised her eyebrows.

"Amber," Cecilia shook her head.

Katherine's skin darkened a shade of pink. "No, just a break from dating. Any human being."

Amber frowned. "That doesn't sound like fun. Besides, you get to live vicariously through me since you never go out with anyone."

"That's not true! I went out with someone last weekend."

"Oh yeah. I forgot. With what's-his-face, Brad? How'd that go?"

"Well, it was like the fifth time we went out. We ended up back at his place and he put me to bed. Told me I must be tired, why don't I go to sleep."

Amber snorted. "What the hell?"

"Yeah, he even tucked me in like I was his daughter."

Amber shivered. "Uggh. How creepy. It's like that movie, what was it, with Nicole Kidman? With the old woman under the veil?"

"Um. . . *The Others*?"

"Yeah." Amber crouched her body down to look like a frail old woman and said in a scratchy voice, "But I aaam your daughter. . . ."

Katherine burst out laughing. "You're insane."

Cecilia was checking out a black and blue sundress when her phone rang. It was Molly, a patient of hers who had recently been diagnosed with a brain tumor. They had performed a surgery but had not been successful in removing all of the tumor. It was an aggressive type and kept growing so quickly that they were running out of time.

She normally didn't give her personal number to patients, but Molly was an exception. She was alone, had no close friends or family around, no support system to help her through this difficult time.

"Hold on a sec, Molly. I need to step outside to hear you better."

Cecilia stepped out into the warm sunshine and was offering words of comfort to Molly when she saw a flash of movement out of the side of her eye. A little girl had wandered from her mother and was standing in the middle of the road, seemingly unaware of the approaching cars. She couldn't have been much older than three. Her dark blonde curls were partially held back by a red and white plaid headband and she wore a red dress with ruffles. She was laughing, doing a little dance, bouncing up and down when a woman on the sidewalk screamed.

"Jessica!"

Suddenly a dark figure appeared and scooped her up and out of the way. Walking closer, Cecilia realized the dark figure had in fact been a man wearing all black and he hadn't made it out of the way of oncoming traffic quickly enough. He was now lying motionless in the street.

*That man just saved that little girl's life and probably sacrificed his own in the process*, Cecilia thought as she ran over to him.

A crowd was forming around the man and she heard someone scream, "*Call 911!*"

She ran into the crowd, shouting to be heard, "*I'm a doctor, please let me through!*"

When the crowd made a path for her, Cecilia froze momentarily when she saw him. That pale face, shrouded by dark hair, was now expressionless and still.

Kneeling down, she pushed his messy hair out of his eyes. "Aiden? Aiden? Can you hear me?"

Slowly, his eyes fluttered open. Bronze orbs of light, luminous in the mid-day sun, met hers.

Gone was the devilish twinkle; in its place was innocent surprise. "Cecilia." He moved to sit up. "Where's the child? Is she OK?"

"She's fine. You saved her. No, don't move. We need to get you to the hospital." Cecilia pushed him back down when he tried to sit up.

Many of the onlookers had begun moving away, already losing interest.

Cecilia heard sirens approaching. "Just stay still. The paramedics are almost here."

"I'm OK. I don't need to go to the hospital." He touched the scrape on his forehead.

"Maybe not. But you're going."

Aiden smiled. "Yes, Doctor."

Sitting in the hospital waiting room, Cecilia called Amber. The girls had been in the dressing room and had no idea what had happened outside.

"We were wondering where the hell you went off to! You scared us, Cecilia!"

"I'm sorry. It all happened so fast. I'm OK. I'm going to stay at the hospital a little while longer to see how he's doing." Cecilia hoped Amber wouldn't ask any more questions about the mystery man and why she was waiting for him at the hospital. She had yet to tell anyone about Aiden. She was beginning to think that wasn't such a good idea. She should tell *someone*, her best friend at least. But she was going to have to leave out a lot of details unless she wanted her friend to think she was crazy and have her committed.

"That's very nice of you. I'm just glad you're OK, CeCe. Call me later, alright?"

"I will," Cecilia promised as she saw a nurse approaching. "Bye, Amber."

The nurse smiled. "Dr. Harper?" When Cecilia nodded, the nurse continued. "Aiden is awake and doing well, remarkably well, in fact. He's been asking for you."

Aiden looked up as she walked in. He was sitting up in the bed, looking better than ever. It was hard to believe he had just been hit by a car. He smiled as she approached his bedside.

"There you are."

"How are you feeling?"

"Never better. I'd love to leave but this one seems to think I need more observation," he said, nodding to a pretty young nurse taking his vitals. She blushed and smiled.

*Wow*, Cecilia thought. *He's worked his magic on her, I see.*

"You were hit by a car an hour ago. They want to make sure you have no internal bleeding, no brain injury."

He touched a small pink line on his cheek. "This is all. Just a scrape. I feel completely fine."

Angela leaned down to him. "That's an old scar. The medics said you had a gash on your cheek," she said, searching his skin for the cut.

"I'm a quick healer," he said then looked up to his right and read the monitor. "120 over 80. Pulse is 65. I'd say I'm good to go. You've taken such great care of me, Angela. I am going to miss you, but I really don't need to be here. You must have other patients who need you more than I do."

"Dr. Rosewater wants to do a CT scan to make sure there is no internal bleeding."

Aiden caught Angela's eyes and stared for a moment. "Do you really think that's necessary?"

Angela smiled down at Aiden. "OK, Dr. Black. Let me just get your discharge approved by Dr. Rosewater."

Cecilia shook her head as Angela left the room.

"What is it, darling?"

She sighed. "You. You used your powers on her, didn't you?"

Aiden's jaw dropped open in mock surprise. "Me? No, I absolutely did not. She just likes me, Cecilia, much like you do, even if you refuse to admit it."

Cecilia began to turn away. "Aiden."

"You stayed. You could have left. You care about me."

"I just wanted to make sure you were OK."

"Right."

A balding short man with wire-rimmed glasses walked in before she could respond. "Dr. Harper?"

"Yes?"

The stout man held out his hand. "I'm Dr. Rosewater. It's a pleasure to meet you! I just read your paper in the *Journal of Neuroscience*. It was brilliant."

"Thank you. I appreciate that," she said, shaking his hand.

Dr. Rosewater turned to Aiden. "And you! How are you, Dr. Black? I hear you were in a little accident today. Saved a little girl's life, in fact. How are you feeling?"

"I'm feeling just fine, actually. All ready to go."

"Well, I really should keep you here a little longer, just to make sure everything is OK. You might feel fine now, but I don't need to tell you that adrenaline could be tricking you. You may have internal injuries."

Aiden shrugged. "You're probably right. But, Jack, let me ask you something."

The doctor looked back at Aiden and suddenly his eyes went blank.

Aiden appeared to be concentrating, staring into the doctor's eyes. A few seconds passed, then Dr. Rosewater appeared to come out of a trance and the blank look disappeared from his eyes.

"You know, on second thought, I think you're fine. Vitals are stable, your color has come back. You're free to go." He glanced at Cecilia. "Just keep an eye on him. Bring him back immediately if anything changes."

"Unbelievable," Cecilia said, rolling her eyes as Dr. Rosewater left the room.

"What?"

"You used your powers on him, too. I thought you said you only used them when absolutely necessary."

"It *is* necessary. I was able to manipulate the machines to give me normal vitals but I don't know if I could manipulate the CT equipment."

"*Normal* vitals? What is normal for you?"

He sat up. "We need to get out of here before they change their minds."

Cecilia didn't move.

He sighed. "My blood pressure and pulse wouldn't read normal to them and I'd never get out of here. My BP, if a machine could even pick it up, would be off the charts, and my pulse, well, it's a little fast. Here, feel." He took her hand and placed it on his carotid artery. She jerked her hand back suddenly. "Jesus! What the—"

"I said it was a little fast." He laughed. "No need for alarm. That's perfectly normal for me, I assure you."

"OK, but—wow!"

"Strange, I know. Which is why I had to rig the machines. Not easy to do, let me tell you. But, there is a limit to how much I can manipulate technology. Which is why we really need to get out of this hospital, Cecilia. Now."

Cecilia stopped for a moment. "So if they took a CT of your brain, what would they find?"

"I don't know, Cecilia. Why are you stalling?" Suddenly, his eyes widened. "Really? You want them to see something strange, don't you? Then they would keep me here and you'd be free of me! Why, Cecilia, I thought we were making progress." He clicked his tongue.

"Do you think I'm stupid? You could just do your little mind tricks on them anyway. Let's go." Cecilia headed for the door, grabbed for the large silver handle.

"But you considered it." Aiden was right behind her.

"Can you blame me?"

"No, I guess I can't." He placed his hand gently on the small of her back to guide her through the long corridors.

# ELEVEN

Lounging on her sofa with the Sunday paper, Cecilia couldn't focus on anything she was reading. She took a sip of her coffee, now cold, and realized she must have been sitting there for a least a half an hour, just staring off into space, thinking. She hadn't slept well the night before. She had been haunted by dreams of Aiden and the scene that kept replaying in her mind: him leaping at superhuman speed into the street, scooping up the little girl, pushing her out of the way into her frantic mother's arms. With his superhuman, god-like speed, why wasn't he able to get out of the way quickly enough? It didn't make sense. But he had saved a child's life. Was he really as evil as she had thought? Or was it just another way for him to manipulate her into trusting him? She was so confused, the millions of thoughts and questions running around her head with no clear answers.

She wanted to believe he wasn't all bad. What choice did she have? He wasn't going anywhere. He knew the truth about what she had done. She could say no, of course, and refuse to take him up on his offer. She felt like she was making a deal with the devil.

*I'm damned if I do, damned if I don't,* she thought. *If I say yes and agree to marry him, spend my life with him, he could end up hurting me anyway. He could use his mind control on me. He could go back on his word and turn me in if he changed his mind. Hell, he could kill me. What was so special about me that he wanted to spend his life with me and not turn me in? What did he care? The other option is to say no and he will most likely turn me in now. He says he has evidence. Maybe it's better to take a chance that he might be telling the truth. Otherwise, I go straight to prison. Better the devil you know than the one you don't. . .*

∞

"You never told me about your mother. What was her name?"

"Casidhe."

"And she was human?"

"Yes. She and my father met when he saved her life. She was in the woods, collecting berries and was trampled buy a horse, or what you could call a horse. They looked a little different back then. He was in awe of my mother's beauty and nursed her back to health. He used some of his healing powers to save her. He asked her to stay with him."

Cecilia narrowed her eyes.

"He did not use his powers of persuasion to get her to stay. He was prepared to let her go. She chose to stay. They fell in love and then I came along. A couple of years later, my sister Zinna was born and a year after that, my other sister Saraid."

The two were sitting on Cecilia's back patio under the glow of the burnt orange sunset, a slight breeze wafting through the palm fronds, orchestrating a slow graceful waltz between the trees.

Aiden had made another surprise visit after Cecilia's long Monday at work. She had been half expecting him this time, though. Having been awake for most of the night, she had had plenty of time to think about her "deal with the devil," as she called it, and had come close to reaching her decision. She wasn't about to put all her trust in a man she barely knew.

Hearing the knock at the door, she somehow already knew who would be on the other side. He had brought a beautiful bouquet of flowers.

Cecilia took a sip of her coffee. "What happened to your sisters?"

Aiden paused, took a deep breath. "They were killed. Along with my mother."

Cecilia frowned. "How?"

"Remember the goddess Elara? She not only put a curse on me to be immortal but she slaughtered my entire family."

"Why would she do that?"

"Let's just say she was very angry with me."

"I'd say. What did you do to her?"

Aiden smiled. "Ahh. . . the million dollar question." He ran a hand through his messy hair. "I fell in love with her sister, Lavena. I thought the feeling was mutual. We were going to come clean to Elara. I felt terrible but I loved Lavena in a way I never loved Elara. Our affair was short, only a few weeks but I knew. She was the one." He took a deep breath, his eyes darkening.

"One evening Elara walked in on Lavena and I in a very compromising position. She lost her temper, cursed me with immortality at that very moment. Said I'd have to live with my mistake and the resulting pain for eternity. Then she took off."

"I didn't find out until the next morning that she had murdered my family right after leaving me. She snuck into their home and stabbed them while they slept." His eyes glistened with tears and burned with a venerable sadness as he stared into space. "The kicker is that the whole thing was a set-up. They were in on it together. Elara sent her sister to seduce me, to test my loyalty and love for her. What really kills me is that Lavena had me fooled. She never loved me at all."

Cecilia didn't know what to say. He looked as if he might cry.

Glancing back at her, Aiden wiped his eyes and smiled. "All these years and the pain never ceases. It appears that Elara was successful in her revenge."

"I'm so sorry, Aiden. That must be unbearable to live with."

"Sometimes it is. I have a hard time letting things go. I have too excellent of a memory." He sighed, pushed a wavy lock of hair out of his face. "But sometimes I can forget about it for a while. When I'm with you, the pain goes away."

Cecilia glanced at the blue and white flowers Aiden had given her. He followed her gaze and smiled. "You should be given flowers every day."

Cecilia smiled. "What kind are they?"

"The blue ones are irises. They are known to symbolize faith and hope."

"And the white ones?"

"Heather. It was a customary for brides in Ireland to wear it in their hair on their wedding day. It symbolizes promise, protection, good luck."

"Interesting," Cecilia said.

"Indeed." Aiden gave her his signature smirk.

"I don't know what to make of this sensitive side of yours."

"I have many sides, dear Cecilia. But, when I told you I would treat you well, I meant it." He paused, taking her hand in his. "Say yes."

"And what happens if I do?"

He pulled out a little black box. "You would wear this ring."

"We'd get married?" *Wow, he's prepared,* she thought.

"Well, yes, of course. We would have a courtship of some length first, so your friends and family don't think you've gone crazy and moved on too quickly."

"That's very generous of you." Cecilia smirked this time.

Aiden leaned back in his chair and smiled, shaking his head. "There's my sarcastic lady I love."

"Hypothetically speaking, if I agree to this, I have some conditions."

"Of course. I'd be disappointed if you didn't. Let's hear them."

"Well, the *courtship*, as you call it, needs to be long and I mean at least a year, maybe more. And not only for the benefit of avoiding suspicion from my friends and family, but so that I can get to know you."

"Fine. We can make it a year, two years. I'm not in a rush. What else?"

"During that time, I do not want to live together. And you have to stop dropping by unannounced."

"Even if I come bearing gifts? Flowers?" Aiden asked.

"Yes. Even if you bring flowers. I need to maintain my sense of sanity. I don't always think clearly when I'm around you."

Aiden narrowed his eyes and cocked his head to the side. "You don't think clearly around me? Hmm. . . I wonder if that's good or bad?"

"I don't know yet."

Aiden nodded. "Fair enough. I promise to call first before coming over. No more unexpected visits, even though it is fun to surprise you. Any other conditions?"

"Not at the moment."

"OK. So what else would you like to know about me?"

"When we were at Chez Francois, you told me you didn't knock me out that first night. Why did I wake up tied to a chair and have such a headache?"

"I thought you might ask. Well, first of all, you had a headache because you drank too much. And like I told you before, I didn't knock you out. Not physically, anyway. Remember how I made your headache go away?"

"Yes."

"Well, I have this ability to. . . get inside your head."

"I've noticed," Cecilia said.

"Once I get a sense of your energy, my intuition is kicked into high gear. You know how you can *feel* a room? Feel the tension in a room when two people have been arguing, even if they aren't saying a word? I'm very sensitive to that, regardless of the thought or emotion. If I focus my attention on someone, I can sense how they are feeling. It opens a door to your mind. I can send energy through that door if I choose to. In the simplest terms, I told your brain that you did not have a headache."

"So, you told my brain that I was unconscious in order to knock me out."

"Exactly. And when you fell, I caught you, brought you over to the chair. And yes, tied you up."

"And your face. You said that I'd never see the evil one again, but was that you? Or are you some sort of shapeshifter?"

"I can change into other things but that face, that was my creation. It's sort of what I'd look like if I aged, I suppose. If I looked my actual age, minus the pointed teeth and black eyes, of course. I am really sorry for frightening you."

"And how old are you?"

"Do you really want to know?'"

"I'm asking, aren't I?"

"One thousand, seven hundred and sixty four."

Cecilia's mouth formed a small "o" and she blinked. "So you were born in. . . "

"250 A. D."

"I need a glass of water." Cecilia started to stand up, but Aiden stopped her.

"I'll get it, sweetheart. Are you OK?" He laughed softly. "I know this is a lot to hear at once."

"I'm OK. I'm just going to need some time to process this."

"Understood." Aiden opened the patio door. "I'll be right back."

She watched him walk into the house, and he turned, pulling the heavy glass door shut behind him, met her eyes through the glass and winked.

The sun was sinking into the horizon and crickets chirped in the distance. Someone was having a bonfire a few houses over. Cecilia could see wisps of smoke in the sky to her right and smell the spicy and warm scent of wood burning. A faint chorus of laughter drifted over, reminding Cecilia of a life she used to have. Backyard barbeques, ordinary family life. It all had seemed so mundane a few years ago but now the thought of a little less excitement and more predictability sounded irresistible.

Then the patio was filled with soft light. Cecilia looked up to see Aiden holding a glass of water. Setting the glass in front of her, he settled back into his chair and looked out into the distance. Neither of them spoke for a long time.

Then Aiden broke the silence. "Is there anything else you'd like to know? Or do you want to talk about something else?"

She paused. "I still don't understand why you changed your face those first two nights. If you wanted me to talk to you, why scare me?"

"Remember the door into your mind that opens once I get a sense of you? Well, the stronger the emotions, the easier for me to get in. If you feel rage or terror, the door opens very wide."

"I see," Cecilia said, her eyes narrowed.

"Are you angry with me?"

"Well I'm not happy with the way you went about it. But, for some reason, I can't stay angry with you. I don't know why."

Aiden reached for the coffee press. "More coffee?"

"Sure." She held out her mug. As he filled it, his eyes held hers. "I have another question."

"Go ahead," Aiden said.

"The day you saved the little girl from the car. What were you doing downtown that day? Was it really a coincidence that we were both there? Me, shopping, and you walking down the same street?"

Aiden held her gaze. "I don't want you to be angry with me, but you want the truth, so here it is." He sighed and leaned forward. "No, it wasn't a coincidence."

"You were stalking me," Cecilia said.

"I told you before that I'd been following you for some time. Old habits die hard, as they say."

Cecilia shook her head. *I wonder how many times he's been just around the corner, watching everything I do,* she thought.

"What's wrong?"

"*What's wrong?*" she repeated. "Are you serious? Don't you understand how. . . how strange this all is for me? To know you've been following me around for months? I'm sorry, but it's just a little disturbing."

"I understand. I'm sorry, Cecilia. I told you before that I wanted you. You captivate me. I can't get enough of you. And, yes the stalking is a little much, but I'm very intense once I set my mind to something. I haven't followed you since then. I just wanted to talk to you, get to know you."

Cecilia shook her head again, then took a sip of her coffee.

Aiden leaned forward and fixed his gaze on her until she looked up. "You look lovely in this light. The glow of the setting sun touching your skin. . . lucky sun."

Cecilia raised an eyebrow at him, but felt her cheeks warm.

Aiden laughed, a rich gravelly baritone. "All business, I see. Alright then. I'm assuming you have more questions."

"How did you get to be the medical examiner for Spring Lake?"

"I went to medical school a long time ago but didn't want to become a practicing physician. I like to solve mysteries. I like to find out how someone died, investigate all the little intricate details of a body, all the inner workings, search for an answer to give to grieving families, give them peace of mind. I moved to Spring Lake about a year ago. I needed a fresh start. After I'm in one place for a while, I need to move on."

"Why?"

"Think about it. I look the same now as I did ten, twenty, a hundred years ago. People start to notice. I have to move roughly every eight years. That seems to be when people start telling me how young I look for my age." He pulled a cherry red Zippo lighter from his pocket.

"Where did you live before?"

He lit the vanilla candle in the center of the table. "Oh, I've lived almost anywhere you can imagine. I've lived on every continent. Even traveled to some of the most remote islands. Served ten years in the Marines. But most recently, I lived in Los Angeles. That didn't suit me well. Too superficial. Beautiful weather, though. Before that, New York. That was better for me. People there don't care if you're different. It takes a lot to get their attention. They've seen it all. Before that, I was in Europe. Now, that," he paused and smiled. "was fun," he said as he tilted his head back, looking wistful. Coming back to the present, Aiden smiled at Cecilia.

His smile turned into a frown when he noticed her expression. "What is it?"

"I was just thinking. . . how do I know you're not going to use your mind control on me? How do I know you haven't been using it on me this whole time?"

Aiden sat back in his chair. For a moment, she thought he looked angry, but then his expression turned to one of concern. "That's a valid question. I thought you might want some reassurance that I'm not manipulating your mind, so I brought this." He pulled a small orange box from his jacket pocket, sat it on the table.

She read the label aloud. "Kombucha tea?"

"That's right. It's been around for a long time and ironically enough, the ancient Chinese called it the Immortal Health Elixir. I found out many years ago that I cannot get inside someone's mind and influence them if this is in their system."

"Really? Why is that?"

"I have no idea. There is some compound in it that blocks me from getting in. You should drink it every couple days or so. It's perfectly harmless and has no side effects. Why don't you make a cup now and I'll try it on you, show you that my power doesn't work."

She thought for a moment. "No, I think I'll drink it some other time and test it out myself."

He laughed. "Oh, I see. Sneaky. Well, I told you I wouldn't manipulate your mind and I meant it. But go ahead and drink it whenever you choose. It's safe to drink every day if you'd like. That way you'll know I'm not able to influence you."

"OK. I will."

The orange sky was turning a dark gray as the sun disappeared. Cecilia shivered as a cool breeze drifted through the air, carrying with it a hint of acrid smoke and the cloying sweetness of marshmallows.

"Good." He smiled, reached for her hand. "So was that a yes earlier? Are you agreeing to spend your life with me, be mine?"

"No, I did not say yes. I'm not crazy, Aiden. I still don't know you! Blackmail or not, I would never agree to marry a man this quickly."

"I respect that about you, Cecilia. You've really surprised me. I didn't expect you to be so. . . strong." He paused. "Keep spending time with me, then. You'll really like me when you get to know me. And then you will want to marry me and you won't feel like you have to."

*I doubt I'll ever want to marry you. Seeing as how this "relationship" started out with blackmail. But, again, what choice do I have? He has the upper hand. If I say no, he turns me in.* "Fine."

Aiden laughed. "I guess I'll take that as a yes."

"It's a tentative yes. I can still change my mind."

"That is true. But this," he said, pulling a little black box out of his front pocket and sat it on the table in front of her. "is my insurance policy that you won't."

It was a tiny voice recorder. Cecilia sat upright in her chair. "You recorded me?"

"Yes, love. I have your confession, but no one will ever hear it once you've agreed to be mine."

She took a deep breath. *Well there it is*, she thought. *He has me.*

"Does this upset you?" he asked.

"Of course it does!"

"You don't like that I recorded you."

She gaped at him. "No, Captain Obvious, I don't."

"What did you expect?" he asked gently. "It had to be done. I'll go now." He leaned in, kissed the top of her head. "Goodnight, angel."

∞

*A tendril of hair fell over one eye as she looked down at him, her eyes scanning his face, down to his chest, then down the length of his body under hers.*

*It was hot under the sheets and Aiden pushed them off in one swift move as he flipped her onto her back and pinned her beneath him.*

*"You're still angry with me," he said as the weight of his body held her firmly in place.*

*"Yes. . . " she breathed.*

*He leaned down, gently biting her neck. "What can we do about that?" He bit harder and she gasped. "Maybe I can make you," he pushed himself into her suddenly. "forget about that nonsense."*

*"Aiden!" Cecilia cried out but didn't try to stop him.*

*"Do you want me to stop?" he asked.*

*Cecilia said nothing for a moment, lost in the pleasure he was giving her. She wasn't sure if she could form a coherent word, much less tell him to stop or push him off her.*

*"Do you?" he pressed.*

Cecilia awoke, sweating and aroused. "Damn it," she said under her breath. He had done it again. Gotten inside her head. Except she wasn't sure if he was giving her the dreams or if it was her subconscious telling her she wanted him. It was as if she had no control over it. She knew she should be angry with him, the cocky son of a bitch who had her confession on tape and was essentially blackmailing her into marrying him, giving herself to him. It was completely irrational but she wanted him. There was some magnetic pull to him, some inescapable force that she was too weak to fight anymore. But she'd be damned if she'd let him know that. She would hide it, pretend he had no effect on her, that she was only agreeing to spend more time with him because she had no other choice. *He knows I dream about him*, she thought. Her mind replayed his words: *I do apologize for interrupting your dream. . . did you enjoy your dream tonight?. . . tequila seems to agree with you. . .*

*Of course he knows*, she thought. *But I won't show it. It's probably pointless, but my pride won't let me.*

∞

"So, tell me about your latest research. Have you found anything interesting?" Aiden took a sip of his espresso. The two were having breakfast at Brewed Awakenings before work.

"Well, there is a drug we're testing to see if it has any effects on slowing the growth of glioblastoma. It slowed the growth of brain tumors in rats, actually doubled their life expectancy. We still have a lot of testing to do, though, to find out if it will have the same effect on humans. It's risky so it's difficult to get the funding."

"I could help with that."

"Yes, I know you could. But, I'd rather do it without your brain-raping."

Aiden's eyes widened. "Cecilia!" he shook his head. She had never seen him look surprised. "You're getting more creative in your description of my abilities."

"Well, let's just call it what it is." She shrugged.

"The lovely term you used isn't really accurate and it's rather harsh, don't you think? I like to think of it as influencing your mind."

"Think of it how you like, but you're still doing it against a person's will."

Aiden sat back in his chair, taking a sip of his espresso. "You're right, Cecilia. But I only do it when absolutely necessary, I don't do it for my own personal amusement."

"And who decides when it's necessary?"

Aiden sighed. "I do." He sat his coffee on the table. "I get your point Cecilia. But I do believe it's a responsibility I have to not abuse my power. It's a gift and I respect it. I don't use it frivolously. I don't know, I've always had this paranoia about it. . . .that the day I start abusing it, the day I start using it just because I *feel* like it. . . well that will be the day it is taken from me."

"You don't understand. Sometimes it feels like a burden. But since I have it, I may as well use it. I just try not to use it in vain."

Cecilia's brows shot up. "Is that really how you feel about it? I thought you got off on the control it brought, the power."

Aiden shook his head. "Not at all."

"But I do need to ask you a favor."

"Anything. What is it?"

"Please don't use your powers of influence as far as my career. Whatever I achieve, I want to know that I accomplished it on my own."

"I thought you might say that. And although I still think you should let me help you, I respect you for not wanting me to. So, I won't help, unless you ask for it, of course."

"Promise?"

He leaned forward and looked her directly in the eyes. "I promise, Cecilia. You have my word. Do you trust me?"

"I trust you."

"Good, it's settled. No brain-raping from me, I assure you."

"Thank you—" Cecilia began when she heard a familiar voice.

"Hey you!" Amber popped her head around the corner of their quiet little booth. Her eyes widened when she saw Aiden.

"I thought I saw your car outside," Amber said. She turned her attention to Aiden. "Who's your friend?"

Aiden stood, held out his hand. "I'm Aiden. And you must be. . . "

Cecilia jumped in. "This is Amber. Amber, Aiden."

"Are you in medicine as well?" Aiden took her hand and planted a kiss on the top.

"Charming." Amber smiled. "Yes, dermatology."

"Ahh. Well, I had no idea there were so many beautiful doctors in this town. Needing medical attention in Spring Lake must be a pleasant experience."

Cecilia cleared her throat and looked at Amber. "So, what are you up to today?"

"Oh, Pilates then I might meet Katherine for lunch. You two should join!"

Aiden flashed a dazzling smile. "Perhaps we will."

Amber beamed. "Well, that would be great! Now I'd better get going." She shot Cecilia a look before kissing her on the cheek. "Bye, CeCe."

"Tell Katherine I said hello."

"Will do. It was nice meeting you, Aiden."

"It was a pleasure, Amber."

After Amber left, Cecilia turned to Aiden. "We are not meeting them for lunch."

"And why not?"

"We'll be barraged with questions that I'm sure neither of us is prepared to answer and I do have to go to work," she said.

"That's too bad, it could be fun."

"I don't think so."

"Your friend is effervescent."

"Yes, she is quite bubbly."

"That's what effervescent means."

Cecilia reached over and pushed him playfully. "Smart-ass."

Aiden smirked. "You didn't tell your friends about me?"

"I didn't know what to tell them."

"Well the cat's out of the bag now, wouldn't you say?"

"It is out and meowing loudly," Cecilia said, rolling her eyes.

"Why? Should we expect the entire town of Spring Lake to know about us within the hour?" Aiden didn't seem worried about this idea.

"No, we can expect *Lakeview County* to know about us by then."

Just then her phone buzzed. It was a text from Amber:
`You're gonna have to spill later!!! Omg he's gorgeous! Why haven't you told me about him??`

"Let me guess—Amber?" Aiden smiled.

"You got it."

"What are you going to tell her?"

"Well, not the truth, obviously. She'd have me committed."

Aiden laughed. "You wouldn't do well in a psychiatric ward. Way too much of a control freak."

"Hey! Look who's talking! Mr. I-Can-Walk-Through-A-Door-To-Your-Brain!" She said this with her hands flailing wildly above her, pointing at her head.

Aiden laughed so hard Cecilia thought he would fall out of his chair for a moment. When his sharp cackles subsided, he sighed and leaned in, taking her hand in his. She looked down, noticing how small her hand was in his, how the texture of his skin was a little rough. He held it gently then pulled it up to his mouth and kissed the top of her hand.

"You're amazing, Cecilia. I've never met anyone like you." His eyes sparkled with sincerity. "If you were my wife, I'd treat you so well. I'd never hurt you, never take you for granted."

She shifted in her chair and reached for her coffee.

He squeezed her hand. "Another cappuccino?"

One thing she was grateful for was that he always seemed to know when to back off. *Maybe*, she thought, *his super-intuition isn't such a bad thing.*

∞

Cecilia moved the phone to her other ear. Amber had called as soon as she knew Cecilia would be getting off work and the two had been talking for over an hour now. Just as she had predicted, Amber was insatiably curious about Aiden and wanted, no – demanded – any and all details.

"There's really nothing more to tell, Amber. We're just friends. We're taking it slow, just getting to know each other. He knows what I've been through and is being very supportive. He's been through a lot, too. We're just being there for each other."

"And part of that involves having his tongue in your mouth?" Amber retorted.

"Amber—"

"Oh, I'm just messing with you, CeCe. I'm sure you're behaving yourselves. But, I don't know how long you can keep that up to be honest. I mean, damn! He's fucking sexy, Cecilia! I wouldn't be able to keep my hands off him for five minutes if I were you!"

"He's really intense," Cecilia said.

"Yeah! And? What's the problem? Can you imagine how that intensity translates into the bedroom?"

"I'm sure. But I'm not ready for that yet and he knows it."

"You gotta hit that," Amber insisted.

Cecilia burst into laughter. "'Hit that? God, Amber. You've been dating too many 25 year olds."

"Too many? No such thing. Well, I'm glad you're happy and he's supportive. That's what you need right now. But remember, if you do go to bed with him, there is nothing wrong with that. No one would blame you. You've been through a lot and if you find a great guy who cares for you, you deserve to let yourself be happy. There is no required mourning period. Just be happy, Cecilia."

"I know. You're right. I'm sure that will come with time."

"I'm sure you both will come with time."

"Jesus! You have the dirtiest mind!" Cecilia laughed.

"That's why you love me!"

"I do love you, Amber. I do."

Elaine Ewertz

# TWELVE

Aiden kept his promise to avoid showing up unannounced at her doorstep but he still made his presence known by calling every day the rest of the week. By Friday, they had plans to go to a quirky new restaurant Aiden had insisted she check out. There was going to be a live band playing and Aiden was friends with the guitar player.

"Oh my God, that's what you are! I can't believe it took me this long! You're a hipster!"

The two were sitting at a table near the stage at Blue Whistle which was already crowded at 9:00 p.m. A band that looked and sounded eerily similar to Weezer were playing.

Aiden laughed. "Oh, is that it?"

"Yes! It all makes sense now. I should have figured it out when I saw you in the fedora. Where are your thick black frame glasses?"

He gave her hair a little tug. "You're quite the smart-ass, aren't you? I have my own style, Cecilia. Those people are dressing like me."

She laughed. "Right. Well you do have a unique style, I'll give you that." She took the last sip of her mojito, draining the glass.

"Another?"

When Cecilia nodded he said, "You'd better slow down, you're making it easy for someone to take advantage of you."

"You wouldn't," she said, watching him as he stood.

"No, of course not. I'll be right back. Don't you go anywhere." He made the horizontal peace sign, pointing to his eyes then hers, indicating he was watching her.

"I wouldn't dare," she said under her breath.

When he returned a moment later, he asked, "So what did you end up telling Amber?"

"I told her we were just friends, that we had met when you saved the girl's life."

"And do you think she bought it?"

"I think she suspects I'm hiding something, but I told her the reason I hadn't told anyone was because I didn't want people to get the wrong impression, think that I was already dating someone new. But she knows me too well. Eventually, I'll have to tell her more. I just can't tell her the truth. I can't tell anyone, that's what is so hard about this. If I tell even my best friend, she'll think I'm crazy."

"I understand this must be hard on you. With time, it will get easier, I promise."

"I hope. I don't want to think about it now, though." She took a huge swig of her drink.

"Whoa there, cowgirl! You're a lightweight."

"I know. Today was just stressful. Is that your friend's band?"

"You mean the one trying their best to impersonate Weezer? No, they are the opener. They should be done with their set soon. Stagefright is up next."

"*Stagefright?*" Cecilia laughed. "Great name."

"I think so. It's kind of a joke because Rob, the lead singer, did have debilitating stage fright at first and still has anxiety issues. But you'd never guess when you see him perform. He's amazing."

Aiden was right. If the lead singer had stage fright, he hid it well. He joked with the audience in between songs and towards the end of their set, he said, "Alright, we're slowing it down. . . .this next song's for all the lovers out there. Grab the one you came with. . . or the one you're leaving with. . . and get on the dance floor!"

Cecilia was leaning her head on Aiden's chest as they swayed to the music. It really was a beautiful song and she found herself swept up in it, forgetting about her worries, even her apprehensions about the man holding her. She felt so safe in his arms, so at peace. Maybe it was the alcohol, but she decided not to analyze anything for the rest of the night, to just let herself enjoy the evening.

They danced for a long time, losing track of time and their surroundings. Neither said a word for what seemed like hours. When Cecilia opened her eyes, she realized the band was long gone and the house music had come on, playing an old Nine Inch Nails song.

She stayed in Aiden's embrace and listened to the erotic lyrics of the song, the words planting images in her mind, images of what might happen if she were to go home with him.

She let herself notice the way his body felt against hers. His hand, slightly rough, grasping her hand firmly, his arm wrapped around her waist, strong and confident, his hard chest rising and falling smoothly under her left cheek. . . Every now and again, the fronts of their thighs would meet and brush together slightly and she thought she could feel Aiden take a sharp intake of breath when this happened.

She wondered if he could tell the effect he had on her, the way her body warmed, how her heart sped up and a chill went down her spine when her mind replayed some of the images from her dreams. The thought of being in Aiden's bedroom. She wondered what his house looked like, if it looked anything like the one in her dream. That would mean she'd have a definite answer as to the origins of those dreams and it would confirm her suspicion that Aiden was somehow placing these images in her head.

Surprisingly enough, she couldn't even muster up any anger at this idea. He was right: she was a neurosurgeon, highly intelligent, science-focused. But she knew she could always trust her gut feeling. And her gut told her that, despite his manipulation of her mind, despite his supernatural abilities, despite his blackmail, she still felt something for him. From the first day in Brewed Awakenings, when she hadn't even known of his true identity, she had been attracted to him. But this could be more trickery on his part. If he could plant images in her mind, what else could he do? Manipulate her emotions? Make her feel as if she could trust him? Her mind was a tangled web of conflicting thoughts and she was unsure whether some of them were even hers.

Suddenly, the house lights came on and Cecilia was abruptly jolted from her reverie.

Blinking in the bright light, she looked up at Aiden. "Wow, what time is it?"

Aiden looked around. "I'm guessing it's two a.m. and they are getting ready to kick us out."

The drive home was mostly silent, except for Aiden singing along to a Johnny Cash song when it came on the radio.

When they arrived at Cecilia's house, Aiden walked her to the door.

"So, did you have a good time?"

"I did, Aiden. Thank you. Your friend's band really is great."

"I agree, but I liked the part after that better." He took a step closer.

Cecilia's heart accelerated but Aiden didn't back off this time. Maybe it was the mojitos or the fact that it was nearly 3:00 a. m., but she didn't back away. Instead, she placed her hands on his upper arms and met his eyes, only inches away.

He looked down at her hands. "Are you going to push me away?"

"No," she said as she held his gaze steadily.

She watched as his eyes displayed three emotions in quick succession: shock, understanding, then desire.

"Then you won't mind if I do this." He leaned in slowly until their lips met.

She was not sure if she was still on Earth; she was certain her feet were no longer touching the ground. She was floating, her body abuzz in warmth and tingling, as if she had champagne running through her veins. She didn't want it to end. His lips were so warm and the way they moved. . . the way his tongue caressed hers. . . it was almost too much. Cecilia wanted nothing more than to ask him to come inside. She wanted him. Now. Once, Aiden tried to slowly pull away. She pulled him back, but not before noticing his smirk. After several more minutes of this, Cecilia disentangled herself from him reluctantly only because she needed to breathe.

"My, you taste amazing, Cecilia," Aiden said, running his hands through her hair and giving it a sharp tug.

Cecilia realized where this was leading and lost her nerve. *No, I'm not ready for this,* she thought. She was still recovering from that kiss, if that's what you could call it. *If he kisses like that. . . damn. . . .imagine. . . .no, stop it!* She forced herself to regain control. She knew she could lose herself in him, lose control around him and she couldn't let that happen. Not now anyway.

"I believe this is the part where we say goodnight and I go home. Am I right?"

"I think so."

Aiden smiled. "You aren't sure though," he said.

"OK, no. . . yes, I'm sure. Yes. It's late and nothing good ever happens this time of night."

"Oh, I beg to differ, love. But, I think it's best that I go, too. You aren't quite ready for what would happen if I stayed."

"And what is that exactly?"

"I would ravage you," he said, taking a step closer. His fingers slowly traced her jaw line, down her neck to her collarbone. "This soft, beautiful skin. . . " He leaned in and kissed her neck. "You smell so amazing. . . and I want to taste more than your lips. . . " he said as his thumb brushed her lower lip gently.

Cecilia swallowed. He grabbed her hips and pulled her close into a strong bear hug. Her heart was beating fast and she knew he could feel it through the thin fabric of her dress. Then, he whispered in her ear, "Sweet dreams, beautiful," before turning to walk back to his car.

∞

Cecilia woke up to growling thunder and blinding flashes of light piercing the window into her bedroom. Rolling over to look at the clock, she clutched her head in pain. *I only had a couple drinks*, she thought. But really she didn't remember. With Aiden, time seemed to travel at a different pace. Sometimes she felt that she were watching him in slow motion; but yet the time flew by and she longed for one more hour with him.

She picked up the engagement ring from her nightstand, put it on, admired the sparkling facets of the diamonds. He had left it with her and instructed her to begin wearing it when she decided to agree to his proposal. When she asked him why, he said it would be more special that way. She wouldn't have to say a word. He would just see her wearing it and would know her answer was yes. She felt a tingle go down her spine when she thought of the kiss at the end of the night.

*Ouch!* Her head pounded as she sat up too quickly. Crawling out of bed, she dragged herself to the bathroom to find the Excedrin. She quickly swallowed two pills and decided to lie back down for a while. As soon as she was about to drift off to sleep, her phone rang.

"Hello?" Her voice sounded hoarse.

"Ahh. . . you don't sound well, Cecilia. I'm coming over." *Aiden.*

"No! I mean, I'm fine. I'll be OK in a couple hours once the headache goes away."

"You know—"

"Yes, I know, you can help with that. But I'd like to get rid of it the old-fashioned way."

The truth was, she'd love for him to cure her headache, but she looked like hell and did not want him to see her this way.

"You're stubborn." She could imagine Aiden shaking his head. "Let me guess, you just woke up and your hair is a mess."

"Well, yeah and—"

"Cecilia, I don't care. I bet you look cute with bed-head. But, run a comb through it if you must because I'll be there in twenty." *Click.*

"Damn it!" Cecilia said.

Twenty minutes later, Cecilia had made her best effort to look human.

When she opened the door, he gave her a once-over. "You don't look as bad as I expected."

"Thanks, I think."

He smiled. "I said I'd call first and I did."

"Yes you did. Come in." Cecilia sighed and began walking to the kitchen.

Aiden caught up to her, took her arm. "Cecilia, turn around, look at me."

When she turned, he placed a hand on either side of her face, looking directly into her eyes for a moment. "There. How do you feel?"

The headache, even the queasiness in her stomach was gone. "Much better. Thank you."

"You're welcome." He kissed her forehead. "Now let's see what we can make you for breakfast."

"You cook, too?"

"I'm a man of many talents, Cecilia."

"I see." She looked down at her pajamas. "I'm going to take a shower."

"Take your time, love. It'll be ready when you come out."

∞

Twenty minutes later, she shook her head, her mouth full of waffle.

"Wow, you're a great cook. Is there anything you can't do?"

Aiden narrowed his eyes, as if deep in thought. "No, not that I can think of."

"So cocky."

"Would you like to hear some music?"

"More Redheads?"

"Coming right up." He closed his eyes for a second then looked at Cecilia, a smile playing on his lips as the music started. It was one of their slower songs, *This Boy's Heart.*

Cecilia closed her eyes, enjoying the song. It sounded like the band was in her back bedroom. It was just the right volume, smooth and serene.

"Beautiful," she said. "The guitar is so clear. It really sounds like someone is in the other room playing."

"I could play for you sometime," Aiden offered.

"You play?" She smiled, rolling her eyes. "Of course you do. I'd love to hear it. The guitar is my favorite instrument. It's just so beautiful. Not only just the way it sounds, but the way it looks, the curves, the shape of it. It's. . . " She struggled for the right word.

"Sensual?" Aiden finished for her.

"Yes, exactly." She met his eyes. Something unspoken passed between them. "I always wish I had learned when I was younger. I took piano lessons instead."

"The piano is a beautiful instrument as well. Well, I could teach you a few things, if you'd still like to learn. I have a small collection of guitars."

"I'd love to see them sometime. But I don't know about teaching me. Are you patient?"

"Patient is my middle name."

"That's a weird name."

He walked around the table to her, playfully tugged her hair.

Finished?" As he cleared the table and loaded the dishwasher, he asked, "Why don't we go to my house today? I'll give you the grand tour. Do you have anything planned?"

"Well, I was going to have lunch with Amber and Katherine." She paused. "Why don't you come with me?"

"I'd love to. It will be good for your friends to get to know this mysterious man you've been spending time with. They can check me out and make sure I'm good enough for you."

"Oh they'll pick you apart for sure. Are you sure you're up for it?"

"I'm up for anything."

"OK then. I'll tell them to expect you."

"Good. I'm going to take a shower." He kissed her forehead and disappeared down the hall.

As Cecilia was heating up water for coffee, the orange box of Kombucha tea caught her eye. She had almost forgotten about it.

Grabbing a mug, she slipped a tea bag into it and poured the water over top. The shower was still running upstairs and Aiden's faint voice drifted down as he sang. She sat at the table and sipped the tea quickly. When she finished, she buried the tea bag in the trash under some napkins and washed the mug.

∞

It was hard not to notice the women staring at Aiden as he and Cecilia walked into Dandelion Cafe. When they approached the table, Amber jumped up and hugged them both.

"Hey you two!" She turned to Aiden. "I'm so glad you could join us!"

"As am I," he said, giving her a smile then turning his attention to Katherine, who was staring, her mouth slightly open.

"I don't believe we've met," he said, holding out his hand.

"Oh, where are my manners?" Cecilia jumped in. "Katherine, this is Aiden. Aiden, Katherine."

"Nice to meet you, Aiden," Katherine said as her cheeks reddened slightly.

"The pleasure is all mine." He winked at her. Cecilia tried to mentally send him a message to take it easy. If he flirted any more, Katherine might faint. Cecilia was relieved to see that it wasn't all in her head Aiden must have that effect on all women.

Two hours later, Cecilia was certain that both Amber and Katherine were in love with Aiden. It was entertaining to watch as he charmed them, asking questions about their lives. He made the three women feel as if they were the only people on Earth at the moment. How he did it, Cecilia didn't know. But he did have an advantage most men didn't have: over a thousand years of practice. *And that's dangerous*, Cecilia thought.

# Thirteen

Cecilia's eyes were on the TV but she didn't even know what was on. She was too distracted by the man sitting next to her on the large plush sofa with his feet up on the coffee table. They had gone back to his house where he had given her a tour—which had taken a solid thirty minutes; his house was opulent, even for a doctor –and showed her his guitar collection. After five minutes of what could be loosely called a 'guitar lesson,' Cecilia grew frustrated. Aiden was patient, as promised, but she had set the guitar back in the stand, giving up. They had decided to watch a movie from his extensive collection, but Cecilia was giving up on trying to pay attention.

"You never talk about your work. What do you do all day?" Cecilia asked.

Aiden gave her a strange look. "I think you know what I do all day, Cecilia. I'm the medical examiner, so—"

"I know, but you never talk about it," she interrupted.

"Well, when I do get to spend time with my lovely, yet very busy girlfriend, I like to spend quality time, not talk about autopsies. But to be honest, I really work on more of an on-call, as-needed basis. I don't do many autopsies anymore. I've scaled back a lot. My assistant does most of them and calls me when he needs me. I prefer to spend my free time pursuing other interests." He gave her a flirtatious look.

She narrowed her eyes. "I'm your girlfriend?"

To this, he said nothing. He grabbed her jaw, pulled her mouth to his and kissed her with ferocious intensity. "Yes, you are." He paused, shook his head. "Oh, Cecilia, why do you keep resisting me? I know you are attracted to me. I know you like me. And that's not me being cocky. I can sense very strongly how you feel, remember? You can't hide anything from me."

"I know, but. . . "

"Stop trying to pretend, Cecilia. There is nothing to be afraid of. There's no reason to deny how you feel. You've gotten to know me more, and you've grown to trust me, even though we have a long way to go. You've seen that I'm not such a bad guy. I simply want what I want and yes, I'm cocky and can be rather pushy about it, and yes, it started out as blackmail, but Cecilia, I want you. I have feelings for you. I will admit when I first met you, I wasn't entirely sure of my intentions. But, I can tell you my intentions are pure. I want you to be mine. And I will not give up. But, none of that even matters, does it? Because, you feel something for me. Admit it so we can stop this nonsense."

Cecilia reached for the acoustic guitar by the fireplace. Handing it over to Aiden, she said, "Play me something."

When he started to protest, she said, "I just need a moment to collect my thoughts. Please play something in the meantime."

He studied her for a moment then started strumming. A few seconds later, his rich baritone filled the room. He began singing the opening lines to "Tangerine" from Led Zeppelin. She recognized it immediately. It had been her favorite song in high school but she hadn't heard it in years.

"I love that song," Cecilia murmured.

"Ahh, you're a Zep fan. I knew I liked you." He tousled her hair, setting the guitar back in its stand. He leaned back into the couch and pulled her in for a kiss.

"You're very talented," Cecilia said.

"Thank you, you're a good kisser, too."

"I meant the guitar playing," Cecilia said.

Aiden looked stunned. "Cecilia! Are you saying I'm not a good kisser?" But his eyes twinkled with humor.

She punched him playfully in the arm. "You know what I meant!"

"Oh, that's how it's going to be, huh? OK, then." He pushed her down on the couch and began tickling her.

"Stop! *Stop*!" Cecilia was laughing uncontrollably, squirming to get out from under him. When he finally relented, she sat up, out of breath. He reached over and took her hand, stroked the top.

"I've never wanted to kiss someone that way before. Before you—well I felt like I was asleep my whole life until I met you."

"You have the quite the way with words."

He leaned closer. "I'm just being honest with you." After a few moments, Aiden gestured towards the TV. "Do you know what is going on?"

"No, I can't say that I do," she said.

"Good. I wanted to turn it off anyway." He pushed a piece of hair behind her ear.

He switched off the television and turned his full attention to her. Smiling, he said, "You're being shy now."

"Well, the other night I did have three mojitos. I was feeling brave."

"Do I make you nervous?"

"Yes!" She was relieved to admit it. "And that's the thing: I normally don't get shy or nervous, but there's something about you. . . I don't know. . . I feel uneasy, but in a good way."

"Hmmm. . . well I'm glad it's in a good way," he said, touching her cheek. "Tell me the truth, Cecilia. Tell me how you feel."

"Kiss me again."

He pulled back. "Not until you admit your feelings."

*OK, this is it. Just tell him. He knows already.* "OK, I like you, Aiden. I'm still not one hundred percent sure about you. But, yes, I'm attracted to you and. . . this hasn't been the usual start of a. . . relationship for me. But I want you, OK? I want you. Now kiss me."

"Much better," he said as his lips touched hers. Cecilia was floating again, her body warming, the sparkling champagne running through her veins, except tonight there had been no alcohol.

Then there was music. A mellow little bluesy number started echoing through the house, bouncing off the walls and tall ceilings. Cecilia opened her eyes for a split second and thought she saw the sparkling chandelier of the foyer sway just a little.

"Nice," she said.

"I think so." In one swift motion, he pulled her on top of him so she was straddling him on the couch.

She studied his dark eyes for a moment then traced his lips with her fingertip. These were the same lips from her dream, the same eyes, the same man. It was a bizarre feeling for a split second, a feeling of deja-vu. Except this wasn't a dream. She was actually in his house, sitting on his lap, their bodies pressed together. She could hear the beating of her own heart, the crackling of the fireplace on the other side of the room. She leaned in to kiss him again, working her way down the side of his neck, stopping to give his earlobe a small bite.

He moaned quietly. "Mmmm. . . do that again, Cecilia."

His smell was intoxicating. She was lost in him, unaware of her surroundings as she bit him on the neck this time, a little harder.

He growled. "Damn. . . I love that. My little vixen."

She turned his head and gave the other side of his neck a little bite, circling her hips, pressing herself into him.

Aiden growled louder, grabbed her by the waist and flipped her onto her back. He pinned her arms down and pressed himself into her. She felt her body opening up, responding to him. Reaching up, she grabbed his hips and pulled him closer so that the fabric of their jeans was the only barrier between them. She felt his hands, large and warm, slide up her blouse, cup her small breasts through the thin silk fabric of her bra.

Suddenly, an image of Rick flashed through her mind. She froze in horror. For days, she had barely thought of her deceased ex-husband. Aiden had consumed her mind. Now, she could feel the longing and desire for Aiden slowly melting away, and the ugly and familiar guilt taking it's place.

Aiden's hands stopped moving. "What is it, sweetheart?"

"We should stop." She tried to push him off but he didn't budge.

"Tell me, Cecilia. What's wrong?"

She sighed. "Just the old demons coming back to haunt me. I'm sorry, Aiden."

He lifted himself off her and helped her sit up. He took her face in his hands and stared into her eyes for a moment.

"What are you—" She sat back and narrowed her eyes. "I've been drinking the tea, Aiden. Nice try."

He let his hands fall. "I'd hope so. That's why I gave it to you."

"But you just tried to do your mind thing—"

Aiden leaned back. "I can't help myself. I care for you, Cecilia. I want to take your pain away."

"I know, but don't you think I should deal with it? Work through it instead of hiding it? Should I just let you sweep it under the rug every time I have an unpleasant thought?"

He was quiet for a moment. "OK, sweetheart. If that's what you want. How are you feeling right now?" He took her hand in his and squeezed.

"I feel guilty." She felt her vision start to blur as her eyes filled with moisture. "I feel guilty for what I did. Who knows if he had already taken enough to overdose. I'll never know. But the thought that I may have. . ." She paused to wipe her eyes. "And I feel guilty for feeling relieved that he is gone! I mean, I would have never wished him dead, but—"

"He was abusive." Aiden squeezed her hand once more then reached over to the table for a tissue and handed it to her.

"Yes." She took the tissue and wiped her face, now streaming with tears. Her face felt hot. "I constantly walked on eggshells. And if he had more than one drink, forget it. I lived in fear. Every day. He would push me, slap me around, call me names. He told me I would make a horrible mother. He told me I was cold and selfish and all I cared about was my career. But it's not true! I loved him so much. I wanted to get him help. I wanted us to be happy again." She leaned forward and cupped her face with her hands, letting the tears fall, feeling her shoulders convulse uncontrollably.

Aiden pulled her into his arms and held her silently for a long time, rocking her back and forth. When she finally stopped crying, she looked up at him and saw that his eyes were wet.

"He hurt you. He treated you terribly. Anyone would be relieved to be rid of someone like that. It doesn't make you a bad person. And you've never really stopped to deal with what he did to you. Not just physically, but emotionally and mentally. You just keep going because you're so strong. You don't have to deal with it alone anymore, Cecilia. You don't always have to be so strong."

She leaned back into him and hugged him tighter. "Thank you," she whispered.

"I've got you. Always," he whispered back.

After several minutes, she gently pulled back. Her eyes burned and felt raw. She pushed stray pieces of hair back, now wet from her tears. Smiling up at him, she felt as if a weight had been lifted from her shoulders.

He smiled back and cupped her face in his hands. "That's it. Everything is OK now. You no longer have anything to worry about, Cecilia."

"It might take me a while to get used to that idea," she said.

"I've got time." He took her hand and kissed the top. "You're tired. Let me take you to bed."

"Yes, please." She yawned as she ran a hand through his hair.

She felt herself being lifted up into the air and cradled against his chest as she saw two black and white paintings on the wall drift past her line of sight: an oddly shaped guitar and a man standing at the edge of the ocean. The last thing she saw was the dark wood of the staircase as her eyelids became so heavy it felt as if there were tiny weights resting on them.

∞

Cecilia woke up disoriented. Her eyes still closed, she knew this was not her bed. She stretched out, felt the cool, soft cotton under her fingers, arms and legs. The bed was too big to be hers. As her eyes slowly opened and the world came into focus, she saw through narrowed slits a bronze sculpture hanging from the ceiling with a circular cage on either side, blades spinning inside the cages. She shivered, feeling the chilly air blow directly onto her shoulders.

Sitting up, she pulled the blanket up to her neck. A column of early morning light lay across the floor and crept up onto the bed. She remembered to compare it to the room in her dream of Aiden. Was it the same bedroom? If it was, that meant he was surely inside her head, planting these erotic dreams himself. But it was not the same room. It was similar only in size and layout.

Everything else was different, the walls a rich reddish mahogany with paintings scattered at eye level. One was of a young woman wearing a flowing white lace dress sitting atop a set of brick steps. Perched on the woman's arm was a raven looking at her with his head cocked to one side. Despite the graceful lines of the painting, the way the bird stared at the woman was creepy. Next to it was a painting of a white sailboat sitting in clear blue water. A gray-haired man stood on the side of the boat, his hand shielding his eyes from the sun as he gazed into the vast expanse of the ocean, a worried look on his face. His skin was reddened from the sun and his clothes looked dirty and torn. Behind him in the distance was a tiny patch of grass and trees that must have been an island. Cecilia wondered if the man would ever turn around and see it, find shade from the hot sun, food and maybe even people who could help him. Or would he just continue drifting at sea?

Cecilia was startled when the bedroom door opened.

"Good morning, beautiful. How did you sleep?"

"Great. Better than I have in a while, actually. Did you carry me to bed last night?"

"I did. You were out. I didn't want to wake you."

She stretched. "I guess I was. Wow, I feel refreshed. Your bed is so comfortable." She hesitated. "Did you sleep. . . "

Aiden smiled and sat down on the edge of the bed. "I slept next to you most of the night. I'm an early riser."

"I see." Cecilia ruffled his hair.

"I behaved myself, if that's what you're asking. I didn't molest you in your sleep."

She laughed. "Well, I hope not. That would be weird."

"Indeed it would. I made coffee. Come," he said as he took her hand.

When she walked into the kitchen, she saw a smorgasbord of every breakfast item imaginable. Fruit, an assortment of

The Devil You Know

muffins, bagels and a French press filled with coffee sat in the middle of the table.

"My God, who is all this for?"

"Us, silly. Eat up," Aiden said, pulling out a high-back dining chair.

Cecilia looked at the clock on the wall. "I've got to get to work."

"Yes, but you can eat first. Have a seat, love."

Cecilia sighed. "I have a few minutes. Thank you, Aiden. You really didn't have to do this." She sank into the plush white cushion and ran her hand over the rustic table. The dark wood was knotted and there were several scratches covering the surface.

"You're welcome."

"How old is this table?" Cecilia asked.

"Older than me," Aiden said, setting a plate in front of her. "Orange juice? Coffee?"

"Both, please. You can't be serious. Really, where is this from? I've never seen anything like it."

He knocked on the table twice with his knuckles. "It was my family's table." He popped a handful of blueberries into his mouth.

Cecilia narrowed her eyes. "From the third century?"

He turned, opened the refrigerator and bent down, grabbing orange juice off the bottom shelf. Cecilia noticed his shoulders start to quiver and when he stood and turned again, she saw that he was smiling.

"You're laughing at me!"

"You are so gullible, beautiful one," he said, pouring her a glass of juice. "I got it from a thrift store in Orlando."

"I knew it wasn't true. I just wanted to see if you were going to lie." She grabbed the glass and took a large gulp of the orange liquid.

Aiden rolled his eyes. "Damn, Cecilia. I was only joking with you." He shoved a platter of muffins at her. "Here, eat one. I made them myself."

125

"Coffee first." She reached for the press and poured, filling up her mug.

"By all means, drink your coffee. You are cranky in the morning without it, aren't you?"

"I'm not being cranky. You're being a pain in the ass!"

"You're feisty," he said, smiling.

"You like it."

"Never said I didn't," Aiden said, cutting a bagel in half. "Cinnamon bagel?"

Later that night, Cecilia insisted on going back to the Blue Whistle.

"Really? I thought it was too hipster for you?"

"No! I loved it. I mean, don't get me wrong, I still think you're the world's oldest hipster. You may have even started the whole trend without even realizing it." She slid closer to him on the couch and rested her hand on his leg.

"Are you saying I'm the original hipster? As in, original gangster?" He pretended to make a gang sign with his hand.

She erupted into laughter, grabbing his hand. "Please stop. Don't ever do that. It's just wrong." She climbed onto him, sat in his lap. "Someone's in a good mood today."

"You make me that way."

"Good. No, I want to go back. Is there a band playing there tonight?"

"Yes, actually Stagefright is playing there for Cinco de Mayo. Let's have dinner first, then we'll go."

∞

Cecilia smoothed her skirt, crossing her legs. It was the shortest skirt she owned, a leftover from her twenties. Aiden had taken her to Derrico's, and after meatball spaghetti and two glasses of red wine, she was feeling relaxed and a little buzzed. Glancing up, she caught Aiden watching her closely, his eyes resting unabashedly on her legs.

"What are you looking at?" she teased.

"Mmmm. . . you have beautiful legs, Cecilia," he said as his eyes lingered.

"Stop trying to look up my skirt!" She laughed, angling her legs away from his line of sight.

Aiden leaned forward. "Do you celebrate Christmas?"

*Wow, that's random*, she thought. "Yes. . . "

"Were you ever one of those kids who just had to peek at their presents before Christmas morning?"

She narrowed her eyes. "I may have tried to peek a couple times, I don't know—"

"Not me. Not that I ever had the opportunity of course, but I'd never do that. It ruins all the fun. The anticipation," he paused, fixing a wicked stare onto Cecilia. "is what really does it for me."

"Oh my God!" Cecilia shouted in exasperation, understanding the metaphor. "You've got to be kidding me!"

Aiden tossed his head back, laughing.

"You're unbelievable!" she said, shaking her head.

"Hey, I'm a man. I can't help myself." He stopped laughing, leaned forward. "What I mean is that I was not looking up your skirt—"

"Yeah, yeah, I got it," she cut him off quickly but smiled in spite of herself.

"You're adorable."

"And you're bad," she said.

"You have no idea," he said as he pushed a piece of wild black hair out of his face and turned his attention to the band.

Stagefright was even better than the other night, if that were even possible. Aiden and Cecilia had been dancing for two hours straight when she stopped, out of breath.

"I have to go to the restroom. I'll be right back," she said, kissing him on the cheek.

"OK, sweetheart. I'll be right here."

In the bathroom, she heard a couple girls in the handicapped stall together. One had obviously been over-served. Cecilia could hear her vomiting while her friend offered words of comfort.

"It's OK, Amy. You just drank too much, silly girl. I'll drive. You can crash at my place, OK?"

"Yeah. . . " the pukey girl groaned.

Cecilia touched up her lip gloss and walked out to find Aiden. But she was stopped when a man grabbed her arm. It was not Aiden.

"Hey, CeCe!"

She turned to see Mike, her high school sweetheart. "Mike! Oh my God! What are you doing here?" She leaned in, hugging him.

"My job transferred me here. This is about the only decent place to go in this small town." He laughed. "I heard you moved to Florida, but I didn't know you were in Spring Lake! Wow!"

"I know! That's crazy. Small world! How have you been? It's been so long." She noticed he looked almost the same as he had in high school when he was captain of the football team. He was still stocky and muscular but his baby face was no longer hidden by his blonde hair which was now cut short.

"I've been great! I'm so glad I ran into you. It *has* been a long time. I hear you're married! Any kids?"

"Not married anymore and no, we didn't have kids."

"Oh, I'm sorry. I didn't—" His face fell.

"No, you're fine. It's OK." Her next words came out in a flurry.

"What are you up to these days? Did you go into the family business?"

"Yep, sure did. Gotta make Dad proud, you know." He smiled and shrugged. "No, I like it. I really do."

"I'm glad, Mike. I'm glad to hear you're doing well."

"I am. And you went and became a neurosurgeon like you always talked about! I'm so proud of you, CeCe!"

She laughed. "Yeah, well. It keeps me busy. I'm working on some research too, so there's never a dull moment."

"Well, that's awesome, CeCe!" He took a step forward and gave her arm a friendly squeeze. "We should get together sometime, go have coffee or something. Catch up."

"We should! That would be great," she said, digging in her clutch.

"Here's my card. Call me sometime."

He smiled, took the card. "I will—"

He was cut off when Aiden appeared by Cecilia's side. "There you are. I was starting to worry." He kissed the top of her head.

"Oh, Aiden, this is Mike, a friend of mine. Mike, this is Aiden."

The two men shook hands, Mike smiling politely but his disappointment was obvious. Aiden's tall, dominating stature seemed to overshadow Mike, make him look small. Cecilia noticed Aiden's smirk as the introductions were made.

After some small talk, Mike excused himself quickly. "Well, it was nice seeing you, Cecilia. Maybe we'll run into each other again soon."

Aiden made a barely audible sound. Then, turning to Aiden, Mike said, "Nice meeting you, Aiden."

"Likewise." Aiden nodded then watched him as he walked across the room. When Mike was out of sight, Aiden turned to Cecilia. "It's getting late. Let's go home."

"No! It's not late. It's only eleven! Let's go back out and dance a little more."

Aiden sighed. "Cecilia, the band is long gone and you have to work tomorrow."

"Yes, but I don't have to go in super early."

When Aiden stayed silent, Cecilia asked, "Is something wrong?"

"No, of course not. I just remember two nights ago and how you felt in the morning. I'm trying to prevent that from happening again."

She smiled, tugged on his sleeve. "But, you can cure me."

He let out a breath and closed his eyes. "No, I can't. You've been drinking the tea I gave you?" Her words were short and clipped.

"Yes. Oh." Although she had not been drinking it consistently, she was not about to tell him that.

"*Oh*," he repeated. "So, we're going home, end of discussion." He held out his hand until she took it.

"OK, Aiden. Don't get pissy with me. You're right. I do have to get up early."

He was completely silent on the drive home and Cecilia didn't feel like asking again if something was wrong. She was getting sleepy and just wanted to fall into bed and drift off.

Walking into the house, Aiden slammed the door. She jumped, startled.

"God, Aiden, what—"

He took a step towards her. "We need to have a little talk."

"I knew something was wrong back there. What is it?"

"Did you enjoy reuniting with your boyfriend?" His eyes had turned from the usual deep brown to pure black.

"Really? That's what this is about? Aiden, he's not my boyfriend. We dated in high school, for God's sake."

Aiden said nothing and just continued to glare at her.

Cecilia walked to him, put her hands on his shoulders. "Aiden, seriously."

"Oh, I am serious. I saw the way you looked at him. You want him, don't you?"

"No!" Cecilia started to walk away, frustrated. But, he caught her arm, turned her back around to face him.

"Don't walk away from me. Is that what you want? Would you rather have him?"

"Let go of me!" She struggled to get free and he finally let go. "No, I don't want him. You're being ridiculous! This is insane. We were just catching up. I'm not allowed to talk to an old friend?"

"Sure you are. But he was more than a friend and you gave him your number, *CeCe*," he said mockingly. "I don't like it. You don't need to be meeting up with him. You know damn well what he wants and it's not to just *catch up*. You know better than that, Cecilia, so don't play dumb with me." His voice became louder with each word.

"I don't even know what to say to this." She walked to the dining room table and sat down.

He followed close behind and stood directly in front of her. "You could start with explaining why you didn't introduce me as your boyfriend. Then you could assure me that you are not planning on meeting him for coffee or anything else."

Cecilia shifted away from him in her chair. "You have issues. You're acting really insecure. Why are you so jealous?"

"I have issues? *I have issues?* You're going to have issues if you don't start treating me with respect, Cecilia."

"Are you threatening me?"

"No, I'm simply telling you what I expect. You are my girlfriend. And you go flirt with your ex-boyfriend right in front of my face? Give him your number?"

"In front of your face? Would you rather I did it behind your back?"

Aiden's mouth formed a hard line. He walked a few feet away then turned again to face her. "You're pushing me too far with your smart mouth. You know exactly what I mean. You were there with *me*. You should have come and found me first and introduced me as your boyfriend, but not stand there and pretend like you were there alone and single."

"You can't be serious! I really don't know what you want me to say. It was completely innocent and you're making a huge deal out of nothing."

"It really concerns me that you aren't taking me seriously right now. You think you can treat me like any other guy, Cecilia, but you're mistaken. I'm not stupid. You were flirting with him. The least you can do is admit it."

Cecilia stood from the table, threw up her hands. "OK, Aiden. You're right! I want him. I want him so bad! I want to go home with him and fuck him! Is that what you want to hear?"

The car keys Aiden was holding crashed into the wall on the other side of the room, causing Cecilia to jump. She felt her feet carry her backwards in an instinctive reaction as he charged towards her.

Her back pressed against the wall, she waited for whatever Aiden was about to do. He walked until he was standing right in front of her, towering over her.

She looked up at him. He was glaring, his eyes orbs of glittering darkness, and her heart sped as she remembered who this man was. *How could I have been so stupid?* she thought.

"Got any more sarcastic remarks for me?"

She wasn't able to find her voice.

"Nothing? Come on, don't disappoint me now. Did you mean that? What you just said?"

"No," she said.

"I know you didn't." He reached to touch her face and she flinched. She thought she saw a quick smirk but couldn't be sure. He leaned in, spoke into her ear. "I really should teach you a lesson." He backed away a couple steps, his eyes never leaving hers.

With him a couple feet away now, she found her courage. "Yeah, well, too bad you won't get the chance. I'm done."

"Excuse me?" he asked.

"You heard me. I'm done! Turn me in, I don't care anymore!"

His face fell. "Oh, you don't mean that."

"Yes I do! Aren't you listening? If this is how it's going to be, forget it. The deal's off. I'd rather go to prison than put up with your bullshit!" She was crying now. "Just leave me alone! I should have never trusted you! You're just going to hurt me!"

"I'd never hurt you."

She huffed. "Right. I'm calling a cab." She began digging through her clutch for her phone.

"Did I lay a hand on you?"

"No, but you scared me and you know it. Knowing what I've been through before with. . . with. . . God, you're fucked up. I don't know what I expected. Who knows what you'll do the next time we have an argument." She pulled out her phone and started pressing buttons.

"I won't do a thing. I'm sorry I frightened you. I'm just upset, Cecilia. I think you can understand why. Now, put the phone down and let's talk about this." He reached out and took her arm but she wrenched out of his grasp. He let his hand fall.

"I'm done talking. Leave me alone!" She walked a few feet away, looking down at her phone, searching for the number.

He sighed. "OK, fine, I'll take you home."

"Like hell you are."

"Is that really what you want?" he asked quietly. "You want to end this?"

"Yes, I do." She wiped the tears from her eyes, hating that she was so weak, that she actually had developed feelings for him. He wasn't even completely human. How did she ever trust him? After placing the call, she grabbed her things and walked past Aiden out the front door to wait for the cab. He didn't follow her.

Elaine Ewertz

# FOURTEEN

Tuesday dragged by torturously. Her office had several no-shows which didn't help her misery. She had hoped it would be like any other day and be slammed, so busy she wouldn't have time to think about anything else.

Finally, her last patient seen, she finished up her notes and packed up to go home where she just wanted a glass of wine and a hot bath. As soon as she got into her house, she received a text from Aiden: I'm sorry. Please call me.

She turned her phone off and tried not to think about him the rest of the night. She slept terribly, waking up every couple of hours, tossing and turning all night. The next morning she received a bouquet of purple hyacinths. When the delivery boy handed the flowers to her, he said, "Someone is saying sorry."

The rest of the week passed by in a blur. She received calls from Aiden but forced herself to ignore them. She needed time to think. And he needed to realize that she was serious. She was not going to let him walk all over her, lose his temper and intimidate her. Yes, he was the only one who knew what she had done. He could turn her in and she would spend the rest of her life in prison. But she was still going to demand respect from him. He had promised to treat her well and he had already messed up, gone into a jealous rage over an ex-boyfriend. If he decided to turn her in, so be it. It was a risk she was willing to take.

On Friday night, she noticed an envelope at her front door when she got home from work. Opening it, she recognized Aiden's handwriting.

*Please talk to me. I don't want to do it. You know what I'm talking about. If you are backing out, tell me now. You told me you had feelings for me. What that true or were you lying? I am sincere in my feelings for you but you know what will happen if you walk away. I am sorry I frightened you. You were right. I was jealous over Mike. I don't want to lose you. I promised I wouldn't come over uninvited, but I will come over soon if you don't call me.*

She took a moment to process the message. There was definitely a threat lurking in those elegantly written lines. *He's apologizing, but he will still turn me in if I back out.* She sighed. *What am I going to do?*

Pouring herself a glass of her favorite Syrah, she stared at her phone, trying to convince herself not to call him. *Call his bluff,* she told herself. *He won't turn you in. He has feelings for you. He won't do it.* But she knew better.

Aiden was serious and it was only a matter of time before the police showed up at her door. Besides, there was a side of her—a side she was still didn't quite understand—that missed him.

She jumped when her phone rang. *I'm not ready*, she thought as she looked at the screen. But it was Amber. She sighed and answered it.

"CeCe! I haven't heard from you in a while. You're in a love bubble, aren't you?"

Cecilia swung her legs up onto the couch and leaned back onto a pillow. "What?"

"You and your hot boyfriend. You two are in a love bubble and haven't come up for air." She giggled. "The sex must be amazing."

Cecilia shook her head. "You have a one track mind. I don't know where to start. It was so good, and then. . .we had a fight. I think it's over." She felt her eyes fill with tears.

"What? No! What happened?"

"Well, I ran into Mike at the Blue Whistle—"

"Wait. Mike? As in, your high school boyfriend, Mike?" Amber's voice raised an octave.

"Yes, and Aiden got upset. I mean, insanely jealous. Accused me of flirting with him, and oh God, Amber, it was crazy."

"How crazy?"

"He just scared me. He didn't even yell. He just threw his keys across the room. I left and haven't answered his phone calls or messages since."

"There's something you're not telling me, CeCe. I know you."

Cecilia felt a tear roll down her cheek. "It's nothing. It's just that I've been through so much and thought. . .I don't know, I—I care for him, Amber. I think I love him. And I don't know why. I shouldn't. I haven't known him long and I'm being stupid—"

"Oh, honey. You are anything but stupid. You must see something in him. If you love him you should give him a chance. Think about it. He got jealous. He cares for you. You are used to a different kind of man. You are used to a passive, abusive, uncaring, selfish man. I'm sorry to bring it up, but Aiden is the opposite of what you are used to."

Cecilia stared up at the ceiling, following the faint white trails stretching to the bay window across the room. "I know that's part of it. I really hadn't thought of it that way. Had too much on my mind. I'm just so confused and nothing seems clear."

"That's love, CeCe. It's painful and hard and hell, I don't know why we put ourselves through all this. But it's supposed to be worth it. If you think he's worth it, don't give up. Only you know, though. You have to decide."

Cecilia was silent.

"You said you love him," Amber said softly.

"I did. But I shouldn't. You don't know, he's. . .I feel backed into a corner."

"He's pressuring you?"

"No, not really. I just feel like I have no choice and I can't walk away for so many reasons."

"Then don't. Listen to your heart."

Cecilia chuckled. "This, coming from my cougar friend? The one who stalks the college campus looking for her next boy toy?"

Amber laughed. "I do not do that! I believe in true love." She paused. "I just haven't met my Aiden yet. But you have. Call him."

After ending the call with Amber, Cecilia poured another glass of wine and walked to the window and looked out into her front yard. She realized she hadn't checked the mail in days. Slipping on her flats, she walked to the end of her driveway and grabbed a handful of envelopes and advertisement flyers from the box. She smelled a cigarette and looked around. Her neighbor Maggie was across the street standing in her driveway holding a dog leash in one hand and a cigarette in the other. Her gray curls were lightly dancing in the breeze along with her house dress covered in red and yellow flowers. Cecilia wondered if there was an age when women just gave up and took to wearing a piece of fabric halfway between a curtain and a dress.

Maggie's little white dog gave a quick bark at Cecilia and began wagging his tail. She waved to Maggie and smiled. She was just about to turn to go back into her house when a short dark-haired man whizzed by on his bicycle only a foot away from her. The smell made her stop dead in her tracks. His cologne drifted with the breeze after him and even when he was out of sight and around the corner, there were still traces of the scent in the air. It was Aiden's cologne.

Going back inside, she tossed the pile of mail onto the entryway table. Her phone was lying on the coffee table and she stood over it, biting her pinkie nail.

She lost the battle and dialed his number.

He picked up after two rings. "Hello?"

"Aiden." She didn't know what else to say.

"Would you like me to come over?"

"Yes, I'd like to talk."

"OK, I'll be right over." *Click.*

∞

"I truly am sorry I frightened you. I panicked when I saw you and Mike together. I didn't know who he was, but it was clear you two had chemistry and I felt like he was going to steal you away from me. And then. . . it was also. . . it felt like a slap in the face, Cecilia. That's the only way I know to explain it."

The two were sitting at the dining room table and it didn't escape Cecilia's notice that she was in the same chair she had been tied to just a few weeks ago. The man across from her was still dangerous, capable of coercing her into submission, but now showing just a sliver of vulnerability. When she opened the door, he had said nothing and simply walked in, given her a hug and said, "I'm glad you called." Although under the surface, there was a thinly veiled message that sounded like *I'm glad I don't have to make good on my threat.*

He took her hand and led her to the sofa where they sat. He turned so he was directly facing her. "I'm sorry, Cecilia. I'm sorry I frightened you. It appears there is a jealous part of me that I forgot existed."

"I understand. I just don't like the way you lost your temper. I meant it when I said I'd rather you turn me in than to deal with that drama, that anger."

"I know you meant it. I respect that about you. You stand up to me and I like it. But I'm a passionate person and I don't know if I can change that."

"But, do you have to throw things, charge at me like that? You knew damn well you were scaring me and I think you were enjoying it."

"I wouldn't say I enjoyed it. But, yes I did it intentionally. I will not lie about that. You were being such a smart-ass! I felt like you were making a joke out of what I was trying to communicate. I had to get through to you."

"I didn't want to be a smart-ass. I realize that is a childish way of behaving. It's just that no matter how I tried to reason with you, you were so convinced that I wanted to get back with Mike! I didn't know what to say to make you understand."

"Well it appears that we both have our weaknesses." He leaned forward, reached for her hand. "What do you say we try? I work on reigning in my temper and you cut back on the sarcastic remarks, although I must say, it would be kind of sexy if it didn't piss me off so much."

She narrowed her eyes, thinking. If she gave in too easily, he would think he could walk all over her.

"You're still deciding. Or, you're trying to make me grovel. Oh, Cecilia. Do you really think you have the upper hand here?"

"I don't know but I *do* have a choice."

"You do. Why don't I help you with that?"

"Oh, no, I don't think so!" She backed away in her chair.

He laughed. "No, no, that's not what I meant." He got up and walked around to her. "Stand."

"So bossy." But she stood.

He surprised her by grabbing a fistful of her hair, pulling her into an intense kiss.

When he pulled away, she was breathless. "Now that's the kind of passionate I like."

"Not the key-throwing passion?" he asked.

"No, definitely not."

He waited, watching her. "So what do you say? Want to give us another try?"

"Oh, why not?"

He laughed. "Well, that's an answer."

"Yes, I do want to try again," she said as she leaned in and nibbled his neck.

His body went stiff. "Damn Cecilia. You know exactly what you're doing."

"Do I?"

"You're driving me crazy."

"Do something about it then," she challenged.

He pushed her against the wall, pinning her. "Oh, I plan on it." He slowly began planting kisses on her neck, her mouth, then back to her neck. His smell, the way his body moved, his hips pressing against her, his lips so warm they almost burned her skin. . . it was exquisite.

"Aiden. . ."

"I've missed this. The way you taste, the way your body feels. . . "

He picked her up so her legs were wrapped around his waist. She kissed his neck and tightened her arms around him as he carried her to the bedroom.

Any thought she may have had left her mind. He consumed her completely, his sparkling dark eyes watching her steadily as they plunged deeper and deeper, and she was so far away.

∞

She rolled onto her back and Aiden lie down beside her, still breathing heavily. She rested her head on his chest.

"Cecilia, you're amazing. You're a goddess."

"Mmmm. . . " she moaned, too weak to form words.

"Are you OK?" He pushed a piece of hair away that had fallen over her eye.

"So much better than OK. Wow. . . "

"I like that response. And I agree. Wow is right," he said, kissing her head. "Play hookey with me tomorrow."

Cecilia laughed. "You know I can't do that."

"Sure you can," Aiden said as he tugged on her hair. "Live a little. I'd like to spend the day in bed with you."

"You're such a bad influence! I can't, I have patients to see. They are counting on me."

"They'll survive. I'm sure someone else can cover for you."

"Maybe but my answer is no. I love what I do, Aiden. If I start playing hookey now, you'll expect me to do it all the time. And that will be a problem."

"I could take care of you, you know."

"Oh, God. Don't even think about it. I don't want to be taken care of. You know me better than that. Do you ever think I would go for that?"

He sighed. "I know you wouldn't. It was worth a shot, though."

She rolled on top of him, pinning him down. "If you say so."

∞

The alarm went off much too early Monday morning. Cecilia had maybe gotten three hours' sleep. She groaned, rolling over, feeling for Aiden. When his side of the bed was empty, she sat up, looked around and realized the smell of fresh coffee was wafting through the house.

She sighed with relief and only wished she could inject caffeine into her veins on mornings like this. She had a surgery scheduled for this afternoon and had to be on top of her game.

He walked in, holding a steaming cup. "Thank you, Aiden," she said emphatically, taking a big gulp. "Ahh. . . the sweet nectar of the gods."

Aiden laughed, sitting down next to her on the bed. "That it is." He kissed her forehead. "Are you sure you can't stay home with me? Maybe try a re-enactment of last night? Last chance. . . " He raised his brows, hopeful.

She groaned and leaned back on her pillow. "That is so tempting but you know I can't." She sat up and sighed. "I have a surgery scheduled later."

"I know, sweetheart. You can't blame a man for trying." He took her hand. "You amaze me, Cecilia. I can't get enough of you. When can I see you again?"

"Tonight," she answered.

"My pleasure." He kissed the top of her head. "Now, it's time for you to get ready, so I'll go. I'll call you later."

∞

"Yes, mom I'm fine, really. I'm sorry I haven't called in so long. Things have been crazy."

143

Cecilia had been taking a short break before her 2:00 pm surgery when her mother had called. The two had always been close, despite her mother's less than encouraging attitude about her daughter attending medical school. Once Cecilia had been offered admission into three Ivy League schools of medicine—Brown, Dartmouth and Colombia—her mother had changed her attitude and become more supportive. Her father had still been skeptical, stubbornly insisting that Cecilia should focus more on getting married and having children.

"I'm sure they have, that's why I'm worried about you. How are you doing. CeCe?"

"I'm a lot better than I was a few months ago. Work is keeping me busy and I'm. . . I'm seeing someone," she said and then waited for the lecture about it being too soon to start dating again.

"Are you? Wow, well, that's good, honey."

"You're not going to tell me it's too soon?"

"Well, it may be too soon, but you're a grown woman and can make your own decisions. Of course, you shouldn't rush into anything. . . "

"We are taking it slow, just getting to know each other. He's helping me get through it. He's been through some hard times, too, so we are helping each other." She hated lying to her mother. *We are not taking it slow*, she thought.

"I'm happy to hear it, sweetheart. Well. . . " she began, sounding impatient. "Tell me about him! What does he do?"

"He's the medical examiner for Lakeview County."

"He does autopsies? Interesting. Well that's good you met another doctor. You two should be more on the same level."

When Cecilia was silent, Linda added quickly, "Oh, CeCe, I didn't mean it like that! Oh, God, I'm sorry. That's not what I meant. I just meant he sounds like he's good for you."

"I know what you meant, Mom. And you're right. He is very intelligent, sometimes I think too much. He seems to read my mind, get inside my head." *If only she knew*, she thought.

"That's a good thing, honey. He gets you. What else? Does he treat you well? Is he kind?"

"Yes, he treats me well. I mean, he has his temper, but—"

"Well, all men do, CeCe. And you are so independent, so stubborn. Try to let him be the man."

Cecilia laughed. "Oh, I do. I wouldn't have a choice, anyway."

"Oh really? Meaning. . . ?"

"He's just so. . .I couldn't emasculate him if I wanted to."

"Good, that's how it should be, honey. You need someone like that. So, tell me, what does he look like? Is he a surfer? Is he nice and tanned?"

Cecilia smiled to herself. Her New York mother thought everyone in Florida was a tanned surfer.

"No, he's not a surfer. In fact, he's paler than me. Big brown eyes, black hair. . . "

"Tall?"

"Yeah, probably 6'2."

"Oh, nice! Skinny-tall, though? You know those super tall men that look like string beans—"

Cecilia laughed. "No, he's in great shape, muscular. I don't know, he's just. . . big."

"Oh, is he now?" her mother asked in a sing-song voice.

"Jesus, Mom! That's not what I meant," Cecilia said, laughing.

Her mother giggled. "I know, honey. It's good to hear you laugh again. He sounds wonderful, CeCe. When do we get to meet him?"

"I don't know. . . I'm taking a trip to Baltimore next month for a conference and I was thinking of renting a car and driving to see you or maybe just hop on another flight. I don't know if he'd be able to come with me, though—"

"Oh, you have to bring him! Your father and I want to meet him."

"OK, Mom. I'll see what I can do." She looked at the clock on the wall. "Well, I need to let you go. I have to scrub in for surgery."

"OK, sweetheart. I'm so proud of you. I've told you that, haven't I?"

"Yes, Mom."

"OK then, you go save lives and let me know when you'll be in town. I love you, honey."

"Love you too, Mom."

She hung up and smiled. Her mother had sounded a lot happier about the news than she had expected.

∞

"Hey, good job in there. That was a rough one." Dr. Patton had finished a surgery about an hour before Cecilia's and had been watching from the gallery.

Cecilia soaped up and scrubbed her arms and hands. "Thanks! Yeah, it was rough but he'll pull through."

"He will. Hey, so are we all set for the trip to Baltimore?"

"Yeah. Everything's good to go. We should run through our presentation again ahead of time, though." She dried her hands and Dr. Patton held the door open for her.

"Oh, definitely."

She was cut off when Aiden appeared by her side. "Thought I might find you here."

"Aiden! What are you doing here?"

"I'm consulting on a case and remembered you had surgery this afternoon. How did that go?"

"It went well. All finished and now back to the office for some paperwork, then I'll be heading home."

"Dr. Harper?" A petite middle-aged woman was approaching from behind.

"Yes?" Cecilia turned around. "Oh, hello Ms. Flores. Is everything OK?"

"Yes, Adam is doing great. I just wanted to thank you again for removing the tumor. You saved his life. Our entire family is so grateful."

"Of course, Ms. Flores. You really saved his life by bringing him in when you did. He may not have made it if he didn't have you. I'll be back tomorrow to check on him but we expect him to make a full recovery."

Ms. Flores shook Cecilia's hand. "Well, thank you again."

When Cecilia turned back around, Aiden was smiling but she noticed Dr. Patton had a strange look on his face.

"What is it?"

"What? Oh, nothing. I'm just exhausted. I've done six surgeries already this week. I need some sleep."

"Oh, I'm sure." Cecilia turned to Aiden. "Let me just go change and I'll meet you in the front lobby in a few."

"OK, sweetheart." He pulled her in for a hug and gave her a peck on the cheek. "I'll see you soon."

"Cecilia, I need to ask you something." Dr. Patton said when Aiden walked away. "How long have you known Dr. Black?"

Cecilia hesitated. "A few months. Why?"

"Listen, I don't want to be weird or stick my nose where it doesn't belong, but, there's just something strange about him. I mean, I don't know. . . " He seemed to struggle to find the right words.

"Strange? Well, he's a little different, I guess, but he treats me wonderfully and I'm happier than I've been in a long time."

"I know. But I just wanted to tell you, and I shouldn't even say anything, but when you turned to speak to your patient's wife just a moment ago, well, Aiden gave you the weirdest look."

Cecilia laughed. "What do you mean?"

"No, I'm serious, Cecilia. It was the scariest thing. He glared at you. Just stared at the back of your head with the most evil look I've ever seen. It was creepy." He paused.

"Look, I'm sorry, I know this sounds ridiculous, but I saw what I saw and I just wanted to tell you."

"OK..."

"Did you guys have a fight or something?"

"No, not at all. We're totally fine. I'm grateful you're watching out for me, but I don't know. I think you just need to get to know him better. He's a great guy. He can be a little intense sometimes. Maybe that's what you saw."

"Yeah, maybe..."

"Everything's fine, Bruce. Thanks for looking out for me, though. I've got to run. See you tomorrow."

She left him and went to the locker room. Changing into her street clothes, Cecilia tried to put it out of her mind. Bruce was just looking out for her, being protective. And maybe he was a little jealous. He had tried to ask Cecilia to dinner a couple times, but she had always declined.

# FIFTEEN

**Friday June 6, 2014**

Aiden took Cecilia's hand as they stepped onto the moving walkway. Glancing out the window, she heard the cheerful announcement overhead:

*Welcome to Baltimore-Washington International Airport! We hope you enjoy your stay in the beautiful Baltimore – D.C. area. Current temperature is seventy-two degrees with sunny skies. Thank you for flying with BWI and we hope to see you again soon!*

"Let's go to the hotel, settle in first," Aiden said, planting a kiss on the top of her head.

Cecilia had asked Aiden to accompany her to the medical conference in Baltimore. Dr. Patton's daughter had become suddenly ill and he had been unable to attend. Aiden had agreed to go with her under one condition: that they drive up to New York to see her parents. Cecilia had protested, wanting to fly because it would be quicker. Aiden had gently but firmly insisted they drive: *We have the time and it's only a four-hour drive, sweetheart. It will give us more time together. We can stop and sightsee a little, make a day out of it. We will still arrive at your parents' home well before dinner time.*

How could she argue with that? And although she was usually too impatient for long car rides, she had to admit it would be nice to spend the extra time with Aiden. This was a change for her, not being the boss, not making all the decisions. As much as she tried to fight Aiden's controlling nature, she found it was a useless battle. More than that, she was surprised to find that she enjoyed having him take charge.

"Sounds good to me. I could use a shower," Cecilia said.

"Mmmm. . . I think I'll join you," he said, squeezing her hand.

"Please do," she said, returning the squeeze.

To this, he suddenly stopped and pushed her against the wall of the long empty corridor, setting their luggage down along the wall. They were almost to the exit of the airport and people might be able to see them, but Cecilia didn't care.

"I want you now," he said, his voice low and gruff. He tucked a piece of hair behind her ear and kissed her neck softly.

Cecilia reflexively pressed her body into his, immediately forgetting that they were in public. "I want you, too, Aiden, " she said, closing her eyes.

He pulled away in a snap. "But," he said, grinning. "That will have to wait."

As he bent down to pick up the luggage, Cecilia slapped him playfully on the arm. "You are so mean!"

Aiden turned and gave her a look of mock disapproval. "Sweetheart, we are in a public place. Making out here is just inappropriate. Can't you wait until we get to the hotel?"

Cecilia slapped him again, laughing. "Asshole!"

"Oh really? I've heard that before."

"I'm sure you have. You earn it sometimes."

He slung a bag over his shoulder, but not before giving her a swat on the bottom.

"Hey!"

He flashed his naughty-boy-caught-with-his-hand-in-the-cookie-jar grin and took her hand. "Let's go."

The grand ballroom at the Baltimore Marriot Inner Harbor was set up with several tables, each with an elegant bouquet of white, peach and lavender roses suspended in crystal vases serving as the centerpiece. The American Brain Tumor Consortium was hosted by Johns Hopkins Hospital and most in attendance were neurosurgeons from various university hospitals, including Cecilia's alma mater, Columbia University. Cecilia had been invited as a speaker to present her latest research on glioblastoma. She had never been afraid of public speaking but this made her nervous because there were so many well-known physicians and researchers there, people she admired, people she would love the opportunity to work with.

"Are you nervous?" Aiden asked.

"Yes, strangely enough, I am. I've spoken in front of crowds before, but this is different. These are the rock stars of medicine here," she gave a little laugh. "I'd love to work with them. I want to impress them."

He turned her to face him and took her hands. "Cecilia, listen to me. They are already impressed by your work. That is why they invited you to speak. And if you are still nervous, remember why you're here. Remember why you are doing this."

"For my grandfather."

"Exactly."

She drew in a deep breath, feeling the nerves dissipate a little. "Thank you, Aiden."

"Come here." He pulled her in for a hug and whispered in her ear. "You've got this."

∞

". . . and because glioblastoma contain various different cell types, this gives us a special challenge in not only determining courses of treatment, but in finding a way to slow the growth of these aggressive tumors. Because they have finger-like tentacles, these tumors are extraordinarily difficult to completely remove surgically. My colleague, Dr. Patton, and I have been researching several drugs over the past twelve months that may aid in reducing the growth rate of GBMs. One drug in particular, Levatryl, which is currently on the market being used to treat hypertension, reduced the rate of growth by three percent in our clinical trials. . . " Cecilia looked around the room and met Aiden's eyes. He smiled and she instantly felt calm again. "This drug can not only be safely administered in conjunction with radiation and chemotherapy but also enhances the effectiveness of chemotherapy. . . "

After her speech, Cecilia joined Aiden in the audience to watch the remaining presentations on various medical studies and current research relating to brain tumors.

He took her hand, giving it a squeeze, when she sat down. "Well done, sweetheart," he whispered.

She breathed a sigh of relief and smiled up at him. "That was nerve-racking."

"You were wonderful." He kissed the top of her hand.

"Thank you," she whispered, turning her attention back to the stage.

She recognized many of the presenters as well known and respected physicians in her field. Many were members of cancer centers and universities that were part of a brain tumor consortium she had always longed to join. She made a mental note to try to speak to a couple of them after the presentation.

After catching up with old friends from Columbia, Cecilia was determined to talk to Dr. Morgan, the director of neurosurgery at Johns Hopkins Hospital and the co-founder of the American Brain Tumor Consortium. The problem was, he was surrounded by people, engaged in what seemed to be a deep and lively discussion.

Aiden returned from the men's room and rested his hand on the small of her back.

"How are you doing, love?" he asked.

"I'm fine." She stood on her tiptoes to kiss his cheek. "I'm waiting to talk to that man right there," she said, looking at Dr. Morgan, who reminded her of her favorite uncle, Andy. A man of average height, he somehow took on the appearance of a teddy bear with his full beard and jovial demeanor.

"Ahh, Patrick Morgan. He's a very talented surgeon. I read his article last year on brain plasticity. I think he might be a genius."

"I think he is. I'd love to talk to him, pick his brain a little, get his take on my research."

"Would you like something to drink? I'm going to grab some water," Aiden asked.

"I'd love some water, too, thank you."

"Be right back." Aiden made his way over to the beverage table.

A moment later, after Cecilia had scanned the rest of the room, she turned back to check if Dr. Morgan was still surrounded. She frowned. He was gone. *Well, he can't have gone far. I'm going to find him,* she thought. She began searching around the room, determined to introduce herself.

Then the avuncular man was standing in front of her, extending his hand. "Dr. Harper?"

Stunned, she recovered quickly and smiled, accepting his handshake. "Yes. Dr. Morgan, it's an honor."

"The honor is mine. Your presentation was informative and inspiring. You and your colleague—Dr. Patton, is it?"

When Cecilia nodded her assent, he continued. "Well, no disrespect to him, of course, but from what I hear, it was you who had the idea of testing this drug on glioblastoma. That was bold and original, but most importantly, it appears to work. That kind of attitude and dedication is just what we need in this field."

"Thank you! Well, we are making progress but we have a long way to go."

"This is true. But, tell me. Why Florida? Why didn't you stay in New York?"

"Oh, that's a long story. I do plan on moving back eventually."

"They always are," he said, smiling warmly, scratching his beard. "Well I hope you do move back to the area. As you know, we have top-notch labs and equipment here, not to mention more opportunities for funding. I'm very impressed that you've made such great strides with the small university in Florida. That speaks volumes, Dr. Harper."

"Well, it has been a challenge, but not an impossible one."

"I hear that this particular type of tumor holds a special interest for you. It does for me as well. My grandfather lost the battle with his tumor when I was ten years old."

"Yes, same for me. I was fourteen."

He gave a sympathetic smile. "These things, while they are tragic, can be used to fuel our passions, our work. And it seems as if you are doing just that. You obviously have passion and dedication, which is why I'd like to ask you to join me at our next consortium meeting. I'd love to have your input and pick your brain on the matter." He laughed. "Sorry, a little neuro-humor."

Cecilia laughed along but was shocked. *He wants to pick* my *brain?*

"Yes, of course! I'd love to. It would mean so much to me."

He smiled, shaking her hand again. "Well, you'll be hearing from me soon, Dr. Harper."

As he was about to make his exit, Aiden appeared at her side and smiled politely at Dr. Morgan. "I don't believe we've met," he said, extending his hand.

Cecilia piped up, making the introductions. "Oh, yes, Dr. Morgan, this is Dr. Aiden Black. Aiden, Dr. Morgan."

As the men shook hands, Cecilia noticed Dr. Morgan scrutinizing Aiden.

"You look familiar. Have we met before?"

"I don't believe so, sir," Aiden replied, a polite smile frozen on his face.

"Hmm. Are you from the area?"

"No, I've never lived in Maryland. I have been in Florida for a couple years now, before that I was in Los Angeles, New York. . . "

"Ah. Well, then. You must just have one of those faces."

"I hear that a lot," Aiden said.

∞

"That was weird how Dr. Morgan thought he had met you before," Cecilia said. They had been on the road for about an hour. The silver Mercedes SUV Aiden had rented was spacious and Cecilia reclined back in her seat, stretching her legs.

"Yes, it was weird. I can't say I've ever met the man, though."

"You've been around for a long time. Maybe you've crossed paths along the way," she said.

"Are you saying I'm old?" Aiden asked, giving her a sideways glance.

"Well, you are old. But you look good for your age, though."

"Oh, thank you! How kind of you, sweetheart!" He reached over, stroked her leg. "Have I told you how proud of you I am?"

"Yes, only about a hundred times since we got into the car," Cecilia said.

"Well, I am. And to think you were nervous about the presentation, meeting Dr. Morgan. It's obvious how much they respect you."

"I can't believe he invited me to their next consortium meeting! Do you know how huge that is?" She shook her head. "All I wanted was a chance to speak with him and now this."

"It only gets better from here, Cecilia. You're on your way." He tugged her hair. "Are you hungry?"

"Getting there," Cecilia said.

"We'll stop in about thirty minutes or so. I believe there is a nice little town up ahead." He glanced over, his eyes traveling from her face down to her left hand, resting on her thigh. His eyes widened. "You're wearing your ring! When did you put it on?"

"The last time we stopped. I. . ." She looked down at her hand, the diamond catching the light streaming in from the window, throwing thousands of tiny sparkles around the car. A flicker of light caught her eye just above her forehead. She sat up and looked into the vanity mirror where wide, pale blue eyes stared back. She felt Aiden watching her and she was surprised to see the woman in the mirror smiling unabashedly, her cheeks flushed.

"So, you've made your decision."

Cecilia peeled her eyes from the woman in the mirror she didn't recognize and turned in her seat to face him. "I decided to put it on today."

Aiden's throaty, sinister laugh echoed throughout the car. He sighed and pulled into the next rest stop.

"Ahhh. . . Cecilia." He leaned closer to her. His eyes never leaving hers, he reached for her other hand, holding them firmly in his own. "I need a straight answer from you, my little minx." He looked up from under dark lashes, his eyes glowing in the sunlight. His demeanor was different somehow. *He looks vulnerable*, Cecilia thought. *Almost like a high school boy asking a girl to prom. Little does he know I already made my decision last night.*

"Would you be my wife, have a child with me?"

"And no one else will ever know the truth about Rick?"

"You have my word. We won't speak of it again. I will never tell another soul."

"Then my answer is yes," she said.

Aiden's eyes suddenly were on fire. He looked triumphant. He got out of the car, came around and opened her door. "Come."

She stood and he took her face in his hands, kissing her forehead.

"You made the right decision, love." He touched the ring on her left ring-finger. It was a three-carat princess cut diamond surrounded by three rows of tiny sapphires on either side.

"Why don't we set a tentative date?"

She realized she must have made a face because he said quickly, "We can always change it."

"Oh. I don't know." She thought for a moment. "I've always thought an autumn wedding would be nice."

"Autumn of next year? That sounds fine to me." He took her hand, kissed it.

"Or this autumn."

Aiden looked stunned. "This autumn? What happened to wanting to take your time, get to know me better?"

"It won't change anything, will it?"

"Cecilia, I don't want you to see this an obligation. I want you to *want* to marry me. I want to earn your trust."

"I trust you, Aiden. The truth is. . . " She took a deep breath. "Over the last few months, I've seen a different side of you. I've started to care for you."

Aiden squeezed her hand. "I care for you, too, Cecilia. I truly do."

"I know. You've shown me that. I mean, you're definitely unconventional, and I don't agree with the way you approached me. It was awful, to be honest. I still don't get why you did it that way. It was fucked up."

"It was," Aiden admitted.

"You had to frighten the living hell out of me, and this little voice still tells me to stay far away from you, that I shouldn't trust you. But for some strange reason, I just can't say no to you. And it's not just the fact that – and let's just call it what it is – you blackmailed me. It's absolutely insane but I trust you. I have feelings for you. I feel like I've known you a long time. As if we met lifetimes ago and are reuniting. " She paused to think. "I want to marry you, have a child with you. No other man has ever affected me the way you have. I. . . I don't know how to explain it. I don't feel like I have to play dumb around you, be the sweet little woman, try not to be too smart, too driven, for fear of scaring you off. I can be what I am and not hold back."

He pulled her close. "I'm so glad to hear you say that Cecilia. And I'm sorry I blackmailed you. I'm sorry I went about it the way I did. I truly am. At the time, I didn't have feelings for you. I was fascinated by you and just had to meet you. Find out the truth. And then you stood up to me, yelled at me that night. You were so brave. It made me respect you even more. I think I started falling for you then."

Cecilia shook her head. "This is the strangest relationship I've ever been in."

"But, you're happy?"

"Yes, very."

"Then, that's all that matters. So, autumn?"

"Yes. Maybe October?"

He pulled her in for an embrace. "October sounds perfect, love. October third. How's that?"

"Wonderful," she said as she sighed and rested her head against his chest.

"Good. Let's get back on the road, shall we?"

∞

As Cecilia stared out the window at the passing lush green landscape, the old faded red abandoned farmhouses, the rusted green tractors nestled in tall grass, her thoughts turned to what her life would be like with Aiden. They were getting married in the fall and she would move into his house in Willow Park, the town directly north of Spring Lake. It would be exciting, starting her new life with Aiden. With each passing day, she found herself falling more in love with him. But there was one thing they hadn't talked about and it was worrying her. She was about to marry an immortal man. He would always look thirty-six years old but she would age like a normal human. Her hair would turn gray, her skin would fill with wrinkles, her body would sag. Would he still love her? Will he still feel the same way he does now when she's an elderly woman? Never mind the fact that her friends and family would notice that he didn't age. What were their options, then? Would they have to move away and never see them again, or at least, never let them see Aiden? *How have we not talked about this yet? Surely, he's thought of it,* she thought.

"Sweetheart." Aiden's voice jolted her from her thoughts. She looked over to see his concerned expression. "Something's worrying you. What is it?"

"I was just thinking. There's something we've never discussed. And I think it's important."

"What?"

"Your immortality versus my mortality. The fact that if I spend my life with you, I will age normally, grow old, and you won't. I'll be seventy years old and you'll still look thirty-six."

"You'll be the ultimate cougar," Aiden said.

"Aiden, I'm serious. Haven't you thought about that?"

"I have, but I'll never stop loving you. Although I do understand how that must make you feel."

"Yes, and our friends and family. . . what will they think? It will only be a matter of time before they notice that you don't age. Imagine if the roles were reversed. You wouldn't want to grow old while I stayed young."

"I understand. We can figure that out when the time comes. Please don't worry about it, Cecilia. That is a long time from now. But, if there was a way to make you immortal, would you do it?"

Cecilia was surprised by his question. Was he able to do that? "I don't know. . . I mean, yes, I'd want to spend forever with you, and don't take this the wrong way, but I think immortality would be depressing. You *were* cursed with it. Sure, it sounds great at first, but is there a meaning to life if you know it could possibly last forever? When you know you are virtually indestructible, don't you start taking it all for granted? Things aren't as special when you have all the time in the world."

"You're right. It is a terrible curse. Never mind the real reason for it, Elara and Lavena's revenge. I don't think they knew just how successful they would be. It still hurts to think about how they deceived me. But the curse was two-fold. Because not only do I have to live forever, but I can never forget the pain. If it had simply been immortality, well, after so many years had passed, at least ten, twenty. . . I'd have gotten over it. The heart heals. We forget the pain. Otherwise, how do we go on? After seventeen hundred years, I should barely remember that day, much less still be as affected by it as I am. Sometimes it still feels like it was yesterday, but then I see your face and I feel better, Cecilia. You saved me."

Cecilia reached over and took his hand. "I'm glad, sweetheart. You saved me, too. I never thought I could be this happy with someone. I thought I couldn't have it all, but with you, I see that I can. I guess a man who was merely human would never be enough for me. As annoying as your super-intuition was at first, I see now that it is a blessing."

"Prevents a lot of arguments, doesn't it?" Aiden smiled. "Women always expect a man to read their minds anyway, so. . ."

She punched him playfully in the arm. "Hey, that's not true!"

"I've been around a long time. It's true, more often than not. I hate to say it."

"Whatever you say," she said, laughing.

His face turned serious. "How are your panic attacks lately?"

"How did you know I was having those?"

"Are you still having them?"

She tried to think of the last time she had one. "I haven't had one in a while. Not since – not since I met you. That's odd, I didn't even realize—"

"You're welcome," he said.

"What? God, Aiden. You scare me sometimes."

"I'm not trying to scare you. Just trying to help."

"Well, it's weird."

"You could say thank you."

"Thank you," she said.

"You're welcome."

Then she thought of something else. "Before, when you asked me if I would choose immortality. . . is there a way?"

"Why, are you reconsidering your answer?"

"No, I still don't think I could choose that."

"I wouldn't want you to. I want you to have a normal life, well as normal as you can have with me. But, no, there isn't a way. Not that I'm aware of anyway. Although," he said as he studied her carefully. "I suppose I could put a curse on you like Elara did to me."

"You could do that?"

"I'm not sure, but it's possible. Elara was a full-blooded goddess, if you will, so her powers were much stronger than mine. And we possess slightly different abilities. My father's abilities, and therefore, the abilities I inherited from him, are different from Elara's. But, some of them overlap. For example, Elara was a shape shifter. She could change form whenever she liked."

"And so can you," Cecilia said.

"That's right."

"How often do you do that?"

Aiden laughed. "Oh, I don't. It takes a lot of energy, makes me very tired. And I haven't felt a need to shift in a long time."

"Not since you first knocked on my door," Cecilia said.

"Yes, I did it then. That was the last time. It's not very pleasant. It's painful, actually. Imagine your face changing bone structure, your eyes changing color, your teeth changing—"

Cecilia shivered at the thought. "I'd rather not."

"Exactly. But my point is, I suppose I could put a curse on someone if I really tried. I could curse you with immortality. But, a curse is a very angry action. The person placing the curse has to be very angry – enraged – at the person he or she is cursing. I would have to hate you. Or at least muster up those hateful feelings to have enough power for it to be successful. And I can't imagine hating you, Cecilia, and I would never want to curse you anyway. Even if you begged me to make you immortal, I don't think I could do it. Because it's irreversible. I do not have the power to undo it. The gods and goddesses who had the ability to place curses did not have the ability to remove them and vice versa. The ancient Celts believed it was designed that way on purpose, so that they would have to think twice before cursing someone. It's not a frivolous thing that you can just do out of anger to punish someone for a while, then change your mind and remove it."

"So, the person – or god – placing the curse has a great responsibility to not use their gift in vain."

"Exactly."

"So, you won't put a curse on me?"

Aiden laughed. "No, absolutely not."

Cecilia yawned.

"Why don't you take a nap?" Aiden looked at the GPS. "We still have another hour or so before we need to stop again."

# SIXTEEN

Cecilia dozed in and out of sleep until she felt the car come to a stop.

"We're here, love."

Getting out of the car and stretching her legs, she read the sign. Sam's Deli.

"This place gets great reviews. It is supposedly the hidden gem of Tuckerville, New York."

"Sounds good to me. I'm starving."

After lunch, they stopped at a Chevron station right by I-95 to fill up on gas. Country music from the outside speakers drifted through the air.

"Hmmm. . . " Aiden smiled and looked at Cecilia. "Now that we have a full tank, where should we go?"

"Did you forget already?" Cecilia looked at him as if he had two heads.

"We've been making great time. Why don't we do something else before we get back on the road?"

Cecilia caught on. "The backseat?"

Aiden laughed. "Like we're in high school?" He turned in his seat, looking at the back of the car. "It's not very big. I mean, don't get me wrong, I'll take you anywhere I can get you, but I'd like to have more room when I ravish you," he said as he reached over and began trailing his hand from her knee, up to the fabric of her dress.

Between his words and the touch of his hand, she felt herself pulled under his spell once more. "Oh, Aiden. . . " She grabbed his hand as he started to inch her dress up her thigh.

He paused, looking at her in confusion.

"People can see us!"

"There's no one out here right now. But we need to get out of here. I'm going to take you somewhere," he said as he pulled his hand back and made a deep male sound of frustration. "Fuck, I want you."

He peeled out of the gas station and after about half a mile, pulled into an empty lot with a brick building nestled behind ornate landscaping.

He got out of the car, walked around and opened her door. "Come with me."

"Where are we going?"

"Where do you think?" He looked at the building then at her.

"We can't just walk in there!" she said.

"Who says? Trust me, Cecilia."

She sighed. "I trust you."

Walking to the front door, Cecilia saw a short woman wearing a green uniform sweeping the floor.

Aiden knocked. The woman came to the door and said through the glass in a thick accent, "Closed! No open today! Is Saturday!"

Aiden smiled and leaned in closer to be heard. "Entiendo. Yo soy hermano del dueño. Me pidió que lo conseguirá unos papeles. Yo tengo la llave pero lo dejé en casa y es un largo viaje. ¿Por favor, me dejaste?"

Cecilia stared at him, speechless. *What the hell?*

The woman shook her head fervently, replying in Spanish.

Aiden laughed briefly then leaned in and locked eyes with the woman. "Abra la puerta, por favor. Y también puedes irte a casa. Para el día haya terminado."

Without a word, she nodded and smiled, opening the door.

"Gracias," Aiden said, smiling in return.

While the woman packed up her things, Aiden took Cecilia's hand and led her to an office in the back, pretending to be looking for paperwork.

"What the hell was that?" Cecilia laughed. "You speak Spanish?"

"Si." He looked behind him. "I think she is gone. I'll be right back."

Walking back into the room, he said, "She's gone and the door is locked. The place is ours."

"What did she say that made you laugh?"

"I told her I was the owner's brother. She said that's impossible because I was the wrong race."

"You used your mind control on her," Cecilia said.

"I had to," he said, stalking closer. "You have a problem with that?"

"Hell, no," she said as she grabbed him, pulled him to her. "Not at all."

"That's more like it." He pushed her onto the brown leather couch. "

"What, no foreplay?" Cecilia pouted.

"Oh yes. I plan to take my time. You're so beautiful, Cecilia. You're a goddess." He walked a little closer so he was standing only two feet from her. "Now, look at me. Tell me what you want."

"I want you, Aiden."

He kneeled down in front of her, between her legs. "I know you do."

He began kissing her inner thighs, paused to give a little bite. She jumped. "Ow!"

She felt the rumble of his quiet laugh. "You love it," he said.

Grabbing his mop of black hair, she pulled until he looked up at her.

"Please, Aiden. . . " she said.

"I love when you beg me."

Five minutes later, she was crying out his name and felt her body clench, that hot, powerful spasm beginning at the tip of his tongue, spreading, blossoming into a flower of fire, the white hot torch burning inside her. She was in another world, surrounded by the warmth of the sun, the chaos of the ocean, powerless under the waves, pushing and pulling her down, then back up again, feeling that her body must have levitated off the couch, if only for a split second. She was at the mercy of the delectable waves of pure ecstasy, the fire-flower dissipating, breaking off into individual petals, traveling from the base of her hips up the length of her spine, to her neck, making her quake with delight.

When she came back to earth, she sat up and met Aiden's eyes.

"Damn, that is the most amazing thing in the world, Cecilia." He stood and Cecilia grabbed him and quickly unbuttoned his jeans, pulling them down.

He pulled her up from the couch then picking her up by the waist, sat her on the desk.

"Lift your arms," he said, pulling her dress over her head. "I want to see all of you."

Tossing the dress aside, he pushed himself inside her and began to move, but paused a couple of times, staring down at her. Cecilia was not having it. She grabbed his hips and yanked him closer.

Aiden's sharp laugh filled the room. "Oh, I see," he said.

"Why do you want to torture me?"

"Because it's fun," he said.

After a while, she opened her eyes and as soon as she saw his face, his eyes heavy with lust, his pouty lips slightly open, a bead of sweat trickling from his dark hairline, his expression turning into one of muted triumph, she lost all control and was riding that chaotic wave of ecstasy again, watching his eyes as they darkened, turned more intense, studying her, seemingly memorizing every look on her face. When she finally stilled, he pulled himself out and grabbed her arm, turning her around.

"Bend over the desk."

Her legs felt weak. "Aiden, I—"

Before she could finish, she felt his large, warm hand close over her mouth and his warm breath in her ear. "Shhh. . . now bend over the desk, love, or do I have to make you?"

She went limp, bending over in front of him. She had no more strength and was at his mercy. And if she was being honest with herself, she rather enjoyed it.

"That's better."

His low voice and the feel of his weight on top of her forced her to give in. He stood back up, taking her hips in his hands and after a few moments, she heard a low groan rumble from his chest as he grabbed her by the hair and pushed her head down, so her cheek was lying flat against the desk. He held her there a moment as he caught his breath. Then he let go and slowly pulled away.

She couldn't move. She was a limp mess and she was sure her legs were too weak to carry her out of this office. He picked her up and sat her on his lap on the couch.

He stroked her hair. "Are you OK?"

"Better than OK. . . " she said, leaning into him, closing her eyes. "You are amazing, Aiden."

He lifted her chin. "No, *we* are amazing. And I'm asking if you're OK because I got a little rough there for a while. I didn't hurt you, did I?"

"No, not at all." She leaned once more against his damp chest.

"OK, good then." He looked up at the wall clock. "Not to ruin the moment, but we'd better get out of here or risk being caught. Let's get freshened up."

∞

They ended up stopping two more times for sex: once in the backseat of the car in a deserted rest area and once in a hotel room after Aiden had used his powers on the desk clerk of a local Hilton. Cecilia had to admit Aiden's powers of persuasion were very useful at times.

When they finally arrived at the residence of Robert and Linda Brennan, and all necessary introductions had been made, the four settled down for an elaborate dinner her mother had made.

"This is exquisite, Ms. Brennan. Cecilia told me you were a great cook, but this is the most amazing Caprese salad I have ever had."

Linda beamed. "Why, thank you. And you can call me Linda."

Aiden smiled, his eyes twinkling. "Well, Linda, it truly is wonderful."

That's a fabulous compliment. Especially because Cecilia tells me you're quite the traveler. . . "

Cecilia watched as her mother was charmed by Aiden as the two talked of their travels around the world. Her father was silent, mostly focused on his food, although every few moments, he would look up and sneak a peek at Aiden with narrowed eyes. It wasn't an antagonistic expression but more of a curious one.

During a pause in the conversation, Aiden glanced at Robert and caught him staring. He gave him a close-lipped smile and a nod to which Robert returned quickly before looking away and clearing his throat.

Cecilia felt Aiden squeeze her hand under the table. "But what we really should be celebrating is some very exciting news Cecilia received today."

"What is it, dear?" Her mother's eyebrows shot up and she smiled.

"Well, we went to the conference yesterday and afterwards, Dr. Morgan approached me about attending the next meeting for the American Brain Tumor Consortium."

"Oh, wow! Did he?" Linda clapped her hands together. "That's a big honor!"

"It is. It was the last thing I expected. So I get to go to Johns Hopkins later this month. It's a great opportunity to get support and possibly more funding for my research."

"Wow! We're so proud of you, honey!"

"We are so proud of you," her father agreed. "It sounds like you are making real progress."

Cecilia smiled. "We are."

Aiden placed his hand on the small of her back. "I am a lucky man."

"That you are," her father replied.

At first, Cecilia thought her father would never warm up to Aiden, but after Aiden mentioned his time in the Marines, her father suddenly took interest and paid him more attention.

After dinner, her father turned to Aiden. "Say, would you want to join me for a cigar?"

"Ah, absolutely. Are you a Montecristo man?"

Robert's face lit up. "Yes! Montecristo Number Two, of course."

"Of course," Aiden agreed. He kissed Cecilia on the forehead and followed Robert to the study. Cecilia decided to go check on her mother in the kitchen. Linda spun around as soon as her daughter entered the room.

"Are the men smoking their cigars?" she asked.

"They are," Cecilia said as she began to help her mother load the dishwasher.

But Linda grabbed her arm. "Oh, honey. He's amazing. So handsome, devilishly sexy, actually, and so smart! And so well-mannered! Cecilia, where did you find him?"

Cecilia laughed. "It sounds like you're in love with him, Mom!"

"Well, aren't you? I mean, he seems like a keeper, if you ask me."

"I think he is, Mom. I care for him very much. I think I could be in love with him, but it just seems so. . . I don't know. . . surreal. We are taking it slow."

"As you should. But all I'm saying is, hold on to this one. Hell, if you don't want him, I'll take him, even if he is young enough to be my son!"

"Mom!" *Oh, if she only knew his true age*, she thought as she laughed.

"What? He's a good looking man. I can't help myself."

Cecilia laughed. "You've had a lot of wine."

"I have," Linda agreed.

And with that, it was official. Both parents not only approved but also adored Aiden. *Did I really expect anything less?* Cecilia thought with a smile.

It was midnight when the men finished their whiskey and cigars. Linda had excused herself to go to bed about an hour before, so Cecilia had retreated upstairs to the guest bedroom where she had called Amber and relayed the news of the day. Aiden walked in to find her sprawled on the bed.

"There you are, love." He bent down to kiss her. "You look exhausted."

"Mm," she grunted. "Time for sleep."

Aiden laughed quietly. "Yes, time for sleep. Here, get under the blanket, you must be cold."

Cecilia awoke a few hours later from a dead sleep. She turned over to drift back off when she heard Aiden mumble something unintelligible.

"What, honey?"

"I never forget. . . you're going to pay. . . " he mumbled.

*I must have heard him wrong. Or he's having a dream,* she thought.

"Forget what?" she asked.

"F- forget what you did. . . "

Her heart skipped a beat.

"Really? What I did?"

"Not you. . . not you. . . but her. . . and you. . . "

"OK." She waited.

"It hurts. . . still hurts. . . it won't go away until I. . . ."

"Shh. . . " she shushed him as she stroked his head. Staring at his face, contorted in pain, she felt something that had been hidden inside her try to break free. She fought it for a few seconds but then the sudden icy pain of resistance was too much to bear and her heart opened and the ice melted, leaving a pool of warm still water. "It's OK, Aiden. I love you."

She felt her head fall to the pillow and within seconds he had stirred and gently pushed her onto her left side as his arm enveloped her torso and his leg hooked hers. She was trapped and fiercely welcomed it, felt the corners of her mouth lift slightly as she held his arm around her body. His breath tickled the back of her neck.

The next morning as Cecilia was stirring creamer into her coffee, she looked over at Aiden. He was reading the newspaper, his hand resting on his coffee mug. "You were talking in your sleep last night."

"Was I? Well, did I say anything interesting?"

"Yeah, it was weird, actually. You said something like, 'I never forget' and 'it hurts, make it stop'."

He reclined back in his chair, studying her for a moment. "That's odd. I really don't know. Maybe it was a nightmare."

"You sounded angry."

"Well, are you usually happy in nightmares?" He laughed. "I honestly don't remember it, Cecilia, so I'll have to take your word for it. I'm sorry if I scared you."

"No, it was just weird, that's all."

"I'm sure it was." He stood, reached for her breakfast plate. "All finished?"

# SEVENTEEN

"*Meow! Meow!* That's exactly how he sounds! He's evil, I tell you! He really is!"

Cecilia took a deep breath. It was going to be a long day. She hadn't fully recovered from her jet-lag yet and was in desperate need of coffee or a nap. Or both.

"Elise, we need to talk about your surgery. I'm not going to beat around the bush here; you need to have the surgery as soon as possible. The faster we remove the tumor, the faster you can go back to having a normal life."

"Yeah, yeah, you said that." Elise drummed her long red and white polka dotted nails on the desk.

"I did. It's true, Elise. How are the headaches?"

"They aren't bad. Well, I had a killer one yesterday but—"

"Wouldn't you like to stop having the headaches?"

Elise began tugging and twisting the bright orange curls on her head. "What I'd like is to get out of this abusive relationship!"

"With your cat, you mean." Cecilia took a breath, trying to remain patient. Elise had a large meningioma in the frontal and temporal regions of her brain, which caused her personality to change and her behavior to become erratic.

"Yes! Tommy-boy! I am Rihanna and he is Chris Brown! I don't know why I keep coming home to him every night!"

"Um," Cecilia muttered, at a loss for words.

"I should put him on the street!"

"Please don't," Cecilia said.

"I'm freakin' serious! I don't know why I put up with it. It really makes me question my self-esteem, you know? I mean, he tries to kill me almost every night, sticking his little demon claws under my feet as I walk down the stairs. Do you know he bit my boyfriend's head the other day? Got up behind him on the sofa and sunk his nasty little teeth right into his head!"

"He does sound mean. Maybe try finding a new home for him. Elise, listen. You're here because we found a large tumor on your brain. If we don't remove it soon, we're looking at permanent damage and you quite possibly won't survive. The survival rate for this type of tumor is very high with an operation, but without—what are you doing?"

Elise had pulled out a small bottle of nail polish and began twisting the top. "Can I paint my nails in here?"

"No, Elise. Please put that away."

"OK, OK, Doc. I hear you." She threw the bottle back into her bag.

"Take the shit out of my head. Just take it."

"We will remove it and you're going to be just fine." Cecilia reassured Elise, shaking her hand.

Harriet bounded into Cecilia's office, the frosted tips of her spiky blonde hair dancing on her head. "Doc! I haven't gotten a chance to see you all day! Congrats on the invite to the consortium! I heard the conference was a success."

Cecilia clicked "save" on her patient notes, before turning to face Harriet. "Thank you! It was amazing. Yes, Dr Morgan approached me after the presentations and talked about my research. I couldn't believe it. They want me to join them at their next consortium meeting next month at Johns Hopkins."

"Wow, I'm so happy for you, Doc." Harriet's astute blue eyes studied Cecilia. "Is there something else?"

"What do you mean?"

"You look, I don't know, *really* happy. I mean, I know you're happy about the conference, but it seems like there's something else you're not telling me." Her eyes lit up. "Are you seeing someone? Is that it? It's a man, isn't it? I know that look."

"What? Oh, God, no. Seriously? Why on earth would you think that?" *Damn, she's good*, Cecilia thought.

"You look radiant. You look better than you have in months and I think there's a man in your life. You have a right to move on and be happy." When Cecilia remained silent, she continued. "C'mon, I've been around a long time, Doc, and I know that look. There's nothing to be ashamed of!"

Cecilia laughed. "I have no idea what you're talking about Harriet, but thank you for the compliment."

Harriet pursed her lips, shaking her head. "Yeah, yeah. You can't fool this old broad." As she began to walk out of the office, she looked over her shoulder. "Your three o'clock canceled by the way."

Cecilia heard her mumble something else as she walked down the hall that sounded like ". . . use that time to call your boyfriend. . . "

Shaking her head, Cecilia turned back to her computer but her a knock at her door.

"Hey there. I heard you blew them away in Baltimore."

"Bruce! How's Samantha?" Dr. Patton had planned to accompany Cecilia to the medical conference to present their research together but his five-year old daughter had suddenly fallen ill with a serious case of pneumonia and had been hospitalized.

"She's better, thank you. She's at home resting now but she's almost fully recovered."

"Oh, good. I'm so glad she's OK. I know you must have been so worried."

"Yes, it was rough there for a while, but we're in the clear now." He lingered near Cecilia's desk, pausing to pass a hand through his wavy ginger-colored hair, appearing to struggle with some internal dilemma. "So. . . I hear you were asked to attend their next ABTC meeting." He let the words hang in the air and Cecilia couldn't help but take notice of the weight of the words. He was upset he hadn't been invited.

"Yes, Dr. Morgan walked up to me after the presentations. I was floored. He said he was very impressed by our research," Cecilia made sure to stress the word *our*. "He wanted to discuss it more."

Bruce took a deep breath. "Well, don't you think it would be prudent for me to attend as well? I mean, not to make this more awkward than it is, Cecilia, but this is a joint venture. We are research *partners*." He itched his forehead, the dusting of freckles on his skin moving back and forth with each motion.

"Yes, of course we are. I'm more than aware of that. I had assumed you would accompany me to the consortium. It is June twenty-seventh, at the—"

Bruce cut her off mid-sentence. "*Accompany* you? Wow, Cecilia."

Cecilia raised her eyebrows. "Well, yes, I assumed we would attend together. Just as we were planning to attend the conference to present together." She paused, studying his angry expression. "Is there a problem, Bruce?"

"Oh, not at all, Dr. Harper. Not at all."

"Good. Because I don't understand why there would be. Everyone knows we are working on this together. I would never try to take all the credit. Your name is on every article, every piece of research, every lab document—"

"Yeah, it sure is but who is getting to go to the prestigious meeting?"

"We are. You and I both, Bruce."

"Right. I'm going to make a phone call." And he was gone.

Fifteen minutes later, Bruce stormed into her office. "Would you like to tell me why your name is the only one listed for the meeting? They don't even know who I am!"

"OK, Bruce. Let's figure this out. I'll make a phone call right now and get this cleared up."

"Don't bother. They told me I could accompany you as your guest. Your *guest*! I should be so honored to accompany you, the big famous doctor who's going to cure glioblastoma! Jesus Christ, you are unbelievable. You go and take all the credit—"

"Bruce. Listen to me. You need to calm down. I did not take all the credit. If you would just give me a moment, I'd be happy to call and—"

"What, call your pal Dr. Morgan? Convince him to give me a pity invite? No thank you. Why don't you just go fuck yourself, Cecilia! You backstabbing b—"

Just then, Bobby, a male nurse who stood at an imposing 6'5, strode into the room. "Is there a problem?" He had always reminded Cecilia of the character John Coffey in *The Green Mile*.

"Please get back to work, Bobby. This doesn't concern you."

"Well, we can hear you from the front office and it sounds like you're threatening Dr. Harper so it does concern me."

"I'm not threatening her. Now, get out of here." He brushed him off dismissively with a wave of his hand and turned back to Cecilia but Bobby placed a hand on his shoulder.

"I'm not going anywhere. Why don't you go to your office and take a breather and come back and discuss this when you're calm?"

Bruce whirled around to face Bobby. "The voice of reason. Thank you so much for your suggestion, but I repeat: Get out of here!"

Bobby took a step closer so that he was only inches from Bruce's face. "Like I said, I'm not going anywhere until you stop attacking Dr. Harper and leave the room."

"Attacking her?" He laughed. "God, she is so precious, isn't she? Let's all treat her like a queen. Everyone is forgetting that I contributed at least half, if not more, to this research. Why is she getting all the credit? Why does she get flown to fancy hotels and invited to prestigious consortiums? Oh, I know why. Look at her. Isn't she pretty? She's nice to look at, right? Let's all watch her prance to the podium and give her little presentation, but we're forgetting who stayed up countless nights in the lab—"

Cecilia's jaw dropped and she suddenly rose from her chair to face him. "Oh, you've got to be kidding, Bruce. You've crossed the line."

"Yes he has and he's leaving." Bobby took Bruce by the arm. "That's enough. Come on, let's go."

Bruce tried for a moment to struggle out of his grip, but Bobby gave him a look. Grimacing, he allowed Bobby to lead him out of the room but not before craning his head over his shoulder to throw one last comment at Cecilia. "This isn't over, you selfish conniving bitch."

∞

"Well, he always seemed a little strange, if you ask me."

"You just didn't like him because he had red hair," Cecilia said.

Amber's girly peals of laughter rang through the phone's speaker. "No, but ginger men are weird. He probably could never get any and that's why he's so angry."

"OK, Amber, whatever you say." Cecilia laughed. "He was always a little intense, I guess, but I still can't believe he went off on me like that. It was insane. Everyone in the office heard him, including some of the patients. I thought he would calm down and come talk to me, but he quit the next morning."

"All's well that ends well. I'm glad he's out of there."

"Yeah, me too, I guess. It's just such a shock. He was never like that. I still don't understand it. And now I have to continue the research on my own. I can do it, but it's going to be a lot more work." Cecilia sighed.

"If anyone can handle it, you can, CeCe."

"I hope so."

"Maybe you should have your sexy doctor boyfriend help you," Amber suggested.

"Oh, I bet he'd love to—"

Cecilia was cut off by a knock at the door.

Hearing the knock through the phone, Amber asked, "Who's that?"

"Probably Aiden. Hold on a sec," she walked to the door, looked out the peephole.

There was no one there. Opening the door, she looked down to find a small white envelope. She ripped it open and inside was a small typed note: You'd better watch your back.

A chill went down Cecilia's spine. Going back to the phone, she told Amber, "That was weird. I just opened the door and no one was there but there was this note." She read the note to her.

"Do you have any idea who it could be?" Amber asked.

"No clue."

"You need to call the police!" Amber said.

"Yeah, I will. I'll talk to you later, OK?"

"OK, girl. Be careful. Call me later."

Cecilia turned the note over in her hands a few times, trying to think of who could possibly have left it at her door. She picked her phone back up and decided to call Aiden first.

*Knock. Knock.*

*Oh, no, not again.* Cecilia's heart thudded in her chest. She crept back to the door to look out the peephole. She breathed a sigh of relief. It was Aiden.

Stepping through the door, he pulled her into an embrace. "How are you, sweetheart? I was in the area and thought I'd stop by—" he stopped, his face changing to an expression of alarm. "What's wrong?"

"Oh, God, Aiden." She pulled away and picked the note up from the hall table, handed it to him. "Look."

Reading the words, Aiden's eyes grew large then he slammed the note down on the table. "Do you have any idea who this could be? Who would threaten you?" He was fuming. "We're going to figure this out, I promise you that."

Cecilia began pacing. "I don't know, I mean, it's just—" Suddenly she stopped in her tracks. "Bruce."

"Who?" Aiden walked closer.

"Dr. Patton."

Aiden's eyes flashed. "The asshole that threatened you at work the other day. Accused you of taking all the credit for the research. Fuck." He ran a hand through his hair, making his inky black strands stand up in a wild mess. "He's not going to get away with this."

"Let's just call the police and report this."

"I'll take care of that. You sit down and relax. That must have really frightened you." Aiden led her to the couch, sat down next to her. He took her hand and leaned in close. "Look at me. Let me handle this. I love you, Cecilia and I'll never let anything happen to you." He reached up to caress her cheek then pulled her in for a kiss. Cecilia was too stunned by his declaration to say anything. He stood and pulled his phone from his back pocket. "I'll be back in a few minutes, love."

*Wow, he said he loved me. I didn't say it back. I want to, though.* Cecilia's head was spinning. It was too much to think about right now, especially after the disturbing note.

∞

"Here you go, sweetheart." Aiden handed her a cup of coffee. He had insisted Cecilia spend the night at his house after the incident with the letter. "Please be careful, love. I really wish you'd let me drive you to work. I'm still not convinced that asshole won't show up."

"He won't, Aiden. And I park right in the front where security guards will be twenty feet from me. I'll be fine."

Bruce didn't show up all day and at 5:30, Cecilia packed up to leave. All she wanted to do was go home to Aiden and snuggle in by the fireplace and watch a movie. She had to make a quick stop by the lab first to grab some paperwork, though. Since Bruce was no longer working with her on the research, she was going to have to take work home with her throughout the week. Aiden had told her to come straight home and not make any stops, but this would only take a couple minutes. Besides, he worried too much anyway.

She found the information on a clinical trial she was following and made her way out of the building to lock up when she felt a hand on her arm. Startled, she shoved it away and darted for her car.

.

# Eighteen

"Wait! Cecilia! It's me, Bruce! Look I'm so sorry about everything, I just wanted to talk to you, please—"

"Get the fuck away from me! I liked your note yesterday, that was great. Now fuck off!"

He hesitated. "My note? Wait, what do you mean?" He was still following her about ten paces behind. "Look, please just give me two minutes. I'm sorry about going off on you at the office the other day. That wasn't me. I don't know what got into me. I'm so sorry! Please. . . "

"It sure looked like you." She opened her car door. "Leave me alone, don't bother me again!" Slamming the door shut, she sped off.

After dinner, Cecilia decided to tell Aiden about running into Bruce in the parking lot of the lab. And just as she expected, he was pissed.

"When did this happen?" Aiden slammed his water glass on the table.

"When I was on my way home a little while ago."

Aiden's eyes widened. "Why didn't you call me? Damn it, Cecilia, you have to tell me things like this!"

"I *am* telling you!"

"Yes, after the fact! You should have called me immediately. Where were you when this happened?"

"I was at the lab, I had to stop and get—"

"You were where?" He cut her off. "I thought you were coming straight home. Cecilia, after that threatening note, you need to be careful. I don't want you going places alone at night without me until we get this straightened out."

"I know, I didn't think he'd be there. I just needed to grab some paperwork. It was weird. He claimed not to know anything about the note, said he just wanted to talk. I told him to fuck off and got in my car and left."

Aiden ran his hands through his hair and sighed loudly. "Jesus, Cecilia, of course he's going to deny writing the note. He's obviously crazy." He leaned forward and took her hands in his. "Promise me you won't do that again. Don't make any stops on your way home, especially places he might show up. Please, just for a while."

"OK, Aiden. I won't, I promise." She squeezed his hands and was relieved to see his face visibly relax.

"Good. I worry about you." He stood and kissed her forehead before clearing the dishes from the table.

∞

Cecilia heard Mama Cass singing "Dream a Little Dream of Me." Was Aiden playing a record in the middle of the night? She was too tired to open her eyes to investigate, stuck in that place between sleep and consciousness.

Turning over, her feet tangled in the mess of the sheets, she fell into a deep slumber, surrendering to that heavenly place of nothingness, melting into her bed, her head heavy on the pillow. Then, in her mind's eye: blood. Lots and lots of blood. (The music grew louder. Where was it coming from?)

A tall man in a hat holding a knife, standing over a slumped body. And at the head of the lifeless body she saw a glimpse of orange. Looking back at the tall dark figure, his eyes shadowed by the brim of the hat, she watched as he stood motionless.

To her horror, his head lifted slowly. His face still mostly concealed by shadows, she recognized its shape. The skin was pale, the jaw angular, and the expression it wore was pure satisfaction and matter-of-fact, just-doing-my-job-ma'am, calm. She took a step back, her eyes never leaving his face. As his eyes came into focus, she realized they were black, two onyx stones in a sea of white, standing out unnaturally against sickly pale skin. It was the same face she had seen through her peephole a few months ago. The song reached a crescendo and she awoke with a start, sitting up in bed. *It's not possible,* she thought.

Aiden rolled over to spoon her and when he realized she was sitting up, he asked, "Are you OK, sweetheart?"

Cecilia didn't respond, just stared at him.

"Aww, honey. You had a nightmare." He pulled her in close, soothing her. "It's OK. . . "

"Aiden, it was terrible, I—"

"I know, sweetheart, let me make it go away so you can go back to sleep peacefully."

"No, wait. . ."

He looked deep into her eyes. "I want to make it go away. I love you, Cecilia. I don't ever want you to feel frightened."

A split second later, Cecilia looked at the clock on the nightstand. "Wow, what time is it? I'm so sleepy. . . " She lay back down and Aiden wrapped his arms around her.

"Sweet dreams, love." He kissed her head.

∞

"It was just weird. I don't know if he had a breakdown or what, but it's just not like him to go off on Dr. Harper like that, then disappear."

"And no one has heard from him?"

"No, that's the thing. He won't answer his phone and hasn't come in to pick up his last check. They tried mailing it but it was returned unclaimed."

"Maybe he took a vacation. He always talked about going to Australia. Maybe he finally went, who knows?"

"Yeah, well, I don't know….after his freak out, he needs—"

The chatter stopped when Cecilia walked into the break room to get her yogurt out of the fridge. To put an end to the awkward silence, Cecilia turned to look at the two nurses. One was smoothing her hair nervously and the other was pretending to be engrossed in a People magazine on the counter.

"Who's going to Australia?" Cecilia asked.

"Oh," the blonde playing with her hair responded. "No one can get a hold of Dr. Patton. It's like he disappeared off the face of the earth."

Cecilia's heartbeat quickened. *I just saw him at the lab a few days ago*, she thought.

Realizing the nurses were looking at her strangely, she quickly composed herself. "I'm sure he'll turn up. You're right, he's probably just taking some much needed time away. Excuse me." She made a quick exit.

∞

"So you've been staying at Aiden's house all week?" Amber asked.

"Yeah, he insists on it, especially after the note and everything. He doesn't want me home alone." She sighed and took a sip of her Riesling.

The two were at El Rico's again where Amber had hoped to see Ryan, her cougar cub, but he was off work that night.

"He really loves you, Cecilia. I can tell. I'm so glad you found him. He seems to be just what you need. You're so strong and independent, but you should let him take care of you. He wants to."

"I know, it's just hard to let go of control sometimes. I'm so used to having to do everything, handle everything. And, honestly, even though it's been less than a year since. . . well, I feel like I'm moving on and half the time I feel guilty and half the time I feel I should be moving on."

"Don't feel guilty. It doesn't do anyone any good if you torture yourself. If you're happy with Aiden, be happy. Don't question it. He was sent into your life for a reason."

Cecilia looked down to hide her reaction to Amber's words. *Yes, that he was,* she thought. "I know. When I'm with him, I almost forget about everything else. It's like he completely takes over and I just get swept up in. . . .*him.*"

"You're in love, CeCe."

"I am." Cecilia smiled.

"And you've said it, I'm assuming?"

"Well, yes, in a way. . . "

"Cecilia Harper! You haven't told him!" Amber set down her margarita glass a little too hard.

"I did! But I think he was asleep, so I'm not sure if he heard me."

"Coward. Has he said it to you?"

"Yes, he did just the other day."

"And?" Amber stared, wide-eyed. "Are you serious? Tell the man you love him, for God's sake!"

"I will, I will."

"Have you guys talked about the future?"

"The future? Well, yeah we have. But we're taking things slow."

"I know, silly, but can you see yourself marrying him one day?"

Cecilia hesitated, not wanting to lie to her best friend, but not mustering the nerve to tell her about their wedding plans. "Yes. Yes, I can see that."

Amber clapped her hands, delighted. "Good! Well, I know it won't be anytime soon, but I will be ready. You two are so great together. I am so happy for you, CeCe."

∞

Cecilia wrapped up another long night at the office. Her tolerance to alcohol had not been improving and she regretted her drinks with Amber the night before. She leaned back in her brown leather chair and took a deep breath, glancing at the clock on the wall. 8:30. Now that she was single-handedly working on her research, long nights were going to be the norm for a while. She jumped when her cell phone rang.

"Hello?"

"Come home to me, sweetheart. I have dinner ready."

"Wow, you are wonderful. I just finished. I'll be leaving in a few minutes."

"No stops on the way. Straight here, Cecilia, I mean it."

"Yes, dear," Cecilia said, smiling in spite of herself. He really was over-protective, but she found it endearing. Most of the time.

"And the night security guard will walk you to your car?"

"Yes. He stays until I leave every night."

"Good. I'll see you soon. Drive safe, love."

## Wednesday June 25, 2014

"But he's gone. No one has heard from him at all for over two weeks now. It's strange, that's all."

"Yes, well, if you ask me, it's for the best. After that stunt he pulled with you, then the threatening note, then his surprise visit at the lab, I don't want to see him near this town ever again."

"I still just can't get over it. He was never like that. He was always so easy-going. I know his daughter was really sick, but I don't know…"

"Didn't you say he tried to ask you out a couple times? Maybe he was finally showing his true colors now that he knew you were taken, and add to that, your success without him at the conference and your invitation to join a prestigious group of researchers. Jealousy has a way of bringing out who someone really is, Cecilia."

"I guess…" Cecilia was not convinced but had to agree that Aiden had a point.

"Come here," Aiden scooped her up and set her on his lap. "Enough about him. Let's focus on us the rest of the night, shall we?"

A bottle of wine later, the conversation turned to their upcoming nuptials in the fall. "When are you planning to tell your friends and family about our wedding plans? You can't put it off forever. It might be a good idea to tell them now, so they have time to get used to the idea, if that's what you're worried about." He was lightly stroking her arms with the tips of his fingers.

"I know. I will tell them. I've just been waiting for the right time."

"Why don't we have a big get-together, a summer barbeque and invite them all here for a weekend? Tell them the news then?"

Cecilia smiled. "As always, Aiden, that is a great idea." She leaned forward, planting a kiss on his lips.

"You love me," he said matter-of-factly.

This caught her off guard. He raised his eyebrows, but stayed silent, giving her his "cat that swallowed the canary" look. When he looked at her this way sometimes, she was unable to form words. The way dimples formed on his cheeks, his eyes twinkled. . . he had a way of making her feel like a silly teen girl all over again, just like he had on their first meeting in the coffee shop.

*Time to man-up*, she told herself. *I already told him at my parents' house when we were in New York, but that didn't count. He had been asleep.* "I do love you, Aiden."

His eyes lit up and gone was the mischievous cat grin and in its place was a warm and grateful smile, full of love and adoration. He picked her up by the waist and plopped her down on his lap. "Show me, beautiful."

Leaning down, her lips met his. She couldn't get enough of his taste, his lips soft and warm, sending tingles from her lips down the rest of her body. Getting lost in the moment, she grabbed a handful of his dark hair and pulled his head over to the side, exposing his neck, where she proceeded to kiss and work her way to his ear, stopping to give a gentle bite. His hands moved up her skirt and she heard a loud rip and then saw fabric tossed across the floor out of the side of her eye. The ripped lace landed on the brick in front of the fireplace.

# Nineteen

**July 4, 2014**

Glancing at all the faces around her, Cecilia could not believe how much her life had changed in the past year. Aiden and Cecilia had invited Amber, Katherine, Cecilia's parents, and two of Aiden's friends –Liam and Kaleb – to their home for a small fourth of July get-together. Liam was an attorney Aiden had met when he had to give testimony last year on a wrongful death case. Kaleb, a young doctor fresh out of medical school, worked with Aiden as an assistant medical examiner. At first, Cecilia's parents had been a little suspicious as to why no member of Aiden's family had attended, but telling them that his parents had been killed in a tragic car accident seemed to stop the questions.

For the first time in months, she was able to smile a genuine smile and not feel guilty about being happy. It took some convincing, but Cecilia had agreed to move in with Aiden this month and not wait until they were married. Aiden had insisted she not live on her own after Bruce's erratic behavior and threatening note. And she had to admit, she did feel much safer in Aiden's house.

She finished filling wine glasses and sat down next to Aiden at their long rustic mahogany picnic table on the deck overlooking the pool. Three antique bronze lanterns were spaced evenly down the center of the table, and whitewash textured wooden vases held bouquets of red gerbera daisies, deep blue iris, and white Asiatic lilies. The hot sun of the afternoon reflected on the water, creating a sea of blue sparkles, dancing in soft ripples with the light breeze.

When she sat down, he squeezed her hand and leaned in, kissed her on the cheek and whispered, "Ready to make our announcement?"

Cecilia leaned against his shoulder and returned the kiss on his cheek.

"Let's do it," she whispered back.

He cleared his throat and tapped his wineglass with his fork. Everyone stopped talking and turned to Aiden, waiting, their eyes wide.

He stood from his chair and looked around the table, meeting each person's eyes as he spoke. "I just wanted to thank you all for coming. It means so much to us to have such wonderful family and friends in our lives and we know you," he said, looking pointedly at Cecilia's parents. "traveled far to get here. Cecilia and I think it's time to come clean about why we really invited you here." He paused and a slow grin of unmistakable joy spread across his face. "We have a little announcement."

Amber squealed and clapped her hands together in anticipation.

He bent down and took Cecilia's hand, kissing the top, before turning back to the group. She smiled up at him, feeling butterflies in her stomach, knowing that in a few seconds all of her closest friends and family would know what they had kept hidden for the past few weeks. Although she had a feeling most of them had figured it out by now.

"Cecilia has done me the extraordinary honor of agreeing to marry me."

Amber squealed again, louder this time. "Aahh! I knew it! Congratulations!"

One by one, everyone stood and began making their way to the other side of the table to congratulate the couple. Cecilia stood and hugged everyone, one by one. Amber held her embrace for the longest time and Cecilia heard her sniffle. "I had a feeling. And I'm just so happy for you, CeCe. You deserve all the happiness in the world." When she pulled away, Cecilia noticed she quickly wiped her eyes. Turning to Aiden, Amber held her arms open. "Give me a hug, you." The two hugged and Amber pulled away and pointed a finger at him. "And you'd better not hurt her. Because I'll have to hurt you."

Aiden put his hands up in mock defense. "I wouldn't dream of it."

Amber laughed. "Good!"

Katherine was next. She hugged Cecilia, saying, "Congratulations. I am truly happy for you." Then turning to Aiden, she held out her hand. "I wish you both the best."

"Thank you, Katherine," Aiden said, shaking her hand.

She gave a quick nod, smiled and turned away quickly.

*That's odd*, Cecilia thought. *He must still make her nervous.*

Liam squeezed past the small crowd, shook her hand and said, "Congratulations. Aiden is a lucky man." Right next to him was Kaleb who nodded his agreement. "Yes he is. Congrats to you both," he said as he shook her hand. Cecilia thanked them and noticed her mother discreetly wiping a tear away.

"Oh, honey. I am so happy for you! You two seem so happy and. . . " She sniffled. "It's just so good to see you like this." She turned to Aiden. "We are so happy our daughter found you, Aiden. Come here," she said as she leaned in for a hug.

Robert pulled his daughter in for a hug, too. "I love you, honey. I am really happy for you, too. He seems to be really good for you and treats you well."

"He is and he does, Dad," Cecilia said.

"Well, then he's good in my book."

Robert turned to Aiden and shook his hand. "Welcome to the family, Aiden."

"Thank you. That means a lot. I love your daughter dearly and I want to take care of her and give her everything in the world."

Robert shrugged, smiling. "Good luck with that. She's a stubborn one."

"Dad!" Cecilia laughed.

"It's true!" Robert said.

"It *is* true," Aiden nodded in agreement. "But I don't give up easily."

"That's a good thing, son." He patted Aiden on the back.

"We have to celebrate! We need champagne!" Katherine did a little girly hop and clapped her hands together.

"I thought we might be needing this," Aiden pulled a bottle of Veuve Clicquot Brut from the silver bucket of ice on the table.

"Very nice," Linda murmured in approval.

"I'll get the champagne flutes." Cecilia practically skipped into the house.

When she returned with the flutes, Aiden took them and filled them to the top, passing them out to each person.

"Mmm. . .this is amazing! Good choice!" Amber beamed at Aiden.

So, have you set a date?" She looked back and forth between Aiden and her best friend.

"Yes, when are you crazy kids going to do this? Don't keep us waiting too long. I'm not getting any younger and we want grandchildren!" Linda added.

"Good Lord, Linda. They only just announced their engagement five minutes ago!" Robert snorted and shook his head.

"I *know*, Rob," Linda said, elbowing him playfully.

"Well, we have played around with a few dates, but we settled on December sixth."

"This year?" Katherine asked.

Amber rolled her eyes at her. "Yes, of course this year. What, do you think they are going to wait another year and a half—" she stopped, then asked, "You're not waiting another year and a half are you?"

Aiden and Cecilia laughed in unison. "No, no. December of this year." Cecilia responded.

After lunch, the women migrated over to the pool and were sitting at the edge, dipping their toes into the water. Cecilia overheard the men talking by the tall bar a few feet away on the deck.

"Congrats, man! I knew you were up to something," Liam said to Aiden. Liam was a couple inches shorter than Aiden but carried himself with the same easy confidence. That was where the similarities ended though. Liam had a deep tan from surfing every weekend – an activity that he couldn't convince Aiden to try—and had long sandy blonde hair and blue-green eyes.

"Yeah, Aiden. You sure can keep a secret! I'm usually the first to know when you have something up your sleeve." Kaleb pulled his friend in for a hug. "Congratulations."

"Thank you both. It means a lot to me that you are here."

"We wouldn't miss it for the world. Now, let's get a real drink." Liam walked over to the bar and grabbed an etched-glass whiskey tumbler out of the mini-fridge. Kaleb followed, his hazel eyes widening when he saw a bottle of thirty year old single malt scotch.

"Damn! You bring this out for a little summer barbeque?" Kaleb shook his head, his short curly brown ringlets bobbing with the movement.

"Highland Park, nice," Liam said, popping the top.

"Oh I have more. Drink up," Aiden urged.

"Of course you do," Kaleb said, laughing.

"Wait, how old are you again, Kaleb? I don't want to be caught serving alcohol to a minor," Aiden asked, studying his younger friend.

Kaleb looked confused for a moment, then laughed. "Not cool, Dr. Black, not cool."

Aiden gave Kaleb a slap on the back. "Just messing with you, kid. Pour yourself a drink."

As Kaleb took a glass and filled it with ice, he asked, "Are either of Cecilia's friends single?"

Aiden laughed. "Seriously?"

"What? I like older women. What about the blonde? What's her name again?" He watched her as Amber talked and laughed with Cecilia, tossing her long blonde waves around.

"That's Amber."

Cecilia noticed the two men glancing over every few seconds from the bar. She nudged Amber. "I think someone is about to pay you a visit," she said as she nodded over to Kaleb.

Amber bit her lip. "Mmm. . . Kaleb, right? He's cute. How old is he?"

Cecilia laughed. "I think he's twenty-six."

"Perfect," Amber said.

"Good Lord," Katherine shook her head. "You have no shame."

"She really doesn't," Linda agreed. "But if I were single, I'd be the same way."

Kaleb returned her stare and said to Aiden under his breath, "She's gorgeous."

"She is. Go talk to her," Aiden said.

As Kaleb began making his way towards Amber, Liam laughed. "This ought to be interesting."

"She will chew him up and spit him out." Aiden laughed, shaking his head. "She's quite the flirt. He doesn't know what he's getting into."

Kaleb strutted casually over to the women sitting by the pool and squeezed in between Amber and Cecilia. The two looked up at him.

"Well, hello there. I was wondering when you were going to come say hi." Amber smiled at him.

"Were you? Well, I decided to make you wait a little." He touched her turquoise bracelet. "I like this. It matches your eyes."

Amber batted her lashes. "Thank you, Kaleb."

"Can I get you a refill?" He eyed her empty glass.

"Are you trying to get me drunk?"

Kaleb laughed. "I'd never do that. Just thought you might be thirsty."

"Yes, that would be great, thank you."

"I'll leave you to talk to your new cougar cub." Cecilia smiled and stood up, starting to walk over to the white linen couch.

"Good idea," Linda said. Katherine followed as well.

Once the women were settled, drinks in hand, Katherine looked at Cecilia. "So, you never told me about your invite to the brain tumor consortium. When was that, last month?"

"Oh, yes! It was last week. It was amazing, meeting these top surgeons that I've looked up to for so long. I've read their articles, papers they've written. . . now to sit next to them is bizarre, but in a good way. I was a little intimidated at first, but they were very welcoming."

"Well, you are on the rise as a top neurosurgeon yourself," Katherine said.

"Hopefully. I have a long way to go, though."

"How's the research coming?"

"Slow. After Dr. Patton's breakdown, I'm on my own. Aiden tells me I should find someone else to assist, but to

Elaine Ewertz

bring them up to speed on everything would take so long. I think I'll just finish it myself."

"Do you think you can handle it?" Katherine asked.

"I think so. It will just take longer."

"And what about Dr. Patton? Has anyone heard from him?"

"Nothing. It's strange, because he never came back to the office for his check and it kept coming back returned in the mail. I did see him at the lab a few days after, though. He ambushed me in the parking lot. Claimed he just wanted to talk, and when I brought up the threatening letter, he looked genuinely surprised." She sighed. "I don't know. It just doesn't add up. It's not like him. But that's why Aiden asked me to move in with him. I was practically living here anyway and I'm safer here."

"Well, I'm glad you haven't heard any more from the looney ginger. He was obviously crazy to begin with if he could do all that. I'm glad you feel safe now. Hopefully you can move on and put the past behind you."

"Yes, definitely," she said before taking a sip of her mojito.

Later that evening, everyone was lounging on the couches on the deck, watching the sunset.

"Would anyone like to go to the lake to watch the fireworks, or just hang here? My neighbor said he can see them from here," Aiden asked the group.

"We could just stay here. If we can see them anyway. . . we don't have to worry about finding parking." Amber looked around at everyone.

"Fine by me," Linda agreed. Everyone murmured their agreement and the little party settled in to watch the fireworks over the treetops of Aiden's backyard.

∞

Cecilia leaned back in her chair and took a deep breath. She had just returned to work after taking off the holiday weekend and faced a mountain of paperwork. Not only that, but the hospital had called her in at 2:00 p.m. for an emergency surgery which had taken five hours.

"Dr. Harper?"

Cecilia turned to see Lizzy staring down at her left hand. *Oh, she sees the ring,* she realized. She had decided to start wearing it to work after their announcement over the weekend.

"Hi, Lizzy, how are you?"

"I'm great," she looked back down at Cecilia's hand. "Is that what I think it is?" she asked, in shock.

Cecilia smiled. "Yes, I'm engaged."

"Seriously?" Lizzy's eyes were as wide as saucers. "Aiden, right?"

"Yes. We were going to do it in October, but decided to make it a winter wedding. We're getting married in December."

Lizzy was speechless for a moment. "I just. . . wow. I'm shocked. I mean, I knew you were seeing someone, but I didn't know how serious it was!"

Cecilia laughed. "I know. Well, it is serious. He has changed my life. Just a few months ago, I was a mess—"

"I remember," Lizzy interrupted. "That's why I'm so surprised."

"But he has helped me to heal and move on. He saved me. We took it slow and got to know each other and well, the rest is history."

"You have seemed much happier lately and I'm glad. Well, congratulations!" Through her smile, Cecilia could still see the shock.

"Thank you!"

Just then, Harriet walked over and looked at Cecilia and then at Lizzy. "What are we celebrating?"

Cecilia put her hand on Harriet's shoulder. "Let's go in the back office and talk."

After Cecilia told her the news, Harriet shook her head in disbelief. "I can see why you don't want everyone in the office knowing! It's personal, but you *are* wearing your ring, so it's only a matter of time before everyone knows. . . "

"I know, but I want to wear it. I shouldn't have to hide it," Cecilia said as she poured a cup of coffee.

"You're right. But, don't you think. . . look, Doc, I hope you don't take this the wrong way, but I just think. . . isn't it a little soon? After. . ."

"After what? I know what happened. And I do realize it's been less than a year. But, I have to move on sometime, don't I?" She looked down and stirred in a spoonful of sugar.

"Of course you do. I know that better than anyone. It's just that, after losing Bill, I just. . . I needed time to heal. And it's still hard! It just seems fast, Doc. I don't want to see you get hurt." She paused. "I'm sorry. I know you're a grown woman and can make your own decisions. I'm just looking out for you."

"And I appreciate that. I really do. But, Aiden has helped me heal in so many ways. Since I met him, my life has only improved and I almost completely forget about all the bad stuff when he's around. I lived with the pain for months. I was so depressed I could barely get out of bed and I had to excuse myself here at the office and run to the bathroom ten times a day to fight off panic attacks and compose myself. He took all of that away."

"Oh, Doc, I get it. I really do. Only you know what is best for you and if you love the man and want to spend the rest of your life with him, then you have my blessing. Come here," she said, pulling Cecilia in for a hug. "You just remind me of my daughter and I'm a little protective."

"I'm grateful that you care so much, Harriet. I really am. And I appreciate your support." She took a deep breath. "Now, let's get back to work before they come hunt us down."

A few hours later, as she finished up paperwork in her office, Cecilia hoped that there were no more emergency surgeries for the day. It was 8:00 p.m. and she could actually get home at a decent time tonight.

She felt her phone vibrate and saw the caller ID: Aiden. "Hi, honey."

"Well, hi love. Are you coming home to me soon?"

"Yes, I just have to check on my patient in the ICU, then I'll be on my way."

"Good. I'd like to take you out to dinner, unless you feel like staying in?"

"No, I'd love to go out. That sounds great, Aiden. I'll be home in an hour or so."

"OK, love. I'll see you then."

∞

"Did you have lunch today?" Aiden asked after the waiter had taken their order.

"I did, amazingly enough," Cecilia replied.

"Well, what did you have? You know I worry about you, love. You don't eat enough."

"Oh, stop, Aiden," she said, laughing. "I eat. I had soup and salad at Panera."

"By yourself?"

Cecilia put her fork down. *Why all the questions?* she wondered. "No, I had lunch with a friend."

"Oh? Anyone I know?"

Cecilia sighed. He was going to be angry. "I had lunch with Mike. He texted me as I was heading out and we met there. It was spur of the moment."

Aiden was silent.

"Aiden, come on. He's a friend and I'm allowed to have friends." She picked her fork back up.

"Yes, of course you are. But, I thought we talked about this. You know after what happened last time, knowing how I feel about you seeing him—"

"Yeah, after last time? When you lost your temper in a jealous rage? I thought we talked about it, too." She picked up her knife and began cutting her steak.

"Don't get smart with me. I'm just surprised you had lunch with him, knowing how I feel about it. I wouldn't do that if the roles were reversed."

"I wouldn't mind if you went to lunch with an old friend. You're more than welcome to anytime. I trust you," she said as she took a bite.

Aiden's eyes darkened. "You know I trust you. I just don't like it. You should have considered that. What I'm saying is, I would do the same for you, if you weren't comfortable with something. I saw the way he looked at you and he wants to be more than friends, Cecilia. It's not that I don't trust you. I don't trust him."

Cecilia swallowed her food and paused a moment. "I understand. But, you can't control me like that. If I want to go to lunch with a friend, I will."

It was a long, quiet ride home. It only took twenty minutes to get home from Chez Francois, but it felt like an hour. Occasionally, Cecilia would glance over to peek at Aiden, to see if he had calmed down. He was still angry over their argument over Mike, but he was going to have to get over it. She saw his jaw tensing, his mouth set in a hard line and his eyes narrowed, focused on the road ahead. But, what confused her was the fact that he almost looked excited about something, a mix of anger and anticipation.

*Who knows*, she thought. *He has such a temper.* Their argument had ended when she called him a control freak. He had gotten very quiet after that. *The look on his face when I said it though*! she thought as she stifled a laugh. It was a true 'I'm pissed and you're going to get it' Aiden look.

His head snapped to the right and he caught her smirk. He said nothing, but to her surprise, smirked back, his eyes sparkling.

She was relieved to pull into the driveway after that oddly quiet ride home. Walking into the house, she threw her bag on the foyer table and started for the stairs.

"Not so fast," Aiden said, and she felt him standing behind her, then his hands resting firmly on her shoulders. He leaned in, whispering in her ear, "Meet me in the bedroom in five minutes."

She turned to face him, starting to protest, but he placed a finger over her lips. "There will be no discussion on this. Five minutes."

Cecilia sighed. "Yes, dear."

Having changed out of her clothes and into a short silk nightgown, she waited on the end of the bed for Aiden. After a few moments, he walked in and slammed the door, locking it. Fixing her with a predatory look, he reached into his back pocket. "I bought you some jewelry, honey." In his hands were shiny silver handcuffs, which he dangled in front of her. "I thought you needed some new bracelets."

Elaine Ewertz

# Twenty

Cecilia swallowed. She had never been handcuffed before. None of her exes had been into the kinky stuff but she had always been curious.

He stalked towards her. "Cat got your tongue?"

"I've never. . . "

"You've never what? Been cuffed before?" He let the cuffs hang off his index finger as he watched her closely. Her eyes darted to the cuffs and then back to Aiden.

"No, I haven't. "

He placed them in her hands. "Hold them. What do you think?"

"They're heavier than I thought they'd be."

"They are solid. Whoever finds themselves in these won't have a chance of getting out."

"And you want to use these on me? Why?"

"I think you know why, Cecilia. It will be fun."

"That's not why. You're angry about me going to lunch with Mike. You want to punish me."

Aiden sat down on the bed beside her, ran his hand up and down her thigh. "You didn't like how I lost my temper when we had a fight over this before. Isn't this better?"

She stood and walked towards the door. "I don't know if I want you to cuff me."

Aiden appeared in a flash, blocking her exit. "And where do you think you're going?"

"Let me through."

He didn't move. She gave him a hard shove but he didn't budge.

"Aiden, seriously. Just move."

"Not a chance."

She backed up and folded her arms across her chest, staring him down.

"You're trying to run from me." He stepped closer. "I wish you wouldn't."

"No, I'm not. You're just so. . . " Failing to find the right word, she growled in frustration.

"You're cute when you pout." He touched his thumb to her bottom lip.

"Dammit, Aiden!" She jerked her face away. "Stop being so condescending."

"I'm not being condescending. I care. I love you. What kind of man would I be if I let you walk out the door?"

"A non-controlling one?"

He cocked his head to the side, his eyes soft pools of brown. "You've never been loved the way you deserve."

"Probably not. But, God, Aiden. You *are* controlling."

"I can understand how it would appear that way to you."

"And you get mad and bring out handcuffs? Some people just talk about their feelings when they are upset. You know, work it out. There are more choices besides throwing things when you get angry or using BDSM to punish."

His eyes grew wide. "Oh, Cecilia. Stop right there. I know you enjoy this. I would never make you do something you don't want to. I sensed your excitement when I walked into the room. And the last time we had an argument and made up this way, you enjoyed it."

"Oh, that's right. You know how I'm feeling at all times. Your godly superpower."

"Yes, I can sense your emotions very strongly. You know this." He furrowed his brow but looked amused. "Are you trying to pick another fight with me? Because your sarcastic little pretty mouth is going to get you into trouble."

"Oh, really? What are you going to do about it?"

"Maybe bend you over my knee and teach you a lesson."

"You're twisted."

"And you like it." He picked her up and threw her onto the bed. "You need to stop pretending you don't. You aren't fooling me."

"You are a deviant."

"I am. And I think somewhere deep inside you, you are too. But if you really don't want this and I'm reading you all wrong, you're free to go." He gestured towards the door. "Go ahead."

She didn't move.

"Last chance."

"I don't want to go."

"I know you don't." He picked up the handcuffs from the nightstand and sat down next to her. He tossed them onto the pillow by her head then slowly crept his hand up under the silky fabric of her chemise.

"Aren't you curious?"

"Yes, but you're doing this to punish me."

"You know I won't hurt you, Cecilia. Don't you trust me?"

"I do, but—"

"Good." He picked her up by the waist and slid her up to the headboard, pulling her chemise up over her head in one swift motion. "Mmm, beautiful. . . now, do I cuff one hand to the headboard, or both together?" Deciding quickly, he put a cuff on each wrist and locked them together so they were in front of her. He sat back to admire his work.

"Perfect."

"You have a thing for bondage, don't you?" She had to admit, she liked the feel of the cool metal around her wrists. And knowing she was at his mercy was thrilling. She felt a chill go down her spine.

"I like knowing you can't get away." He looked her up and down. "All mine."

He rose from the bed. "I'm going to get something. Don't go anywhere." He turned to the large dresser by the window and pulled out an eye mask.

Putting it over her eyes, he said, "Much better."

A few seconds later, Cecilia heard music. It was a little scratchy, like it was being played on a record player. It sounded like an old Stones song.

She felt his weight return to the bed and then a moment later, a drop of hot liquid on her stomach. She flinched in response. What was that? It smelled like vanilla. . . oh, a candle. Every few seconds, she felt the hot wax drip onto another part of her body: her abdomen, then her thighs. . . then she heard his voice, low and soft. "What was it that you called me back at the restaurant?"

Giggling, Cecilia twisted and squirmed but didn't answer.

"I asked you a question, love. What did you call me when I was trying to talk to you about seeing your flirtatious ex who wants what's mine?"

*A control freak, and I'm obviously right*, she thought. "That's not fair, Aiden. You were making a big deal out of—"

She jumped again when she felt the hot liquid fall onto her inner thigh. "Oh, Cecilia. See, you're in no position to argue with me now. Kind of ironic, isn't it? After you accused me of being, what?"

"A control freak," she responded, pouting.

"Yes. And now I have no choice but to live up to that label. I wouldn't want to make you into a liar."

Then, one more hot liquid drop onto her other thigh. It was an odd sensation. The quick burn was mildly painful, but she enjoyed it. Her nerve endings were alive and on edge, waiting for the next sudden shock of delicious almost-pain that would quickly turn into pleasure. She flinched when she felt him come close again, but there were no more burning drops of wax. Just his warmth of his body and his slow, relaxed breathing. Then, she felt his lips, softly kissing her, working his way up her leg, from her ankle to her upper thighs, stopping right before the area she wanted him most.

For a few seconds, she felt nothing. Then, she felt another drop of hot wax on her stomach.

"Aiden, please. . . you're just going to torment me all night, aren't you? You're so mean."

Hovering over her, he leaned down and whispered in her ear, "I know you enjoy this, sometimes even make me angry on purpose because you know what I will do to you when we get home. Don't think you've fooled me. I've been around a long time, love."

She squirmed in the cuffs and began kicking her legs. "Why would I make you angry on purpose? That's insane."

"Hold still," he commanded. "You're a terrible liar. You like our little game, don't you?"

"Maybe."

"You like that I'm a deviant in bed," he said, trailing his fingertips down her stomach.

"Yes. . . "

"I know." Then silence. A split second later, she heard the bedroom door open. *Where is he going?* What seemed like several minutes passed.

*What the hell? Is he going to leave me here, handcuffed and blindfolded?* She tried to relax, but began to seriously wonder whether he was coming back.

Just as she was beginning to squirm and try to rub the side of her face against the pillow in a futile effort to remove the eye mask, she heard soft footsteps on the rug near the bed and smelled his distinct scent.

"Aah!" She squeaked a small scream when she felt the icy cold drops of water on her collarbone. She shivered. Then, she jumped when she felt what must have been ice being gently grazed from her throat down to her stomach. She trembled, her entire body on alert for the next sensation, goose bumps covering her arms and legs. She needed Aiden to touch her. She almost couldn't bear it.

She arched her back and whimpered. "Please, Aiden. . ."

The low rumble of his devious laugh made her jump. It was the first sound he had made since re-entering the room. "But, I'm just getting started, love. I love watching you tremble for me." He began kissing her neck then trailed his fingertips down her torso.

Then he abruptly stopped. *No!*

"Aiden! Oh, please. . . don't stop!"

"Has anyone else ever made you feel like this?"

"No—"

"Not even Mike?"

*What the hell? Please, don't bring him up*, she thought. "No, what are you—"

"Just making sure. Because I don't like to share." "I only want you, Aiden," she said, her body alive with sensation and longing.

"Do you mean that?"

"Yes!"

Then, she felt his rough hands grab her arms and flip her onto her stomach and he gave her behind a hard smack. Ow!"

"Good." He flipped her back over and heard the zipper of his pants.

Then, the eye mask was gone and she could see him. After having been blind for the past hour, she was struck by his muscular chest and arms, his rosy, pouty lips and the look of sheer triumph and cockiness in his intense brown eyes.

"You are not going to see him again. I know you don't think it's fair, but that's too bad. You can have all the friends you want, but not ones that want to get into your pants. Because you," he said as he gave her hair a sharp tug. "are all mine." She felt the heat begin to build again, the delicious tingle starting at the base of her hips. "Do you understand?" he said as he moved rhythmically.

"Yes. . . "

"Good girl."

She cried out as her back arched and nearly levitated off the bed. The little explosion, bursting inside her like fireworks, reached the base of her spine, then raced up and down her body for a few seconds, then down to her toes where the sparks dissipated.

A few moments later, Aiden propped himself up on his arms and gazed down at her tenderly.

"How you doing, sweetheart?"

She was limp, unable to move a muscle. "Mmmm. . . " she moaned. "Can't move. . . "

He stroked her cheek, moved a tendril of hair away from her eye. "I suppose I should uncuff you now. Although you do look amazing in your new bracelets. Silver really suits you."

Looking down at her wrists, she said, "I like my new bracelets. Thank you, honey."

Aiden smiled. "You're welcome. I knew you'd like them." He rolled over and stood up, retrieved the key from the dresser and came back to the bed, unlocking the cuffs and setting her free.

Elaine Ewertz

# Twenty One

**October 18, 2014**

Amber set her phone on the table. "That was Alison. Everything is on track, CeCe."

"Good. I am so glad we decided to hire a wedding planner. One less thing I have to stress about." She leaned back in her chair and sighed. "I can't believe I'm getting married in less than two months." Reaching for her ginger lemon iced tea, she studied the plastic cup. It was clear with a thick purple straw, a big dandelion covering one side and the words "Dandelion Cafe" written in yellow and purple letters below the flower.

"Your big day is going to be perfect. Listen to this." Amber read from a pamphlet. "The Casa Monica. This 1888 landmark has an old-world charm that will captivate and provide the perfect start to a beautiful marriage. Enjoy the tropical, fountain-filled garden then hold your reception in one of the majestic ballrooms. Make your exit in our getaway car – a vintage Model A Ford. Won't Aiden love that?"

She flipped the page and shoved it across the table to Cecilia. "That's beautiful. I hope you get the one in this picture. The cream color is perfect."

"That is great! Aiden will love that." She shoved the brochure back to Amber. "Don't show him that. I want it to be a surprise. He'll be over the moon."

"I know! I think it suits him. Even the whole getting married in historical St. Augustine thing. There's something about him that just seems, I don't know, old-world, like he was born two centuries ago."

*Try seventeen*, Cecilia thought. "He is an old soul, that's for sure. But, I think it's a good balance for me." She looked around the tables at the outdoor cafe. Men in board shorts and women in bikinis and sarongs sat with their surfboards propped up against the white brick wall. Cecilia could smell the fresh breakfast breads and pastries each time the large glass door swung open at the bakery next door. On the other side of the cafe was a surf shop and a man who looked to be around twenty-three walked out wearing bright orange board shorts, his long blonde hair twisted into dreads.

Cecilia cleared her throat when she noticed Amber staring. Amber quickly turned back to Cecilia. "Oh definitely! He looks after you, takes care of you. And whether or not you like to admit it, you need someone like that. You've always been so independent, self-sufficient, which, don't get me wrong, it's not a bad thing. I just like that you found someone who understands you, seems to intuitively know what you need. I love you two together."

"So do I," Cecilia said, smiling. She could hear waves crashing and kids playing down on the beach several hundred yards away.

"And you two are going to have the most gorgeous babies! I can't wait to be Auntie Amber. Wait, you are going to have kids, right?"

Cecilia laughed. "Yes, I think so. I was never ready for them before, but Aiden and I are definitely going to have a child. Maybe just one, though. That would be enough."

"Oh come on, you can't have just one!"

"They aren't potato chips, Amber." Cecilia laughed again. "But, let's just focus on the wedding first, shall we?"

"OK, OK. I just love the thought of cute little Aidens and Cecilias running around." She looked up at the sky. "It's so beautiful today. Why don't we walk down to the beach?"

"You just want to check out the cute surfer boys," Cecilia said.

"Yeah, so?"

"I thought you were seeing Kaleb, Aiden's friend."

"Oh, honey, that ended a month ago. I thought I told you! He couldn't keep up with me. Besides, all he wanted to do was play Xbox. I don't think you should be allowed to play that after twenty-five." She rolled her eyes.

Cecilia laughed. "Let's go."

She had some time to kill before dinner and Aiden was at Liam's helping him build a deck on the back of his house. There was nothing that man couldn't do. She had to remind herself that he had been around for a long time and had an unfair advantage. Anyone living for nearly two millenniums would probably pick up many skills along the way.

∞

After a few hours of hanging out on the beach, Amber had two phone numbers from men who looked almost young enough to be her sons and Cecilia had the beginnings of a sunburn. She wanted to go home, shower and make dinner for Aiden. And Amber had a date with a thirty-eight year old cardiothoracic surgeon she had met through Katherine. Pulling into the driveway, she stared at her house for a while before turning off the engine. She was still getting used to the McMansion. Actually, she wasn't sure why she called it that. It was just a mansion. The marble floors, the six fireplaces, the crystal chandeliers, the four-car garage, the tennis courts were a little overwhelming at first. It seemed showy. What would her friends think? It was almost embarrassing. But when she had mentioned this to Aiden, he had told her that he had earned every penny the honest way so why shouldn't he enjoy it?

Aiden had amassed a fortune over the years. He told her that at one point, he lost everything during the Great Depression, but that he had made it all back within ten years. Setting her keys on the foyer table, she smelled something delicious in the air. Was he already home? As she made her way into the kitchen, she noticed flickering candlelight in the dining room and saw Aiden standing at the stove.

He turned around, his eyes warm and golden, and smiled. "Hi honey, you're home."

It didn't matter that she saw him every day. Cecilia was still taken aback by him. He was wearing a white Henley shirt and snug faded gray Levi's. But, it was mostly those intense brown eyes that held thousands of years of secrets and knowledge, yet displayed an unmistakable vulnerability. It was such a compelling contradiction. Even as powerful and experienced in life as he was, she knew he was still afraid of being hurt, just like anyone else.

She walked quickly around the black marble island and hugged him. "I thought you'd be a little while longer. I was going to make you dinner. Did you finish the deck?"

"It's all done. I couldn't wait to get home to my beautiful bride-to-be. What did you and Amber end up doing?"

"We had lunch then walked on the beach for a while. She's working with Alison on planning the wedding. She asks me what I want but won't let me get too involved. She says she wants to handle it so we don't have to worry about anything."

"She's a good friend. And she's your maid of honor so let her take care of it if she wants to. Is the Casa Monica booked?"

"Yes! I can't wait, Aiden. It's so beautiful. We can have the ceremony outside on the Pavilion if the weather's nice or if it's too cold, we can have it inside."

Aiden pulled her in for another hug. "That sounds perfect, love. You deserve the wedding of your dreams." He pulled back suddenly. "What about the music? Has that been decided yet?"

"I think she said something about hiring a deejay."

"What about having a live band? I could ask Justin if Stagefright would play."

"Ooh! That's a great idea!"

He kissed her forehead. "I'll ask him. Now let's eat."

∞

Cecilia took another bite of her pasta. Aiden had made linguine in white wine sauce, asparagus and baked potatoes and it tasted amazing. She decided she would have to start working out more. Being married to Aiden was sure to pack on the pounds.

Bringing a second bottle of sauvignon blanc to the dinner table, Aiden asked, "Do you know anything about your ancestry?"

"No, not really. I know that my family is Irish, but that's about it." She took a sip of her wine.

"Hmm. You should really look into it, find out who your ancestors are. It might be interesting." His eyes sparkled in the soft dancing glow of the tall red candles in the center of the table.

"I've never really thought about it, but you're right, maybe I should."

"You actually bear some resemblance to Elara. Wouldn't it be weird if you were related to her?"

Cecilia laughed. "I doubt it. What are the odds of that?"

Aiden shrugged. "Pretty weak odds, I'd think, but you never know."

"Yeah, well, I hope I'm not related to her because it sounds like you're still pretty upset about what she did to you and your family."

Aiden's eyes widened. "Should I not be? Should I have gotten over it by now?"

"No! No, that's not what I mean. Of course, you have every right to still be upset about that. I'm sure it's impossible to forget, even with all the centuries that have passed."

"It is impossible to forget. I'd still like to have my revenge. If I could find one of her descendants alive today. . . .oh, what I would do to them. . . " Aiden's eyes turned dark.

"Really? I mean, I understand, but revenge won't do you any good. Even if you met a descendant of Elara, that person had nothing to do with it. It doesn't seem fair to punish that person."

Aiden narrowed his eyes, stared at Cecilia for a moment before speaking. When he finally spoke, his voice was menacingly low. "Doesn't seem fair? That's ironic, considering that what was done to me was far from fair."

"I know, but at some point you just have to. . . move on," Cecilia said carefully.

"It's awfully hard to move on when you have no closure. I never found out what happened to Elara and Lavena. They disappeared after destroying my life and the lives of my family. Even my father, with his superior mental abilities, was unable to find them and even using his powers of influence on anyone he met, no one had seen them. It's quite possible they committed suicide. Rather cowardly, if you ask me."

"I know having no closure is painful. But, do you really think it's possible after all these years? You're just tormenting yourself, Aiden."

"I do think it's possible. Justice will be served. I don't care if it takes another millennium."

Cecilia let it drop. There was no point in trying to reason with him. It was clear he was still suffering from his loss and wanted revenge. And it was clear that nothing she could say would change his mind. Maybe over time, he would let it go and find some peace.

After dinner, they retreated to the back patio to sit on the wooden swing. Cecilia leaned into him, resting her head on his shoulder as they rocked back and forth, gazing at the stars. She began running her hand up and down his thigh, feeling the warmth of his skin through his snug jeans. When she glanced up at him, she noticed he looked far away, as if he were lost in memories of the past.

"What are you thinking about?"

"Ahh. . . lots of things. When you've lived as long as I have, there is never a shortage of memories, both good and bad, to think about at any given time."

"It doesn't look like you're thinking of the good ones right now. Why don't I help take your mind off it?"

"You already do, Cecilia. With you, I know there is hope for a happy ending."

He wasn't getting her hint. She was still learning that subtlety didn't work with men. So she decided to make her intentions a little clearer. She continued to stroke his thigh, but this time, she let her hand go up farther.

"I was thinking of something a little more. . . physical," she said, looking up at him with a mischievous grin.

His eyebrows shot up. "Oh really?" He began running his hand up and down her leg, stopping just at the hemline of her dress, then leaned down and kissed her passionately. "I like the way you think." He stood up abruptly. "Come here." He held out his hand and when she took it, he pulled her violently to him, picking her up and throwing her over his shoulder.

Carrying her through the French doors, he gently tossed her onto the sofa and climbed on top of her, pinning her down. "Is this the kind of physical you meant?"

"It's a good start," Cecilia said.

"Oh, it is only the start, don't worry, love." Aiden tightened his grip on her wrists and began planting kisses on her neck, working his way to her mouth.

She let herself succumb, felt the fizz coursing through her veins, making every nerve ending come alive. Then she noticed music playing. Had that been playing the entire time? It was a dark sounding song from Kings of Leon and the singer was crooning about wanting to see someone crawl. The sound of the guitars and the singer's raspy voice only heightened her arousal. As if Aiden's touch and the weight of his body pressing into hers wasn't enough.

His hands pushed her dress up to her hips and grabbed the thin fabric. He appraised the black lace, murmuring, "Nice," and tossed them across the room and they landed next to the fireplace on top of a tall porcelain vase.

An hour later, Cecilia lay limp on the floor next to the coffee table. She could feel beads of sweat on her forehead cooling under the ceiling fan and she felt weak and unable to move. "You wear me out," she said, reaching over to Aiden and resting a hand on his chest.

"Just doing my job," he said, squeezing her hand.

"You do it well," she said as she sat up. "I'll be right back."

As she made her way to the bathroom, she thought of how sore she was going to be the next day. *Might need to just sit on some ice*, she thought, smiling.

Turning off the faucet, she thought she heard two men talking in the living room. *That's weird*, she thought. She turned off the fan and stood, listening. It definitely sounded like Aiden was not alone. Maybe Liam or Jakob had made a surprise visit. She grabbed a robe from the closet in the bathroom and wrapped it around her. As she walked down the hall, she heard the front door close.

When she walked into the living room, she didn't see anyone, so she went to the kitchen, where she found Aiden standing at the sink, drinking water from a glass.

"Here's some water, love," he said, handing her a glass.

She looked around. "Where is he?"

"Where is who?"

"I heard you talking to someone out here. Did someone stop by?"

Aiden furrowed his brows. "No. No one is here, sweetheart." Then he smiled and reached over, playing with her hair. "I really did a number on you, didn't I?"

She put her hands on her hips and cocked her head. "You did, but I know I heard someone while I was in the bathroom—"

Aiden laughed suddenly. "Oh! Liam called and I had him on speaker. That must be what you heard. Sorry, sweetheart, I didn't think you'd hear that."

"Oh," Cecilia said. She still wasn't convinced but it had been a long day and the two had just had a long sweat session, so maybe she was imagining things. "Yeah, you must have worn me out," she said, shaking her head.

Aiden laughed. "I think so, honey." He pulled her in for a hug. "I love you sweetheart. You should get some sleep."

She yawned. "Yeah, I am tired all of a sudden. Must have just caught up with me."

# Twenty Two

**December 6, 2014**

"Do a spin for me!" Amber held up her iPhone and snapped a picture.

The soft, glowing icy blue organza grazed the floor as Cecilia did a twirl on her tiptoes. Her gown was a satin corset with white lace overlay and a square neckline. A small delicate bow adorned her waist and from there, the pale blue organza flowed into soft waves that tumbled to the floor.

It was an Irish wedding tradition for the bride to wear blue instead of white and she had chosen to honor her Irish roots as well as Aiden's. Her jewelry was simple but stunning, a twelve karat diamond necklace with a glittering sapphire in the middle and princess cut diamond studs for earrings. She had decided to braid her hair and pull it back in a bun. A strand of delicate white heather and blue irises—the same type of flowers Aiden had brought her on their first date—were interwoven into her thick brown hair.

As she twirled, she took in the beautiful Rose Room at the Casa Monica. It was a room provided by the hotel for the bride to prepare for the ceremony and was filled with lush green tropical plants and flowers. The men—Aiden, Liam, and Cecilia's father—were across the hall in the Blue Room. Cecilia had not seen Aiden all day. She and her mother and best friend had taken a limousine to St. Augustine the day before and had stayed the night at the hotel. Aiden and the other men had taken another limousine to St. Augustine the morning of the wedding. The ceremony was set to start at four in the afternoon with a cocktail hour and reception to follow. Then, the newlyweds were driving to the airport and hopping on a plane to St. Barts.

Linda smiled at her daughter. "You look so beautiful, Cecilia!" She sniffed. "Oh, I wasn't going to cry, but I just can't believe it. I've never seen you so happy and so in love. And you just look so. . . " She trailed off as she dabbed at her eyes with a tissue.

"Oh, mom," Cecilia said as she hugged her mother. "Don't cry."

"I know, I know. I just can't help it. You've just made me so proud. You're just so strong. Stronger than I ever could be. And you're so good at what you do, becoming successful at such a young age. . . and now you're marrying this wonderful man that we've all just fallen in love with." Linda pulled away slightly and held Cecilia at arm's length, giving her a warm smile. "You deserve it all, sweetheart."

Cecilia felt her face grow warm and her eyes begin to tear up at her mother's words. "Thank you, mom." She wiped her eyes. "Now, let's stop this. We're going to have mascara running down our faces."

"I'm about to cry, too! Wow, CeCe! You are stunning!" Amber stared at her friend. "Wearing blue was such a great idea. It makes your eyes and skin look radiant!"

"Thank you! I'm so glad you're here. And that you agreed to be my maid of honor. Again." Cecilia laughed.

"I wouldn't miss it for the world. I love you, girl. And I'd be your maid of honor twenty more times, but I think this is going to be it." Amber grabbed Cecilia and hugged her.

"I know this is going to be it," Cecilia agreed.

"Now let's stop with the mushy-ness and get down to business. You have a man to marry! Let's do some last minute touch-ups before you walk down the aisle."

"Good idea," chimed in Alison. Their wedding planner had been on the other side of the room on the phone with the hotel's kitchen making sure the food would be ready for the reception. She was also a makeup artist, so she had offered to do their makeup free of charge.

As she touched up Cecilia's lip gloss, she said, "The music is set to start any moment now. So, Linda, you will walk out first, meet Liam in the hallway, join arms, and walk through the French doors. Remember: *sloooow*. Then, Amber, you will do the same with Kaleb, then once we hear the opening note of your song, Cecilia, it's all you."

"Got it." She picked up her glass of champagne and took a deep breath. "Why am I nervous? It's just Aiden out there. . . and twenty of our closest friends."

"Exactly. No reason to be nervous, honey. You know everyone out there and they all love you." Linda placed her hand on Cecilia's arm.

"You're right." She took a large gulp of champagne. "It's just that sometimes I don't think he's real. Like it's too good to be true. I just need to calm my nerves a little." She took another large gulp, emptying the glass.

"Damn, girl! Well, that should help!" Amber laughed and grabbed the bottle and another glass. "Here, I'll join you for one."

"Oh, hell, me too." Linda held out an empty glass as Amber poured.

"To a long and happy marriage," Amber said, holding up her glass. The three clinked glasses just as the music began.

"It's time!" Alison sang.

Cecilia hugged her mother again before Linda left the room to walk with Liam down the aisle. A few moments later, Alison gave Amber her cue.

Amber checked her hair in the mirror, then turning back, said, "See you on the other side!"

Cecilia took a deep breath. *Here we go*, she thought.

Alison was standing just outside the door watching the processional. "OK, about time. Everyone is in their places. . . OK, Cecilia. Ready?" She took her hands and smiled.

"Yes, let's do this."

"Great. You look amazing. Now go marry your man!"

Cecilia laughed as she stepped into the hallway where her father was waiting and the two linked arms. He leaned in and kissed her on the cheek. "I love you, sweetheart."

A man of few words, Robert was one of those rare people who only said exactly what he needed to say and somehow it meant so much more this way.

"I love you, too, Dad."

Then he whispered in her ear, "Ready?"

She nodded and leaned in, kissing him on the cheek.

Stepping out into the sunshine, Cecilia paused to take it all in as she heard the first chord of her song, then a soft female voice was telling her lover he was the breath that she breathed. They had agreed on Amber's suggestion, a sweet acoustic song by an Indie band they both loved.

Just outside the French doors, a stone walkway was nestled between two lush rows of majestic palms. Beyond the walkway about ten yards ahead, stood a set of weathered white wooden doors that must have been salvaged from an old farmhouse. A small bouquet of white flowers had been placed on each side, fastened to the door by a black cast iron plaque.

Walking slowly, arm in arm with her father, she felt the comforting warmth of the sun touch her bare shoulders, a light breeze gently drifting through the layers of the delicate fabric of her gown, then weaving through the blue and white flowers of her bouquet. Three rows of white chairs were aligned on either side of the aisle, where her friends and family now stood, smiling, watching her entrance.

Then she saw him.

He stood motionless, his hands clasped in front of him. He smiled brilliantly, his eyes sparkling. She returned his smile, feeling her cheeks warm. He looked his usual dapper self, but even more-so in his midnight blue tuxedo, crisp white waistcoat, white satin tie and icy blue handkerchief in his breast pocket to match Cecilia's gown. He had tamed his wild hair slightly, but it was still semi-messy, in true Aiden style.

When she made it to the altar, Aiden stepped forward and took her hands. As she looked into his dark eyes, any doubt she may have felt about marrying him disappeared. She felt electricity flowing through her veins and her thoughts turned to the wedding night. They hadn't made love in a week – on purpose – and she couldn't wait to be alone with him.

She was quickly jolted back to the present when she heard the officiant begin to speak. He was a tall, slender man who looked to be in his late forties. He wore gray wire-frame glasses and spoke in a voice so jovial, it instantly made everyone in attendance smile.

"Good afternoon everyone. Welcome to the wedding of Cecilia and Aiden. My name is Andrew Sullivan and it is my honor to be officiating this wedding. Before we begin, please turn the volume of your phones up as high as possible, so that when somebody gets a phone call during the ceremony we all know whom to blame." Aiden and Cecilia laughed quietly along with the guests. "Alternatively, please silence your phones. The ceremony is about to begin."

Aiden squeezed Cecilia's hands as they gazed into each other's eyes while Andrew spoke. When it was time for the ring exchange, Aiden turned slightly to Liam, who handed him a delicate platinum band.

"Cecilia, my bride," Aiden began. "My heart is in this ring. My love is in this ring. I give you this ring as a symbol of my love. I promise to be your faithful husband, to love you when the sun shines and when the rain falls, in sickness and in health. When you look at this ring, think of me and remember that I love you always." His eyes alight with warmth, he took her hand and slid the ring onto her finger.

Amber took a step forward and handed Cecilia Aiden's ring. Holding his hand in hers, Cecilia began. "Aiden, my heart is in this ring," she said as she slowly slid the ring on his finger. "My love is in this ring. I give you this ring as a symbol of my love. I promise to be your faithful wife, to love you when the sun shines and when the rain falls, in sickness and in health. When you look at this ring, think of me and remember that I love you always."

Andrew spread his arms in a gesture of finality and proclaimed, "I now pronounce you husband and wife. Aiden, you may kiss your bride."

∞

The reception was held outside on the Moroccan-style pool deck, with rustic brass Tiki torches and heat lamps positioned near each table in case the guests got a little chilly. Round tables draped in rich white cloth with indigo candles and white heather and blue iris centerpieces were scattered around the sparkling pool. The band was set up in between the two sets of French doors.

"May I have everyone's attention, please?" Rob, Stagefright's lead singer called out to the guests.

Cecilia held Aiden's hand as they stood just inside the French doors and waited while Rob introduced the bridal party. Aiden leaned down and kissed her. "Are you ready, baby?"

"Let's do this," she said as she smiled up at him.

"Announcing for the first time. . . Mr. and Mrs. Aiden and Cecilia Black!"

As Cecilia and Aiden walked out onto the deck, everyone stood and applauded. Giddy with joy, she looked up at Aiden, who quickly swept her into an embrace and kissed her passionately, drawing more cheers from the crowd. Then, Natalie Cole's soft, warm voice filled the room and the two began their first dance.

"Everyone's watching us," Aiden whispered in her ear. "Let's give them a show."

Before Cecilia could respond, he was twirling her nimbly around the slate-gray stone tile. She giggled, following his lead as the turquoise water whizzed by her line of sight, then the flickering candles and the faces of her loved ones zoomed by. Although she had never been much of a dancer, his skill on the dance floor made her feel graceful by proxy.

"I had no idea my husband was such a talented dancer," she said, breathless after three spins in a row.

"It's unfair, really. I've had a lot of practice," he said as he dipped her low and paused for dramatic effect at the end of the song which earned them a standing ovation.

After dinner and three more hours of dancing, it was time for the final farewell. The guests lined up along the gates behind the pavilion where a buttery cream-colored Model A Ford was waiting.

As soon as Aiden spotted it, he turned to Cecilia, his eyes wide. "Did you know about this?"

"I may have," she said as she watched a wide grin spread on his face.

"You're amazing Cecilia." He stared at the car. "What a beauty. I always wanted one of those."

"Well, we get to ride in it to the hotel."

"Hmm. . . I wonder if they'll sell it," he mused.

Cecilia shook her head, laughing. "You would try to buy it!"

He shrugged. "Hey, it doesn't hurt to ask."

∞

The honeymoon so far had been one Cecilia could only dream of. After spending their wedding night at a local St. Augustine hotel (where the two had spent most of the night christening every area of the hotel room; the bed, the sofa, the shower. . . ), they had risen at the crack of dawn to catch a flight to St. Barts.

Eight hours later, they checked into the Hotel Guanahani and spent the day lounging on the beach. It was a warm eighty degrees with very little humidity, which was a nice change from Florida. It was just what Cecilia needed. The two decided to order room service for dinner and have a low-key evening. Aiden had booked a scuba diving trip for the next day and kept coming up with new ideas for the remainder of their two week stay.

"So, tomorrow, scuba. Maybe the next day, we can rent some jet skis. . . have you ever been kite surfing?"

"No, I haven't. That all sounds great," Cecilia said, stretching out on the couch.

"You look so relaxed, love. I don't think I've ever seen you this way."

"I know. I don't think I've ever felt this way," Cecilia said, laughing. "At least not for a long time."

Aiden scooped her up and tossed her onto the bed. "Well, I love seeing you this way," he said, lifting up her sundress and kissing her legs.

Just then, there was a knock at the door.

Aiden sat up. "That must be dinner," he said as he walked to the door. "But, you are dessert."

∞

The next morning, Cecilia awoke to the scent of rich, earthy coffee wafting through the air. She smiled and rolled over groggily, running her hands over the luxurious white cotton linen. Just then, Aiden walked in with a tray carrying a small coffeepot and two mugs.

"You're wonderful, " she said, sitting up.

"Only the best for you, *wife*. I love saying that." He took her face in his hands and kissed her.

"I love hearing it, *husband*," she said, smiling.

"Relax and enjoy your coffee, love and I'll take a shower, then we'll go exploring," he said, filling her cup.

"OK, sweetheart," she said, stretching.

"Are you sore?"

"Yes! You wear me out, Aiden! You're like an Olympic athlete. I don't know if I can keep up."

"Aww, honey. I would say I'm sorry but I'd be lying. We'll just have to build up your endurance. You slept well, though, didn't you?"

"Yeah, better than I have in years."

"You're welcome," he said.

She grabbed a pillow, laughing, throwing it at him.

"Arrogant, much?"

"Hey, what can I say? When you've got it – " he said, shrugging, as he strode to the bathroom.

She leaned back into the pillows, feeling more content and peaceful than she had felt in years. There was something about being with Aiden. . . he made her feel on edge—always keeping her on her toes with his unpredictability and challenging her with new experiences—but also so blissful and serene.

The water was still running in the shower when she finished her coffee, so she decided to get up and figure out what to wear for the day. Picking through her clothes in her suitcase, she glanced over at Aiden's bag and saw a small notebook hidden under a pair of jeans.

*Hmm. . .*she thought. *Wonder what that is. I shouldn't peek. . . a marriage is built on trust after all.* But her curiosity won and she opened the brown leather journal. The pages were blank but she saw jagged edges near the seam, suggesting pages had been torn out. As she was about to put it back, a piece of paper fell out onto the rug. Picking it up, she noticed the paper was old; it was yellowed and frayed at the edges. It was a drawing of a woman that looked like it had been drawn in pencil. She was beautiful with long flowing dark hair and fair skin. Cecilia's heart skipped a beat. *It looks just like me!* she thought. But, it didn't make sense. It was too old. There was no way Aiden had drawn this since meeting her.

"What are you doing?"

She jumped and stood up quickly, holding the picture.

"Oh! This fell out of your bag and—"

Aiden raised his eyebrows. "It fell out? On its own?"

"Well. . . I was moving your bag and this notebook fell out then the picture. . . "

He stalked towards her slowly, his face serious. "Are you lying to me, Cecilia?"

"No, I'm not lying. I was not going through your things. I wouldn't do that." She held up the picture. "Who is this?"

He gazed at her a moment longer, his eyes narrowed. Then he said quietly, "That is Elara."

"Really? Did you draw this?"

"Yes, I did, a long time ago."

"She looks just like me!"

Aiden nodded. "There is a resemblance."

"A resemblance? We could be twins!"

"Yes. You do look alike. But you are much more beautiful," he said as he touched her cheek.

She jerked away. "Stop it! Why do we look so much alike? I don't get it, Aiden. What is going on?"

He let his hand drop to his side. "What can I say? I like brunettes."

"Why are you lying to me? I don't like this. I don't know what's going on, but—"

"Calm down, Cecilia. There is nothing going on. You are being paranoid and unreasonable. Let's just enjoy our honeymoon. Come here," he said, reaching for her again.

She slapped his hand away. "No! Not until you give me some answers! You expect me to believe it's a coincidence that

I look exactly like the woman you were in love with, the one that betrayed you?" Her heart accelerated and she backed away from him. "Oh my God. What you said before. . . Am I related to her? Because you said that if you ever found a descendant of hers, you would—"

Aiden stepped closer. "Cecilia. Stop this. You're being ridiculous." He stared into her eyes. "Look at me."

"Oh, no, you're not going to use your mind control on me! You're not going to make me forget about this! Get away from me!" She ran out onto the balcony and slammed the door behind her.

But, Aiden was right behind her, sliding the door open.

"Don't run from me. I'm not going to hurt you. You're acting crazy. And you've been drinking your tea, right? So, I couldn't influence your mind even if I wanted to." He took her hand. "Please think about this. I thought you trusted me."

The truth was, she hadn't drank any of the tea in weeks. She trusted him. Why would she keep drinking it? She had married him for God's sake; if she didn't trust him by now. . . But, she now regretted that decision more than ever.

"Of course I've been drinking it." She decided to lie. Maybe he wouldn't even try it.

He took her face in his hands, stared into her eyes. "Then, there's nothing to worry about, is there? It hurts that you don't trust me, Cecilia. I thought we were past that."

Five seconds later, Cecilia blinked and gazed into the eyes of her handsome husband. "You're right, this view really is amazing. Good call on having coffee on the balcony," she said, glancing out to the water. "This is the best honeymoon a girl could ask for." She leaned in and kissed him. "I should hop in the shower. Thank you for the coffee, sweetheart."

"Anytime, love," he said, smiling.

Elaine Ewertz

# AIDEN

Take me down where it's too dark to see
Nothing but black not a light to flee
A flight on a spiral, a wave of a staircase
Are you brave enough to try
your feet meet with air
You really could fly
Or get caught in the stare
The wind sweeps you up
Fooled into trying
You think you're flying
but where the dumb meets the brave
is a riddle I've yet to solve
Crawling through the cave
You pour the misery over like
a thick sauce of years past
She didn't make this for you
she doesn't even know you exist
but when you get the chance
please ask her was I missed

# TWENTY THREE

**April 8, 2015**

"I love you, Aiden," she says softly in my ear, wrapping her arms around me, pulling me close. I feel her warm, sweet breath on my neck.

*I know you do.* "I love you, too, sweetheart."

She smiles at me. "I'm going to make dinner now. Anything special you'd like?"

"No, honey. Surprise me," I tell her as she makes her way to the kitchen.

Leaning back in my leather chair, my mind drifts to the events of the past year. It seems my plan has worked. Everything is falling into place and it couldn't be more perfect. I remember last year when I first met her parents in New York after the medical conference. She told me she loved me when she thought I was asleep. I knew I had her then. The thing that continues to delight me, even after a year together, is that each and every event leading up to our marriage was seemingly orchestrated by some magical force, without even the need for my hand to guide things along. It was meant to be.

From the moment Dr. Aiden Black had stepped into the exam room and pulled back the sheet, revealing Mr. Rick Harper, deceased ex-husband of Dr. Cecilia Harper, I had known luck was on my side. It was a happy coincidence, a random mistake from a young doctor, who had only wanted to go back to her old house and collect the remainder of her belongings since her divorce from her abusive husband.

She had, in her mind, innocently slipped her former husband a little Xanax in an effort to prevent another attack, another set of bruises, another broken bone, another night of screaming and endless tears. How could she have known he had already downed a fifth of Jack and a few Xanax himself? Oh yes, it had been the too-perfect cue for me, the Medical Examiner of Lakeview County and immortal demi-god, to step gingerly into Cecilia's life and get the ball rolling on my long-awaited revenge. It is rightfully mine. Cecilia has no knowledge of her ancient ancestry. She has no idea that we are already linked, and were already a part of each other's lives well before she was even born.

Music drifts from the kitchen, interrupting my thoughts. Cecilia is listening to "Mr. Brightside" by The Killers and from the sound of it, she's having a hell of a time in there. I get up and peek into the kitchen and see her dancing around, a spatula in her hand. I smile, watching her for a moment. She's adorable.

I sigh, settling back down into my big leather chair. It wasn't hard to track her down. Once I found her family in New York – dear Mr. and Mrs. Brennan and a few cousins – I learned that their only daughter had become a neurosurgeon. So she was smart. I was instantly turned on. I love a challenge and it would definitely not be easy to work my way into her life and think of a plan for revenge. Her ancient ancestors – Elara and Lavena – had taken my life from me. They had set me up, made a joke out of the love I had for them both. And then Elara, that deceitful witch, had slaughtered my entire family, save my father. He had been away fighting a battle and had sensed very strongly that something was amiss. He had returned to find me on the floor of our home, sobbing uncontrollably over the lifeless bodies of my beautiful, loving mother and my two innocent sisters. My father had gone on a wild rampage of revenge, using every power at his disposal to locate Elara and Lavena. They had been nowhere to be found.

To this day, I still don't know what became of them. They may have committed suicide, taken the coward's way out. I must admit, it would have been the smart thing to do, knowing what my father is capable of. I am all for justice, but only if the punishment fits the crime. Yes, I cheated on Elara with her own sister, but it wasn't in vain. I truly fell in love with her and had every intention of coming clean. Murdering my entire family and then casting a spell on me to live for eternity, well, that was too much.

I've been searching for years for any descendants of Elara and luck finally showed up in the form of a wickedly intelligent, albeit naive, brunette.

I pull out the letter from my pocket. My father is in Australia this month, and along with telling me of his latest project – saving a species of birds that is on the verge of extinction – he begs me not to kill my wife. Even knowing who she is, he doesn't believe I should take revenge.

*My son, I ask you again. Please, do not punish this woman for the sins of her ancestors. She is not Elara. There is very little of Elara's blood in her veins. It is unfair to punish a woman who knows nothing of this. Do you not think I would love to see justice? Elara killed my wife and my daughters. But, this is not the right way, Aiden. This will only bring you more pain. Remember what I've taught you. Remember the man I've taught you to be.*

I sigh and shake my head. *She* does *know of this and – she's about to walk into the room.* I fold the letter and shove it back into my pocket.

"How does lasagna sound, sweetheart?" Cecilia peeks her head around the corner and smiles at me.

I smile in return. "That sounds perfect, love."

She dances over to me and kisses me on the forehead. "I'll bring you a glass of wine."

"You're the best." I swiftly pull her onto my lap. "Come here, my beautiful wife."

She snuggles into me and I can feel her desire. She wants me. I caress her body from her neck down to her long legs. She arches her back and I pull her head down to me and kiss her. "Don't worry, I'm going to ravage you all night. Now, make me dinner." She stands and I give her a playful swat on the bottom.

"Yes, dear," she says, winking, as she makes her way to the kitchen.

A couple of years ago I found Cecilia's grandparents. They were living in a small but well-maintained cottage-style home in Westchester County, New York. Walking up their sidewalk, staring at the rust-red brick exterior, I had a feeling I should leave. When her grandmother, Alice, answered the door and I looked into her eyes, I immediately sensed death. She didn't have much time left. I heard her grandfather, Howard, call out from another room, "Alice. Who's that at the door?"
Alice turned back to me and smiled, weakly and demurely. "How can I help you, son?"

Something about her sweet nature, her shy and innocent demeanor, wouldn't let me harm her. Instead, I looked deep into her eyes and planted the thought that she would live to see more grandchildren and die a peaceful death with family by her side. It was the least I could do. She was on the verge of death after all. It would be a waste of my time to seek revenge on a feeble elderly couple, even if they were related to the evil Elara and Lavena.

Then, as I was searching the Brennan's home, I came upon a picture of the beautiful Cecilia. She could be Elara's twin. It's amazing how centuries later, there is still a family resemblance. This was my sign that she was the one. I had to find her, get to know her, find out if she was anything like Elara. If she were even close to being as two-faced and deceitful as my ex-lover, my plan was to kill her immediately. I honestly expected to meet an arrogant, manipulative bitch. After all, her ancestors were nothing but liars and murderers. It was time that her bloodline paid for their sins, finally got what they deserved.

My second sign that I should make Cecilia pay was that she was married. But, I was disappointed to learn that she had no children. That would have been perfect. I could have killed not only Cecilia, but her disgusting offspring that would, no doubt, carry on the family tradition of being lying, entitled trash. I followed her from New York to Florida when she and her husband moved so that he could attend graduate school. I watched them for months, witnessed their domestic troubles and then their inevitable divorce. Then, Rick went missing. Failed to show up for work and then Cecilia suddenly looked distraught. She looked so guilty.

It amazes me that no one suspected anything. Beautiful women get away with so much. The jackpot was when I heard that he was dead. I decided to use my powers of persuasion to "become" the district medical examiner. I had to do the autopsy myself to prove it was homicide. On the surface, it appeared that it was an accidental overdose, but I knew better.

But, instead of file the report as suspicious and requiring further investigation, I filed it away as an accidental overdose and then began following her every day from October to March.

Although she appeared upset, she was getting over the death of her husband a little too quickly for my liking and going about her daily life thinking she was off the hook. Then, I learned that she had been ordered to pay alimony and it all came together. She had killed her deadbeat husband in order to avoid paying him for months or even years to come. But, as I watched her with each passing day, I became intrigued with her. She is so strikingly beautiful and intelligent, so ambitious and hard-working. I had to get to know her, talk to her. When I saw her in the coffee shop, I intentionally bumped into her so she would have to speak to me. I wanted to look into her eyes, touch her skin. She was so shy around me. The effect I had on her was obvious. She was attracted to me. I knew at that moment that I couldn't kill her. Not yet. I should have hated her, but all I wanted was to kiss her. I am half-human, after all.

The first two nights I knocked on her door, she had been so frightened that I knew that she was living alone. So, the next night, I snuck into her house while she was out drinking with her friends. I waited in the closet for hours, then when I heard her return home and go to bed, I could feel her dreaming of me. I decided to add more spice into her dream and get her a little hot and bothered and then give her a rude awakening, frighten her again so my power to get inside her head would be even stronger. She surprised me by being so brave and even sarcastic, although she must have thought I was going to kill her on the spot.

That's when I decided to offer her the deal I had carried around in the back of my mind since learning of her husband's death. It was the perfect blackmail. I counted on her vanity, her pride, and therefore her unwillingness to confess her mistake and go to prison. And I was right. Not only was she determined to live her life normally and not pay for her actions, she was also so enamored with me, so drawn to me like a magnet. I admit I had a little to do with that, the naughty dreams she had of me every night. But, the rest was all her. She couldn't help herself. And she's such a sexy little number. I wanted to have a taste of her, have a little fun with her along the way.

So, I have to continue to be careful not to tip her off to my plan. She truly believes I love her and I know without a doubt she loves me. Well, I will admit that I have had a hand in that, have used my "brain-raping", as she calls it, to help things along. I'm a little disappointed, though. It was too easy. I thought she would have given me more of a fight, but all's well that ends well, as they say.

There was one snag, but I took care of that. Dr. Patton, her nerdy red-headed colleague, was beginning to sniff around a little too much, putting his nose where it didn't belong. That pedantic, hair-brained hack tried to get in the way, telling Cecilia about a look I gave her when her back was turned in the hallway at the hospital. Fucking idiot. I heard every word he said. I could feel his mistrust of me, his suspicion. It was clear he thought I was no good for her and he was determined to show her.

So, I did something I truly despise doing: I changed. I shape-shifted into Dr. Patton's wife, Amy. The woman weighs 220 pounds, God help me. I thought I was going to keel over with a heart attack within thirty seconds. I stole her car from the hospital parking lot and drove to the Patton residence. She is a nurse at the hospital so the story was perfectly believable. His "wife" told him she had overheard Cecilia talking to another doctor about him, saying that she really deserved the credit for their research, that she had done all the work anyway and Bruce had barely contributed.

He believed his portly wife (me) without question and it really got under his skin. I wonder how the conversation must have gone that night, when the real Mrs. Patton came home from work. Confusion must have been abundant in the Patton home that evening.

The icing on the cake was when little Samantha Patton fell ill with pneumonia and Bruce stayed home from the conference, which allowed Cecilia to attend by herself and, in essence, receive all the attention and credit for their work. This sent the asshole over the edge. I really regret that I didn't find a way to be at their office the day he lost it. Now that would have been entertaining. To see his face turn bright red as the rage and jealousy overtook him. The final step was to get rid of him. Everyone just assumed he went off the deep end and disappeared in shame and humiliation.

It's just as well, because his thin, pale mutilated body is really buried deep in the ocean where no one would find him if they looked for a thousand years. I have only killed a small handful of people in my lifetime, which is impressive considering how long I've been alive. I never enjoyed murder; I only did it when absolutely necessary. I despise injustice and the few that I killed in the past all had it coming to them: two were child molesters and one was a serial rapist. Bruce wasn't a bad guy, but it had to be done or else my plan would have failed.

Being part human myself, I couldn't help but gloat a little so I planted the images in Cecilia's mind while she was sleeping. I was still high off the adrenaline and not thinking clearly. When she awoke in terror, I knew I had made a mistake. Even though I was only a tall, dark shadow in her dream, she would have figured it out quickly, so I erased the images from her mind. I hope no one else is stupid enough to try to stand in my way because I really do not enjoy killing another being, especially if the reasons are weak and self-serving.

Oh, Cecilia. I can hear her dancing and singing in the kitchen as she cooks. Every few minutes I get up to take a peek at her. I love watching her move, her long, graceful limbs working deftly in the kitchen. I love sensing all her shifting moods. Right now, she's content and happy. I'm looking forward to spending the next several years with her. I'm going to enjoy having her as my wife, loving me, devoted to me, making love with me every night. I love how submissive she is. Especially because it's such a stark contrast to her strong, independent, capable nature outside the bedroom. She allows me to take charge and control her body. I can feel the effect I have on her when I simply walk into the room. Her mood completely changes and she practically starts panting.

Although she thinks she's hiding it. She is so tightly controlled but I see through it. She gives it up to me so easily now. I almost wish she would resist me sometimes. Now, that would be fun.

I'm going to have no problem impregnating her with my child and if all goes according to plan, that will happen soon. Once our child turns nine, he inherits my abilities. They won't be as strong as mine, being that he will be a quarter-god, but he will still have supernatural abilities humans can only dream of. I wonder why she hasn't asked me about this. There are many things she hasn't asked me about.

I hear a clap of thunder and glance out the bay window to my right, where the heavy midnight blue curtains are pushed to the side. A sudden storm has begun in sleepy little Willow Park.

"April showers," I mutter as I stand and walk to the window. Just twenty minutes ago, the late afternoon sun was sinking but now charcoal clouds sit atop a fading gray canvas, hovering overhead ominously, as if imparting a warning. I like watching the palm trees sway in the chaos of wind, rain and lightning, the world at the mercy of mother nature. It's thrilling, the idea that some unseen presence can hold so much power over the entire world. It can choose on a whim to create a warm, bright sunny day or a violent storm, capable of tearing roofs off, destroying homes, knocking trees over like they are made of tissue paper. And there isn't a damn thing a human being can do about it except take cover and hope for the best.

I take a long glance before pulling the curtains closed and turning back to face the room. I can hear Cecilia in the kitchen, singing quietly to herself, and the occasional clatter of stainless steel pots and pans, the soft tapping of what must be a wooden spoon against a saucepan. The rich smell of tomato sauce and ricotta cheese wafts into the living room. Sitting back down in my chair, I study the platinum band on my finger, spin it around a few times. I feel an involuntary smile spread over my face.

My lovely bride is in for a big surprise one day. She will pay for not only her ancestors' sins, but for her own. But, until then, I plan to enjoy my time with her.

After she's gone, I will still have an eternity to live, but I will have a son or daughter by my side. And if something should happen to me, my child will carry out my legacy.

Ah, what love does to mere humans. They fail to see what is right in front of them. Love really is blind.

## TO BE CONTINUED. . .

ELAINE EWERTZ PRESENTS. . .

A SNEAK PEEK

INTO THE NEXT INSTALLMENT

IN THE **AIDEN BLACK** SERIES:

# SHADOW HOUSE

**COMING SOON**

# ONE

Jakob took a swig from his whiskey. "Well, you heard about the woman in Tennessee who slaughtered her entire family and took off. They finally found her last week. She was at a gas station in Virginia."

I nodded. "Larissa Myer. I just saw it on the news last night. Her doctor will have us believe she is suffering from *post-partum depression.*"

"A thousand dollars says she gets off for reason of insanity."

*Please.* I couldn't hold in my sound of disgust. "Or reason of beauty. . ."

Jakob laughed. "Oh I don't think she is pretty enough to get away with that!"

I set my drink down on the bar top. "Wait and see. Beautiful women get away with so much. They get away with murder. Literally. Go back in history and count the cases. Thousands of them. But, if a man so much as bats an eyelash at a woman, he goes to jail. Boggles the mind. I may sound like a misogynistic prick, but it's the truth and no one talks about it."

Jakob shrugged. "I'll agree that does happen a lot but I don't see what's-her-name, Larissa, getting away with anything."

*He's young*, I thought. I was about to continue the debate when I noticed Cecilia making her way towards me.

"We'll see," I said to Jakob before turning to Cecilia.

"Aiden," she said to me, leaning in for a kiss. "What are you two talking about over here? It looked like a heated discussion from where I was standing."

Jakob smiled at her and winked. "We were talking about beautiful women," he said.

"Oh—" Cecilia raised her eyebrows. "Well—"

Before she could finish, Amber came racing up behind her and tugged on her hand. "Hey! I was wondering where you ran off to. Katherine wants to get a group photo." She looked at me and Jakob. "You too! Come on, over by the pool," she said before bouncing back over to the water's edge.

"Well?" I glanced at Cecilia, who was pretending to be annoyed at her friend.

She groaned but was still smiling. "More pictures? Jeez, Amber, I think you've taken enough to fill an entire book today."

"Yeah, yeah," Amber called from several feet away. "Just get your asses over here and get it over with then I'll stop. Last one, I promise."

I took my wife's hand and kissed the top. "Let's oblige her, sweetheart. She's right; there's no use fighting it."

∞

Cecilia plopped down on the sofa and let out a long, ragged breath. "What a long day!"

I slid a coaster in front of her and handed her a mug. "That it was, love. Amber seemed to enjoy her birthday, though." Sitting in the leather chair opposite her, I watched as she sipped her tea.

"Yes, she did. I'm glad." She closed her eyes. "Mmm. Chamomile. You know me so well." The steam rose up from the mug in wispy silver streams, reached her eyelashes and then floated up to her soft brown bangs. I heard a *ting* when her wedding band touched the side of the cup. Her ivory hands were such a beautiful contrast to the deep red porcelain of the mug.

"What are you looking at?"

I looked back up at her face and saw she was giving me a mischievous half-smile.

"Why, I'm looking at my beautiful wife. Aren't I allowed?"

She sat her tea down and came over to me, sitting in my lap. "You're so good to me, Aiden. I don't know what I'd do without you."

I ruffled her hair. "I am, aren't I?"

She poked me in the ribs. "And so modest!"

I pulled her in close. "You must be exhausted love. Why don't I run you a hot bath? We can go to bed in a little bit."

"That would be great. Thank you, honey." She kissed my cheek and stood up.

After running the bath and tossing in some Epsom salts and bubble bath, I called down to Cecilia. "It's ready! Come on up, love!"

When she reached the top of the stairs, I kissed her forehead and hugged her. "It's all ready, sweetheart. Enjoy."

About thirty minutes later, I heard the bathroom door open and saw a sliver of light at the top of the stairs. *She must be going to bed*, I thought.

But she didn't. Our bedroom was to the left of the bathroom. By her footsteps I could tell she was walking the opposite way. I listened and heard a doorknob being opened quietly. I shook my head. *She forgets I have superior hearing.* I sat up quickly. She was going into the room I told her was off-limits. I must have forgotten to lock it. What the hell was she doing?

It was so quiet in the house I could have heard a pin drop. She was being very careful, whatever she was doing. I could feel the heat rising in my chest. I forced myself to take a deep breath. I knew she had been going in there when I was gone. Earlier today it looked like the antique clock had been moved slightly across the floor. I thought I was imagining it but now I knew otherwise. The only reason to move the clock—which was really heavy, by the way—is to get to the armoire behind it. What concerned me is what she would find behind that clock.

With this thought, I tip-toed up the stairs and stopped at the third step from the top, peeking around the banister. The door to my off-limits room was closed halfway and I could feel her there, much the same as how I always get a strong sense of her emotions, her mental state. Except—and I must admit, this happened often—her emotional state surprised me. Her vibration (the best way I can describe it) floated down the hall and to me and it was angry. She was angry. I expected her to be nervous about getting caught, knowing she was doing something wrong, knowing she was in the one room in the house I explicitly asked her not to go into, but she was angry. Ironic, if you ask me. She has no right to be upset. But she's going to have some explaining to do.

My nosy wife heard me coming by the creaking wood floors—I was no longer trying to be quiet—and then her emotion turned to fear.

I pushed open the door and she was standing in front of the armoire—this time the huge, dusty clock had been pushed even farther away—holding an envelope. She dropped it to the floor as soon as she saw me.

"What are you doing in here?" I asked her.

"I thought I smelled smoke," she said.

*Well, I didn't expect that,* I thought.

I couldn't help but smile. "You thought you smelled *smoke?*"

"Actually, yes, I—"

I cut her off. "And do you *smell smoke* often?" *I know she's been in here before,* I thought. *Let's see if she tells the truth.*

She furrowed her eyebrows. "No. . .what kind of question is that? I thought I smelled smoke and. . ."

"And you decided it must be coming from this room. Well, that makes sense." I was being sarcastic but I didn't care. I had to find out what she was hiding from me. I walked closer to her. "What did you have there?" I looked down to the floor, where she had dropped the envelope.

Her mouth formed a small "o" and she bent down to pick it up. "Well," she began. I noticed her hands were trembling but she straightened her back and looked me square in the eye. "I'm sure you already know what's in this." She handed me the envelope. "This is your secret room, after all. I'm hoping you can explain how you have this."

*Shit. Why the hell did I forget to lock this door? I'm slipping. She's starting to get to me.* I opened the flap and a small plastic card fell onto the floor. Picking it up, I saw a face I hadn't seen in a while. His face pale as a sheet with tiny orange dots scattered haphazardly across and a tuft of ginger hair on top of his head. To the right of the picture was his name and address.

Cecilia stood frozen, staring at me. I glared at her. I couldn't think of anything to say. It was no matter anyway; I could erase this from her memory in two seconds and she would forget the whole mess.

"You—you killed him, didn't you?"

"Who? This guy?" I held up the ID. "Everyone knows he went off the deep end after you got all the credit—and rightfully so, if you ask me—for the research on glioblastoma." I tossed it onto a nearby table and walked closer to Cecilia so I was only a foot away. I reached out and took her hands. She looked down quickly and tried to pull away but I held tight. "Honey. Look at me. We both know I'm not a murderer. This is silly. I did not kill Dr. Patton. You know that. So stop this. Come on." I took her hand and led her to the bedroom.

She wrenched free of my grasp and shook her head as tears began to form at the corners of her eyes. She went to the window on the other side of the room and then turned back to look at me. "Then why do you have—"

"Cecilia, I can explain that. But, first, I need you to look at me and tell me you trust me. I'm your husband." I walked over to her and she backed away. She was up against the window and had nowhere to go. I only had a few seconds. I took her hands, held her gaze and concentrated on removing every trace of the last twenty minutes from her memory.

Reaching inside her mind, I swiped all the memories of her walking to the off-limits room after her bath, her opening the armoire, her finding the plain white envelope with Dr. Patton's drivers license inside and finally I erased the memory of this conversation and replaced all those images with blackness. To prevent any confusion, I then planted images of her walking to the bedroom after her bath and us standing and talking by the window.

She blinked a few times and looked around the room. Then, she smiled and wrapped her arms around me. "I love you, honey. I'm exhausted. Let's go to sleep."

"Sounds like a plan to me, love."

I watched her dig in her dresser for her pajamas. "Where are those shorts with the butterflies on them?" she said to herself. Glancing over to the bed, I noticed a pair of small baby blue shorts with yellow butterflies strewn across the fabric. I came up behind her and handed them to her.

"Oh, thanks, honey," she said. But she had an odd expression on her face. She looked almost afraid or suspicious. But then she quickly smiled before turning to the bathroom.

"Is something wrong, honey?" I asked.

She turned, her soft pajama shorts in her hand. "No, of course not. Everything is great, husband." She smiled and flitted over to me, kissing me on the cheek. "I'm going to get ready for bed. Be right back, sweetheart."

As soon as the bathroom door closed, I sat down on the bed to think. *The Kombucha tea. There's no way. She threw it away right in front of me when we returned from our honeymoon. She told me she trusted me not to use my gifts, my ability to get inside her head and influence her thoughts. I watched her toss it in the trash and then I took it out later that night. It's not possible.*

I stared at the bathroom door with the yellow sliver of light underneath, the over-the-door mirror hanging in the center. Looking at my reflection from across the room, I was startled at how small I appeared in the mirror. Then I met my own eyes. Dark pools of brown stared back at me and for a moment they looked like someone's else's eyes. Whose, I didn't know, just not mine. They were vulnerable. They were not the eyes of a man in control.

# Songs that Inspired the Novel

Intro  ~  The xx
Crawl  ~  Kings of Leon
High Ball Stepper  ~  Jack White
Glory Box  ~  Portishead
Personal Jesus  ~  Marilyn Manson
Bruises  ~  Band of Skulls
Wedding Song  ~  Yeah Yeah Yeahs
Physical (You're So)  ~  Nine Inch Nails
Top Yourself  ~  The Raconteurs
Back to Black  ~  Amy Winehouse
The Funeral  ~  Band of Horses
Cecilia  ~  Simon & Garfunkel
Folsom Prison Blues  ~  Sugar + the Hi-Lows

# ACKNOWLEDGMENTS

I would like to thank the following people, places and things for helping me in this quest—writing my first novel. It has been my dream since I was a little girl to write a book using my wild imagination with all the characters and ideas that just need to be made real. Or at least put on paper. Dreams do come true.

So, thank you to the following people for their unending support, love, encouragement, inspiration, belief, honesty and patience: Dad (you are always there for me, cheering me on, believing in me. Thank you), Stephen (my sweetheart. You mean the world to me. Thank you for your love, support, encouragement and for believing in me), Cherry Ann (you inspire me more than you could ever know. Thank you for your Virgo brain and for always being there for me and talking me through things when my neuroses gets the best of me. You are an angel), Angela (you are an amazing friend. Thank you for being there. And thank you for going to nursing school so you can reassure me that I'm *not* having a heart attack when I was anxious about whether I'd ever finish this), Teresa A., (thank you for your editing genius and your words of advice), Keaidy B. (the first real author I ever met! You've inspired me so much and helped me to understand what it means to truly believe in myself and the crazy stories and characters dancing around in my head. Thank you), Lisa B. (you were one of the first people to read and comment when I shared pieces of this book as I was just starting to write it and all through the process. Your support and encouragement means so much!), Tammie (you are my muse! You always contacted me at just the right time, sending photos from your travels with inspiring and beautiful words), Mom, Emily, Evan, Teresa, my entire family, Jayden C., Declan C., Stacey C., Megz, Nikki B., Michelle B., Jasmine M., Henry Louis, Christy and Scott at The Lost Parrot (you're bartenders. I'm a writer.

Do I need to explain why I'm thanking you?). Thank you to Dr. Connelly at North Orlando Spine Center for putting my head on straight (literally!) and for your support and encouragement, thank you to the rest of the staff at NOSC for your support. Thank you to the greats: George Orwell, Stephen King, Edgar Allan Poe, Aldous Huxley, and Kurt Vonnegut.

There are many more people that I'm probably forgetting but please forgive me. I thank you. There were others I was going to thank but I see you have unfriended me from Facebook and we all know what that means. But, thank you? I don't know. This is awkward.

Oh, also thank you to loud neighbors for forcing me to put on classical Pandora to drown you out. Your fighting and airing your dirty laundry (figuratively) is so inspiring.

Thank you to the following places: Starbucks, Panera, libraries, the beach and dive bars.

Thank you to these things: Coffee, wine, incense, Soundrown, Pandora, music (specifically Jack White, Amy Winehouse, Johnny Cash, The xx, Sugar + the Hi-Lows and Band of Horses), Peanut M&Ms and Sharpie Fine Point Pens.

# About the Author

Elaine Ewertz is the author of the Aiden Black trilogy including *The Devil You Know* and the upcoming sequel, *Shadow House*. Her first passion is writing fiction, namely the psychological thriller variety. Elaine has written stories and poetry ever since she learned how to write. She lives in Central Florida with three Betta fish and has a day job in healthcare. Elaine loves hearing from readers so drop her a line at eSquaredPress@outlook.com and be sure to check out eSquaredPress.com for news and updates on upcoming releases as well as random musings from Elaine.

50651798R00164

Made in the USA
Charleston, SC
04 January 2016